1

Ireland, January 7, 1839

The land lived and breathed and stirred his soul; he knew it as intimately as he knew himself. And yet as Rían Kelly crested the hill and stared in horror at the valley below, he did not recognize the place of his birth and the village that had been his home throughout all of his twenty-seven years.

He dismounted a horse as black as his own raven locks and saw his bewilderment and fatigue reflected in the steed's eye. Draping the reins loosely over the horse's neck, he tried not to think about the froth that dangled from the animal's mouth or his need for water and food and rest when there was none to be had.

They had ridden hard through the night on a journey that should not have taken more than a few hours. It was impossible to believe, in fact, that only the day before he stopped on this very hill to gaze at his beloved Cait. He struggled to find her house now as he remembered the last time he'd seen her; he'd kissed her good-bye and held her in his arms as he promised to return before nightfall.

For some reason, something had gnawed at him as he left her and he'd stopped and looked back to find her standing outside the stone house she shared with her mother. Her image had seared into his brain like a physical imprint that would never leave him. She'd stood in the front yard, her slender arms draped over the gate. Her hair was straight and long; parted in the middle, she kept the warm brown locks on either side of her face braided. On that day, she'd pulled the braids back, where they were joined at the nape of her neck and allowed to cascade over her thick tresses. The wind had nipped at the simple ivory dress she wore, causing it to billow while the sun's rays had warmed her hair to a chestnut shine.

He'd had a sudden impulse to return to her, to scoop her into his arms, to feel her slender, firm body beneath that dress and to weave his hand into those braids until they came undone. He'd wanted to look into her blue-gray eyes once more; eyes that mirrored the stormy waters that surrounded all that was Ireland.

Instead, he waved. And when she blew him a kiss in return, he'd clicked his heels and turned his steed and headed toward Dublin.

The weather had been unseasonably warm; the sun's welcomed emergence rapidly melting a heavy snow that had occurred only the day before. But the wind had steadily increased as he neared his destination, bringing with it much colder air.

Mere minutes had passed before he was racing back down the steps of the building housing the Dublin Metropolitan Police Headquarters, desperate to reach his horse and frantic to return to Cait before it was too late.

He'd barely climbed atop his steed and clicked his heels when a storm the likes of which he had never witnessed before slammed into the city.

His horse was thrown into the side of a building, Rían's leg nearly crushed as it lay pinned between the animal and the stonework. Then the wind whipped again, lifting them both into the street where they were scuttled along like God's hand was at their backs.

He heard a thundering crash behind him and as he peered over his shoulder, he watched in horror as a church steeple dissected itself from its roof and spun through the air until it became impaled in a building a block away. Windows were similarly disengaging themselves, flying through the air as if possessed by demons before smashing into people and buildings. A tree became uprooted directly in their path and had his steed not risen onto his hind legs in panic, the roots might have clipped his muzzle.

Rían tried vainly to rein in the terrified animal but whether it was racing at full speed or the wind was catapulting them along, the effect was the same: they were unable to stop or even to slow themselves. He had no choice but to hang on with every bit of strength he possessed or risk being blown into the sky with all manner of debris.

Screams assaulted him from every angle and yet he never saw the sources of the cries; they seemed to be completely disembodied.

Then the sky turned as black as midnight and a torrent of rain smashed into them. He spotted a stable and managed to steer them toward it before the roof lifted cleanly off and spun above them with such violence that it was torn into a thousand pieces that sailed in all directions.

Somewhere in the dark recesses of his mind an inner voice directed him to move inland. He struggled to get a clear sense of where he was and where he needed to go but streets that had been familiar only moments earlier were now totally unrecognizable.

He didn't know how he managed to get out of the city. A sense of duty urged him to return; as a county inspector, he knew every hand would be needed to assist the survivors. But a stronger, more urgent voice spurred him onward toward home.

The winds and the torrential rains clawed at him and the night sky soon encompassed him. He found himself in a living hell of rising waters, downed trees and whole villages swept away.

From the best he could gauge, the storm overtook him sometime around the midnight hour. Buffeted from all directions, he was no longer able to distinguish between east and west and he had no choice but to trust in his horse to bring him home.

When the first vestiges of light arrived, it found him soaked to the bone, shivering and spent. And as his horse moved steadily onward with a driven sense to outrun the horrors, Rían stared around him with mounting alarm. Creeks he had passed only a day earlier had morphed into raging rivers they could not cross; and as the waters grew before his eyes, so did the debris they carried—clothing, roofing, furniture, crops. And then the bodies came, bloated and lifeless: horses, livestock and an occasional person sailing past them so quickly he could not snare it.

And he didn't know what he might have done if he'd managed to. He saw no other living human beings; no families searching for loved ones, no one assessing the damage around them.

He felt like it was the end of the world.

And now he stood on the last hill before the village, his energy drained beyond human endurance, staring into the valley where his home once stood—and where Cait had waved good-bye.

He scrutinized the terrain as if she might magically appear before him. It no longer mattered if every village between him and Dublin was wiped off the face of the earth. It only mattered that Cait was alive, she was well and she was waiting for him.

His eyes landed on the village church. It had been built near the top of another hill and now it towered, lonely and desolate, above a seething river that had not existed a day prior. Though he wanted nothing more than to sleep for days on end, he managed to place one foot in front of the other until he was slowly, painstakingly, making his way toward the lone structure. His horse followed though he would have understood if he'd simply collapsed. Perhaps it thought a warm dry stable, fresh water and good hay was awaiting it at the end of their journey; but Rían knew the stable was destroyed, the water was polluted and dry hay was too much to ask.

When he spotted Father Fitzpatrick, he thought his eyes were deceiving him. Then others came into view: men, women and children of the village, gathered together on the steps of the church; lamenting the memories, the livelihoods and the futures that were swept away with the waters below.

When they in turn spotted him, they rushed at him like one massive being. They all spoke at once, as if one lone county inspector had the power to change the course of their lives.

He ignored their pleas, their cries for help and their desperation. He had only one thought; only one mission that had driven him home without rest.

"Where is Cait?" he asked time and again, only to be met with silence, stunned eyes and traumatized expressions. "Where is Cait?"

He felt a strong hand on his shoulder, squeezing it tightly. As he turned in that direction, he peered into Father Fitzpatrick's tired, lined face.

He shook his head and Rían tried not to hear the words he spoke. "No one has seen Cait, Rían," he stated in a tone so flat, it was as if the emotions had been wrenched from him and only a void remained.

"That cannot mean she's not still alive," Rían insisted, turning to peer below.

The villagers gathered in silence around him as they peered toward Cait's home but not even the roof or stone walls had survived to peek through the waters.

He forced himself to form another question "Was there a stranger spotted before the storm?"

He turned to look in each of their faces. Their eyes told him they understood his question. It was the reason he'd left for Dublin. Four women had been murdered in recent days; four women who each bore the same description: long brown hair, gentle eyes, slender, petite and in their twenties.

And it was the reason he had raced from the Dublin Metropolitan Police Headquarters within minutes of arriving. They had not sent a dispatch to him, urging him to Dublin for crucial information on the cases. They'd known nothing about the string of murders.

Which meant he'd been sent on a wild goose chase as a monstrous storm bore down upon them. He'd unwittingly left the villagers to fend for themselves. And he'd left his beloved Cait alone with a killer.

2

North Carolina, August 23, 2011

The insistent ringing of the telephone sounded offensive and as Ryan O'Clery opened his eyes, he had difficulty orienting himself. The skylights above the bed revealed a hazy sky in muted shades of pewter and as he sat up, he glanced at the clock on the nightstand. It was still thirty minutes before his alarm was set to go off.

The phone stopped ringing and he stared at the dresser on the other side of the room where his cell phone lay charging. Whoever it was had a lot of nerve calling at this hour of the morning, he thought.

He ran his hand through thick black hair, combing back the locks that threatened to spill onto his forehead.

He'd been dreaming of her again.

The dreams had been with him for as long as he could remember. They were different scenarios, different settings, but she always looked exactly the same. Her hair was very long and straight and in this dream, she had the warm brown tresses sun-streaked with chestnut gathered into an elaborate bun. He was mesmerized by the tendrils that escaped the confinement and teased the nape of her neck; captivated by the strands that might have brushed her brow had she not swept it to the side.

When she pulled her hair into a bun or a twist or any manner of upward styles, it seemed to be an invitation to free her mane from imprisonment. Now it teased him as if she was meant for the pure pleasure of his fingers strumming those silk strands.

It was New Year's Eve; he didn't know how he knew this about his dream but he did. The house was full of revelers. Music was wafting through the rooms from a small but lively band and the sound of laughter sometimes rose above it as if someone had told a particularly amusing story. Excitement was building as the New Year approached and in the final moment before the celebration reached its crescendo, he grabbed her petite hand in his and whisked her away from the others, down the hallway and behind a closed door.

She giggled as she was pulled along, her laughter like bells pealing. It was sweeter than any musical instrument, more spellbinding than any song.

She wore clothing the likes of which he couldn't imagine in the twenty-first century. The golden hued dress descended to the tops of her shoes. The bodice was form fitting, accentuating breasts that enticed him with the simple act of rising and falling with each breath. Her waist was so small he could place a hand on either side and his fingers could touch in the middle of her back. At her hips, the dress flared into folds that tantalized him with every subtle swing and sway.

And then he stopped her just inside the door and took both her hands in his. His eyes locked with hers as he dropped to one knee. Her eyes widened and for a moment, he was so hypnotized by them that he couldn't speak. Her eyes had always done that to him; they changed colors like a chameleon, appearing gray at times and green or blue at others. They were the colors of the waters that surrounded Ireland; tumultuous and calm, restless and pensive, stormy and placid, all in one breathtaking moment.

And as he gazed into them, the words lingering just on the tip of his tongue, they looked back at him in a way he'd never witnessed in the harsh light of reality. They portrayed a love so deep, he couldn't fathom it; admiration so wide he knew he didn't deserve it; and trust so steady that he knew he could not fail her.

It was then that the telephone had awakened him. And now as he leaned against the pillows stuffed from an uneasy slumber against the headboard, he knew it didn't matter. He knew what he had asked her and how she had answered.

The phone began ringing again and this time with a cross curse he tossed the bedcovers to the side and flung his long, lean legs over the side of the bed. He caught a glimpse of himself in the dresser mirror as he approached: muscular arms, wide shoulders and a flat stomach on a frame that often felt too tall; thick, black hair that brushed the back of his neck and grazed his ears; and vivid green eyes that poorly concealed his irritability.

"*What?*" he said as he answered.

"Detective O'Clery?"

"What do you want?"

"Another body's been found. This one along the banks of the Lumber River."

He ran his hand through his hair again as if he could comb the unruly locks. It was going to be a long, hot day. "Where?"

3

The sun had barely burned through the haze and his shirt was already stippled with perspiration. The insects were out in full force, the heat and humidity of the August day acting as an irritant to them as they buzzed around his head. He slapped at a tiger mosquito, looking briefly at its squashed body against his forearm as he brushed it away. Mosquitoes before breakfast, he thought. Hell of a day.

He knelt beside the body as he thrust hands that were too large into medical gloves that were too small, the sweat on his palms meeting the inner powder to create a decidedly uncomfortable mess. His eyes were focused on the work at hand; he started from the feet and made his way upward to the face, as he always did.

The feet were petite; one wore a muddied shoe with a two-inch heel while the other was bare. The legs were scratched as though from brambles and the thin skirt might have been long but it was bunched just above the knees. The frame was diminutive and it wasn't until he reached the breasts that he saw the first splatter of blood. She still wore a sleeveless blouse, the straps remaining in place against pale shoulders. And as his eyes traveled upward, he knew there was but one wound: the jugular had been sliced through. Blood pooled on the ground beneath her head, soaking long, dark brown hair into the grass and the muddy bank.

He didn't want to look into her face, as if the woman of his dreams would be laid before him, her life snuffed out and his intense dreams turning into a hellish nightmare. He could feel the eyes of the other officers upon him and he forced himself to grit his teeth as though the scene didn't bother him.

He looked into eyes that were open, the dark brown pools almost black as they stared lifelessly at some point in the sky. It wasn't her and he breathed a sigh of relief. The nose was too wide, the cheekbones too fleshy, the dark hair forming sideburns that appeared almost masculine.

It wasn't her.

He came to his feet.

The county courthouse stood before him, a modern, clean brick building that straddled two blocks and faced the bridge that wandered over the Lumber River. A group of spectators had formed on the courthouse steps and another group lined the crime scene tape that had been erected fifty feet from the body.

It was the third homicide in as many days and if this one was to be like the others—and he suspected it would be   there would be scant evidence to go on.

The first one had been found along the railroad track, the body nearly obscured by underbrush. She'd been discovered by landscapers working on an adjoining property; men who were hauling the debris from a manicured lawn to the public property alongside the tracks. She also had long brown hair but her eyes had been as blue as the Carolina skies and her skin as pale as alabaster.

The second was spotted at the edge of a cemetery by mourners at a funeral. She, too, had long brown hair. Her eyes had been light brown and she'd had tattoos stretching from a thin shoulder to her wrist in a column of butterflies.

All three had their jugular veins laid open. Neither of the two prior ones had shown any signs of a struggle; there was no evidence under their nails, no sign of sexual molestation. He could see this woman's nails clearly from where he stood. They were immaculate and something told him there would be no blood or tissue underneath to suggest that she'd resisted him.

It was as if someone simply swooped down on each woman, slit her throat and disappeared.

The crime scene techs had arrived and Ryan allowed his eyes to wander the surrounding terrain. Footprints trailed from the body along the shore and as he followed them, it was easy to see it was only one set with one women's shoe on and one off. The imprints were shallow as if the woman had been running. He studied the underbrush further down the river's banks, following the trail of prints until they merged with brambles separating public property from a private residence. A lone shoe dangled from roots that sprouted upward through the muck. He called to a nearby tech, pointing out the shoe and directing him to photograph and catalog it.

He was just about to follow the prints deeper into the brush when his cell phone rang.

"Aye?" he answered.

"Ryan O'Clery?"

"You telephoned me. Who else might you be expecting?" He slapped at another mosquito.

"This is Wanda from PD. You have a message."

"Is it urgent?"

"It's some reporter from Atlanta, asking about the two women killed earlier this week."

"Atlanta?" He'd been in America long enough to know Atlanta was a good five or six hours' drive. "Why?"

"It's become national news."

"Oh, that's just grand. I won't be talking to any reporters, national or otherwise."

"I thought you might know this one."

"Why?"

"The last name's Reilly. That's Irish, isn't it?"

He didn't know whether to retort angrily or respond with biting wit so he remained silent. It was the craziest thing, he thought. People always spoke as if Ireland was the size of a small town and everybody there knew everybody else. Like they all met around the supper table each evening or shared the same bath facilities.

"Anyway, here's the number," Wanda continued. "You ready to copy?"

"Aye." He half-listened as she rattled off the number, his eyes following the trail through the underbrush. He didn't make a move to write down the number and he wouldn't be asking her to repeat it. He'd told her he wouldn't be speaking to the media and he meant it.

When she was done, she added, "And the chief wants to see you when you're done there."

Lovely. "I'll be in straight-away." He clicked off the phone. Just lovely. He'd be wanting to know how close he was to settling the cases and he was no further along than he'd been three days prior.

He didn't relish the thought of going to work each day with "notify next of kin" at the top of his to-do list and three days straight was beginning to annoy him. He wasn't good with sobbing women and children. He had to exert patience while he asked tough questions and anyone could attest to the fact that he had scant patience to begin with.

He'd spent the first day looking closely at the victim's family, her personal situation and any enemies she might have had. When the second murder occurred, the task of finding a link between the two victims got added to all the other boxes he had to check. Now this. This meant they were definitely dealing with a serial killer and the circumference of his investigation had just grown substantially.

He swatted at a pesky horsefly buzzing around his face before spreading apart the tangle of brush.

4

Ryan laid the map of the town across Chief Johnston's desk. "The first was found here," he said, writing a '1' with a heavy black marker. "This stretch of the railroad track is close to the historic downtown area, about three blocks south of the public library. I'm using this as my Ground Zero."

He glanced up as the chief nodded before writing the number '2' and continuing, "The second body was found approximately ten blocks away. Still on the same side of town. Almost a direct line of sight as the crow flies." He marked the last spot. "While today's was found not quite ten blocks north and maybe eight blocks to the west."

"Go on," Chief Johnston said as Ryan fell silent. He had a kind face but Ryan knew it hid an iron resolve just behind the smile, a tenacity that could easily erupt in anger and impatience if he thought someone wasn't pulling their weight. He had heard his voice bellow with irritation many a time and had promised himself to stay clear of it.

"All three were found on public property. All three were killed with a single slice to the jugular." He indicated the area on his own neck. "The first two women, best we can determine thus far, did not know one another. I've begun the investigation on the third. They all have very similar characteristics. All Caucasian. All with long brown hair, very similarly styled. Their eye colors varied. All about the same height, same weight, same build."

The chief locked eyes with his.

"Doesn't take a rocket scientist to know we're dealing with a serial killer here," Ryan said. "I've searched the records and there have never been any others matching this modus operandi."

"Any conclusions?"

"Aye. It leads me to believe this isn't a resident. Possibly someone passing through. Or someone just out of prison, perhaps, just now returning to this area."

"Suspects?"

"None at present. We have toxicology tests in progress and I'm awaiting the results."

"What else have you done?"

"I've canvassed residents surrounding each of these areas." He drew a circle around each one so they overlapped. "I also have the identities of all three women. I've interviewed the families of the first two and will be speaking to the third family when we're done here."

Chief Johnston walked to the window and glanced outside. The parking lot was just beyond; the sun beat heavy on the asphalt pavement. In another hour, Ryan figured he could fry eggs on it. The chief turned back to him. His eyes were narrowed and his brows furrowed. "I'm due at the mayor's office to report on this. We can't have a serial killer running loose in this town. You have to know we need this wrapped up *yesterday*."

"Aye. I do."

"What do you need?"

"I need men to go door to door. Perhaps someone heard something; each crime scene showed evidence of the woman running away. Someone might have heard a scream, a cry, anything out of the ordinary. I need men to interview the neighbors of the women, friends, acquaintances."

"How many?"

"As many as you can spare, quite honestly."

"This is our highest priority."

Chief Johnston's administrative assistant poked her head through the doorway. "Detective O'Clery." Charlie Meade was tall and willowy with short blond hair and large blue eyes. She always seemed to linger when Ryan was around, dropping hints of places she wanted to go and things she wanted to see. He'd never bit at the bait; he preferred to keep his private life private.

"Aye?" he said now.

"That reporter from Atlanta called again."

He turned back to the chief. "I won't be talking to the media. I've got my hands full with the investigation and I won't be detoured."

Chief Johnston nodded. "All media inquiries come to me."

With that, Charlie reluctantly ducked away.

"I'll need men to fan out from each of these locations, walk block by block if need be, looking for any evidence. Particularly down by the river. The ground is soft there and if she was running from something, there should be footprints behind her. I didn't find anything but that doesn't mean there's nothing there."

"I want a report morning, noon and night. You got that?"

"I do," Ryan answered. "And you'll have it. And we'll soon have our man. I'm certain of it."

5

The storm door slammed behind Ryan as he made his way down the steps to the grill. In one hand he carried a bottle of Connemara whiskey and a glass. His other hand balanced a plate of three oversized beef patties and the same number of skewers filled with chunks of vegetables.

He set everything on the table and lifted the grill lid. The mingling aromas of charred apple wood and wine barrel wood wafted up to him. He closed the lid and opened the whiskey bottle. It was good peated single malt Irish whiskey, his favorite kind. The local liquor store didn't normally carry it but they'd ordered a case just for him and he'd picked it up just this afternoon. He poured a half glass and swirled it around, enjoying the fragrance before he lifted it to his lips.

There was nothing like Irish whiskey, he thought. It had been a long day and a hot one and he was looking forward to some tasty ground steaks and a goodly portion of drink.

He hadn't intended to cook all three patties this evening. He wanted two but there were three left in the package and what's a man to do? So he'd marinated all three overnight in a special sauce he'd conjured up himself. Then he'd chopped up the vegetables and marinated them in a separate mixture of olive oil and herbs. He'd have two patties and two kebobs tonight and with any luck at all, he'd have the time to stop in for lunch tomorrow and finish up the leftovers.

The sky was taking on a stormy appearance but as he enjoyed his drink and watched the clouds, he determined it wouldn't rain before his food was done. Once the grill was ready, it wouldn't take long.

He set his drink on the table and raised the grill hood again. He was getting hungrier by the minute. He left the hood open, reached for the plate and readied the patties. He was just preparing to plop them onto the fiery grill when a voice rang out.

"Detective O'Clery?"

He hesitated, his plate still held in one hand while the grill sizzled beside him. He thought his eyes were playing tricks on him. A woman had stepped through a break in the hedges and was standing there watching him.

She had very long brown hair with chestnut highlights; it appeared thick but perfectly straight. There was something about the way she held her head, her chin slightly lowered so her eyes were cast upward as she looked at him. She was of medium height and as he drew his eyes downward, he took in a royal blue cotton blouse with a neck deep enough to expose just enough cleavage to entice him. His heart quickened as his eyes drifted further south to a pair of form fitting jeans that ended in open-toed shoes with enough heel to show off her slender ankles. A dragonfly was tattooed on one ankle.

"Ryan O'Clery?" she said expectantly.

She had an American accent but she'd pronounced his name in the Irish manner; instead of pronouncing the 'y' as an 'i' in the American manner, she'd pronounced it as an Irish 'e'. Yet he knew he'd never laid eyes on her before—at least not in the flesh. He would remember if he had because her image had been seared into him night after night. It was as if she had stepped right out of his dreams and materialized in front of him, right there between the grill and the garden hose.

She took a step forward, her head still slightly downward and her eyes peering up at him quizzically. "Are you Ryan O'Clery, by chance? Detective O'Clery?" Her eyes were the color of a stormy sea; gray and blue with flecks of gold that swirled and danced like crashing waves.

Her chin wavered a bit and he found himself unable to tear his eyes away. She bit her lower lip. When he continued staring at her, she reached into a purse that hardly looked large enough for bills and a driver's license and pulled out a card. Holding it out to him, she said, "I've been trying to reach you. My name's Cathleen Reilly. I drove in from Atlanta—"

"You're the reporter," Ryan said. His voice sounded disembodied to him.

"I was hoping to ask you a few questions—"

"Only the chief can comment on ongoing cases." Her face fell and he realized how abrasive he had sounded. It was as if his mouth was moving without direction from his brain. "But are you hungry?"

6

He didn't remember going back into the house for a bottle of wine, but somehow it was in his hand and he was opening it without taking his eyes off her. She sat on the other side of the patio table, her legs crossed. She dangled one shoe and now he was mesmerized by the way it swung gently away from her now naked heel. The tiny dragonfly held him rapt and he longed to touch it.

"I was told you were a man of few words," she said. She didn't look at him but seemed interested in the layout of the back yard, her eyes sweeping over the gardens that gently curved and wound their way around the perimeter. "Nice place you have here."

"I can't take the credit for it," he said, pouring the wine. He handed the glass to her. "I'm only renting. The lady who lived here has gone to a nursing home." He nodded toward the row of gardenias against deep pink crepe myrtles. "She planted all of this. Obviously, she was quite good at it."

"I see you've found your voice," she answered.

He looked at her in silence.

"You're Irish."

"Aye," he answered. It occurred to him that the meat might be burning and he turned his attention to the grill. Moving the meat to the side, he placed the kebobs on the grate.

"How did you manage to wind up here?" she asked, taking a sip of wine.

"My sister." He turned the vegetables though he realized as he did it, it was premature. Glancing up, he saw her watching him expectantly, a soft smile on her lips. "I come from a family of law enforcement officers," he said. "For generations, it's what we did, all of us in the same county there in Ireland. But my sister wanted to attend college here in America. And the family didn't want her to be here alone."

"So you came to keep an eye on her." Her smile deepened and he thought he caught a twinkle in her eyes.

When he spoke again, he was surprised to find his mouth had gone dry. "Turned out, she was quite capable of tending to herself. She graduated from the University of North Carolina at Chapel Hill. Met a military man stationed at Fort Bragg. He's a good bloke, even if he is a Norseman. They married and have a set of twins. Cute little lasses, they are." He felt like he was talking too much; it seemed he'd already said more in the past few minutes than he'd spoken all day.

"And you?" The smile hadn't left her face, nor had her eyes left his.

He gazed at her upturned lips for a moment before forcing himself to turn the kebobs again. "There was a job opening here for which I was qualified."

"I see."

He moved the food onto a platter and placed it in the center of the table. Then he transferred a beef patty and kebob to her plate and one of each to his own. He started to pour himself a bit more whiskey but realized he hadn't touched his glass since she'd appeared.

"This is tasty," she said. "What kind of marinade did you use? I can't quite place the spices."

"It's just something I whipped up myself."

"Do a lot of cooking, do you?"

"I do now."

The smile twisted into a mischievous grin. She never looked
at him straight-on but always tilted her head and peered at him
out of the corner of her eye. It was a coquettish look, he decided
as he squirmed uncharacteristically in his chair.

"That sounds like a story there," she said.

"My story would no doubt bore you."

She reached across the table suddenly and grasped his hand.
Her touch was hot and electric and he almost dropped his fork
out of the other hand. She squeezed his ring finger. "You were
married until recently." She held his hand a bit higher and tapped
on the white band of skin.

"Aye."

"Divorced?"

"Aye." It felt strange for him to say it. The truth was he was
so freshly divorced that the papers had not yet arrived. But the
day had come and gone, the day he'd marked with a large "x" on
the refrigerator calendar, the day the judge was to sign the papers
and their separation would become permanent. But he didn't
wish to explain this to her; he didn't feel the need to bring up the
memory of a wife who had hurt him deeply, a woman he realized
now that he never truly loved, a life that would have always left
him wanting.

"Children?" she asked.

"No. Not that I have anything against children," he heard
himself saying. "It just—never happened. Thankfully now that
we're apart." He added the last bit as if to announce to her that
there were no encumbrances. "And you?"

"What about me?" she asked. Her voice moved over him
like fine silk and he had a suspicion that she knew what it was
doing to him and she enjoyed it.

"You're American but you have an Irish name," he stated.
He'd wanted to ask about her own marital status or marital status
be damned, come to think of it, but there his tongue went again,
wagging without his brain.

"My father's family immigrated to America a long time ago.
During the potato famine or something like that."

"You don't care how they came to be here?" he asked.

She shrugged. "It doesn't matter, does it?"

"If you don't know who you are, how do you know what you'll become?"

She picked the vegetables off the skewer with long, slender fingers. It became clear that she didn't intend to answer him and he realized he didn't care. She could have sat there in total silence or read her grocery list aloud and he would have been equally captivated.

~~~~~

They were bites away from finishing their meal when the sky opened up. There might have been a warning, had he been by himself and able to observe his surroundings; but by the time he noticed the trees bending deeply and the gray clouds roiling, the rain had descended on them in a torrent. Within seconds, their food was floating.

A tiny shriek escaped Cathleen's lips as she vainly tried to keep the rain off her head.

Ryan jumped up, grabbed her wrist and in one fluid movement, had her on her feet. They raced for the back door, managing to rush inside just as a wicked clap of thunder sounded, followed almost instantly by a white streak of lightning.

Once inside, he closed the door, plunging them both into relative silence. He turned around, an offer to get her a towel on his lips. But when he laid eyes on her, the words froze. She was completely drenched. Her hair was hanging in folds from which water streamed until it formed a puddle on the hardwood floor. Her thin blouse was plastered to her body and seemed to highlight the black lace bra beneath. It further accentuated a slender waist before giving way to jeans that she now appeared to have been poured into. Her feet were soaked and as he took in the petite toes peeking out, he found himself staring at the pink polish and a Celtic toe ring before his eyes moved back up her body.

By the time they reached her eyes, he felt as if he was on automatic pilot. His mind was completely blank, his emotions swept away. He stepped toward her at the exact moment he reached out and pulled her to him, the wet blouse teasing his chest. He didn't look in her eyes but closed his as his lips locked onto hers.

They were everything he'd dreamed about; full and moist and soft. But she wasn't kissing him.

He stopped and took a step backward, separating them. She stood perfectly still and stared at him with eyes that had grown round and huge. Her face had lost its color and as she continued staring at him, he realized she was in shock.

Horrified with his own boorish behavior, he stumbled over his words. "I am so sorry. I've never done anything like that in my life—"

She rushed at him and for the briefest of moments, he didn't know if she planned to slap him or pummel him or push him to the side to rush out the door. He staggered backward to get out of her way but when she descended on him her arms encircled his neck, pulling his head down to hers. When their lips met again, hers were slightly open and she met his mouth with a passion he had only dreamed about but had never fully experienced.

Ryan's arms wrapped around her; pulling her to him so tightly he had to contain himself to keep from bruising her. She tasted sweet and fresh, the raindrops mingling with perspiration and a fragrance that was both soothing and wild and which seemed to envelop them both in a sensual cocoon.

His large hand found her face, the palm cupping her chin while his fingers stroked her jaw. Her skin was as soft as silk and moist from the rain; and as her lips parted further to allow him in, he thought he could never get enough of her. As one hand wandered to her hair, weaving his fingers through the long tresses, a mingled scent of citrus and florals wafted upward, growing in intensity as he fondled her locks.

He pressed his body against her, tightening his hold on her as his other hand explored her back, kneading her skin through the thin, wet blouse. Her breath was coming in short shallow bursts now and he could feel her heart quickening as he pressed ever closer. When she sighed softly, he opened his eyes and when she moaned, he reluctantly drew back from her, his muscled chest rising and falling and yearning.

Her face was flushed, the heat rising in her cheeks in a way that tantalized him. Her plump lips remained slightly parted and as he gazed at them, he realized he might have bruised them despite his efforts to control his passion. As his eyes found hers, he discovered them staring at him in a way that disarmed him. The gold flecks he had seen earlier appeared to have grown and now they nearly glowed as she looked at him. They were tumultuous, the colors dancing under her long, curved black lashes. But it was the raw emotion in them that gripped his soul; he'd seen desire before and had witnessed passion but there was something more—something deeper. It was trust, he realized with a start. As if she was standing before him, naked to the soul and she was entrusting herself to his care.

In his peripheral vision, he could see her chest rising and falling with her jagged breath and each rise threatened to take him closer to the peak of desire.

Somewhere in the back of his mind, the storm registered; the thunder and lightning and the driving rain against the window panes. His senses began to heighten as they stood there in silence, their eyes locked.

His body seemed to respond through pure instinct and he moved forward in one fluid motion and lifted her off her feet and into his arms. As he cradled her there, he bent again to her lips; pressing his mouth against hers, he felt the heat rising in her body as he drew her nearer. Her arms were encircling his neck, drawing him ever closer to her and he wanted to lose himself in her soft embrace, to feel his soul sucked into hers, never to return.

Reluctantly, he pulled back again. He glanced into her eyes as she continued looking at him silently. His legs began moving of their own accord as he carried her through the house and down the hall toward the bedroom. The door was standing slightly ajar and he kicked it open as he swept through.

He laid her gently on top of the bed; she let out a short burst of breath as her body sank into the thick down comforter. Then he was pulling off each alluring shoe and raising each ankle to his lips as he kissed her ankles and calves. At last his fingers were able to caress the tender dragonfly that had driven him to distraction. Her jeans soon joined her shoes and his mouth moved upward until she was writhing beneath him.

By the time her blouse and undergarments had joined her clothing in a wet heap, he could no longer look into her eyes. He no longer trusted his own control and as he climbed atop of her and smothered her with kisses and teased her with his tongue and his fingers, he knew he would never forget this moment even if he lived an eternity.

7

She was gone when he awakened.

He knew he was alone in the house the moment he opened his eyes. The house felt vacant, the soul sucked out of it as if her departure had drawn the life out the door with her.

He might have been tempted to think it had been just another of his vivid dreams but his skin was still hot and sore and nearly bruised from a night of passion more intense than anything he had ever before experienced. His muscles ached more loudly than if he'd run a marathon and as he remembered their fervent lovemaking, the heat rose in his cheeks and he realized that in a manner of speaking, they had both run that marathon.

The storm had continued until the wee hours of the morning, their ardor rising with the storm's thrust until the thunder and the lightning had felt like an extension of their own emotions. Now a reluctant sun tried to rouse itself through the haze of a Carolina summer and he lay in bed for a time just looking at the sky through the bedroom window.

When his alarm sounded, he rose with a deep groan and shut it off. Then he sat on the edge of the bed and stared at his legs as he remembered her hands on them. They had been soft and petite but firm when they needed to be and she had driven him completely and utterly wild.

Finally, he rose and donned a pair of running shorts. He grabbed a pair of socks and his running shoes on the way out the door. By the time he reached the kitchen, he was looking for a note of some kind but saw none. She had gathered the towels they'd used through the night and placed them in a neat stack atop the washing machine. As he sat in the recliner and put on his socks and shoes, he eyed the linens through the open laundry room door and remembered how torrid their lovemaking had become. It had grown so heated, they had moved to the shower at one point but the tepid water had done nothing to cool their ardor and they had gone another round under the gentle stream.

He had washed her hair and afterward had towel-dried it, or at least taken it from a soaking mass to mere dampness before their passions had taken hold of them again… And he would give his right arm to relive every single minute one more time.

He made his way out the back door and stopped at the edge of the patio. The grill top was open and now the grill was filled with water, the charcoal and wood briquettes soaked through. Their plates and glasses were still where they'd left them on the table the previous night. And he realized as he stared at their water-logged food, he'd barely touched his dinner and she had barely touched hers.

The air was thick and muggy and clung to him; the storm had done nothing to cool things down but seemed only to have exacerbated the heat and humidity. Before he lost his resolve, he began to jog, making his way through the same break in the hedges from which she'd appeared before bursting into a run as he hit the street.

8

Ryan had barely stepped over the threshold at the police department before Charlie called to him.

"Chief wants to see you a-s-a-p," she said, spelling the letters to emphasize them.

He half-nodded and started down the hallway when she called to him again. Moving closer to him so she could speak in a softer voice, she said, "There's a dance tonight at the recreation center. Shagging."

"Oh." He waited for her to continue.

"It's kind of a Carolina dance," she said.

"I see." He kept his eyes wide and his expression pleasant, as if he had no clue why she had started this conversation. "I assumed it wasn't the Irish type."

She made a sound somewhere between a giggle and a laugh.

"Well then, if you'll excuse me."

The smile faded from her face and he turned as if he hadn't noticed. It wasn't new, this thing of women flirting with him; sometimes in subtle ways and sometimes not.

He continued past officers gathering to discuss cases they were working on or their plans for the day, past ringing telephones and citizens filing complaints, past witnesses and suspects. He barely heard the hubbub; he knew it was loud, it was always loud, but now it seemed but a whisper against his thoughts.

He saw her sitting in the chief's office before he had reached the doorway. She was seated with her back to him. Her long hair was accented with two long braids that began in front and were pulled to the back, where they joined together. He fought a sudden wild impulse to pull her into his arms and run his fingers through those braids, to weave them against his fingertips until they came loose and spilled over his hands.

Instead, he tapped lightly on the door. As the chief glanced up, he stepped inside and avoided looking at her.

"Ah, there you are. Detective O'Clery, this is Mrs. Reilly."

He stopped in his tracks and stared at her. He could feel his cheeks grow so hot they felt scorched and at the same time, he sensed the blood draining from his face. His legs felt as though they had turned to liquid.

She turned toward him, her eyes veiled by her long lashes. Her face was neither pale nor flushed but appeared as normal as if they had never met.

"*Mrs.* Reilly," he heard himself saying.

"This is Detective O'Clery—"

"Yes," she said, remaining seated, "we met yesterday."

"Mrs. Reilly is here," Chief Johnston continued, "because the cases you're working sound very similar to some murders that occurred in the Atlanta area." He stopped as if waiting for a response from Ryan but got none. After a moment, he cleared his throat and perched on the edge of his desk. "She may have some information that could be of use to us. I'd like for you two to have a chat, find out the details about the Atlanta killings—"

Ryan turned on his heels and left the room. As he made his way down the hall, he could feel their eyes boring into him.

"He doesn't talk much," he heard the chief saying as if in apology, "and he often rubs people the wrong way. But he's the best detective we've ever had—"

The voice abruptly stopped as he reached the front door and pushed his way through it, nearly hitting two officers approaching from the other side. One appeared ready to express displeasure but seeing Ryan's face, he clamped his mouth shut.

Ryan was nearly to his police car when he heard her calling his name. He fumbled with his car key, his anger building so rapidly that he felt as if he was all thumbs.

"Ryan," she said as she reached him. "Let me explain—"

He turned on her with such fury that she instinctively backed up a step. "You might have told me you were married," he growled, his normally deep voice now on the verge of sounding gravelly.

"You didn't exactly give me the opportunity—"

He finally unlocked the door and with a muttered oath, he flung it open.

"Wait a minute," she said, grabbing the top of the doorframe.

He caught a glimpse of her eyes filling with tears and he quickly looked away as he got in and started the engine.

"Just because we had one night together doesn't mean you own me," she said, her voice trembling.

"Apparently, a piece of paper doesn't do it for you, either," he retorted.

With the door still open, he threw the gear into reverse and stepped on the gas. With a startled cry, she released her hold on the door and jumped back just in time to avoid being dragged through the parking space.

"The chief told you to talk to me!" she screamed as he stopped long enough to slam the door closed and put the car in drive.

With a curse, he thrust it into park and got out. He towered above her but she didn't slink back the way others normally did. Though her chin wavered, she tilted it upward and returned his hot stare with tear-streaked cheeks. He could feel the eyes of other officers on them now as he approached her, his face growing so fiery that he began to perspire.

"You know what you need to do, *Mrs. Reilly*," he bellowed, "is go home and tell your boss to send a man here to do the job."

"I'll have you know," she came back instantly, "that I am a *senior* correspondent and I've put in more television time than anyone else at the station!"

"Oh, so you're one of those!"

"One of what?"

He gestured with his hand as he tried not to stammer over his words. "One of those—people—who place a microphone in front of a victim's family so they can see their faces broadcast around the world on the worst day of their wretched lives!"

"There are some victims who have something to say to the world!"

"Then go find them—somewhere else!"

"I am staying here and I'm going to do my job!"

"Then you'd better get yourself a hell of a bodyguard!"

She took a step back and her voice grew quiet. "Are you threatening me?"

Out of the corner of his eye, he realized several of the officers were making their way toward him. Glancing toward the station, he caught the image of Chief Johnston standing at his office window. He did not appear happy.

"I'm saying," he said, trying to get a grip on his temper, "that you fit the profile of each of the murder victims."

"Are you telling me," she said, her voice tremulous, "that a woman isn't safe in your town, *Detective*?"

"That is not what I'm saying, *Mrs.* Reilly!"

The nearest officer raised his hand as if to get Ryan's attention. When Ryan looked him in the face, he mouthed the word "Chief", pointed at Ryan and then gestured toward the police station. Lovely, he thought, now I'll be brought on the carpet for sure. He turned back to Cathleen to find her chewing her bottom lip in an attempt to get a grip on her emotions. "My job is to find the killer and bring him to justice, *Mrs.* Reilly. And if you'll pardon me, you're keeping me from my duties." Before she could retort, he climbed back in his car, jammed it into gear and slammed his foot down so hard on the gas pedal that it took off like a race car.

As he drove away, he bellowed in the confines of his vehicle, "What kind of a fecking farce did the fate fairy fetch for me this time?"

9

By noon, his mood had gone from bad to worse. The anger had subsided but a melancholy rose up to take its place that he was having difficulty shaking. He notified the next of kin to the third murder victim, a terrible task that would have depressed anyone. Yet he stayed to gently but doggedly ask the questions that needed to be asked even though his gut felt like it was being twisted inside him.

He spent the rest of the morning going from one hotel to the next, inquiring about any guests who had checked in prior to the murders and who were still registered. He could tell from the way the desk clerks gave him a wide berth that his dark mood was written all over his face but he didn't care.

The town straddled Interstate 95 and most guests were passing through on summer vacations, staying only one night. No one had arrived around the time of the first murder who was still checked in. He had several more hotels to speak with but as the noon hour approached, he decided to go home and make an attempt to compose himself. The chief had called his cell phone several times and he hadn't answered but he knew he couldn't put him off much longer.

So he'd pull himself together, stop in the police department and get the chewing out over with and get back to work.

He parked on the street in front of the house. The moment he opened the front door, he had a strange feeling that he wasn't alone.

He closed the door and listened for a brief moment. He thought he heard a faint voice so he made his way toward it, moving down the hall and stopping at the doorway to the den. Just inside the door were several boxes, stacked one atop of the other. The television was on and the weatherman was showing the projected path of Hurricane Irene, which was heading toward the Atlantic coast. The aroma of food cooking wafted toward him but from his vantage point, he couldn't see inside the kitchen.

Before he could make a move in that direction, he felt someone crash into him from behind. Two tiny arms wrapped themselves around one thigh but they were so short the fingers didn't meet; as he peered down, he felt like his thigh was the size of a tree trunk.

"Guess who!" came a high-pitched, happy voice.

Before he could respond, a diminutive face peeked around his leg at him. He caught a glimpse of red-orange hair that looked surprisingly like the shade of a carrot and two large green eyes.

In one quick movement, he twisted around, grabbed the young girl and hoisted her into his arms.

"Uncle Re, I love you!" she screamed, planting a kiss on his lips.

"I love you, too, lass," he answered, kissing her rosy cheek.

"Uncle Re! Uncle Re!" another voice shouted. He barely had time to turn toward the kitchen before another little girl almost identical to the first scurried toward him, her arms outstretched. The facial characteristics made them appear almost like identical twins, but this one had golden red hair. Shifting the first one to one hip, he grabbed the other with his free hand and heaved her onto his other hip. Now they both kissed him simultaneously, smothering his cheeks with their soft little lips.

"Oh, aren't you two a sight for sore eyes?" he said. "I needed my two best ladies today."

He walked through the den, effortlessly carrying the two four-year-olds, to find his sister standing at the island separating the kitchen from the den, wiping her hands on a dishtowel.

Claire was a tall woman with shoulder-length hair that was such a deep red it almost appeared to be burgundy. Her eyes were a startling green. She was neither willowy nor buxom but somewhere in between; three years his junior, it often felt like she was thirty years his senior.

"Emma and Erin, go wash your hands for lunch," she said in a soft but firm Irish accent. "Wash all the way up to the elbows now."

He reluctantly deposited them on the floor. As soon as their feet touched the tile, they were off and running, chattering non-stop to each other as if the other twin wasn't talking at all. Though born in America, their mother's influence was obvious, as they both spoke with melodious pseudo-Irish accents.

"What brought you here today?" he asked.

She nodded toward the boxes. "When Auntie passed away, you became the official keeper of the family records. They came in the post yesterday."

He glanced at the boxes. "They could have waited until I got to your place," he said gently. "You shouldn't have bothered yourself moving them."

"It was no bother." She cocked her head to study him. "I had a funny feeling you were needing me today."

"Did you now?"

She didn't answer but continued to study him. Her eyes were astute and after a minute, he stepped around the island and pulled her to him. He closed his eyes and held her, resting his chin on the top of her head.

"You've always known when I needed you."

"Aye, Re. We're joined together, you and I." They stood for a moment in silence before she pulled away. "Are you sad on account of the divorce? It's only natural, you know—"

"It isn't that."

"Well, what is it then?"

He could have gone to his grave with his secret inside him, had she not already known he was troubled. And she always knew. She'd known since she was six years old and he'd never been able to keep anything from her. "You remember the dreams I've always had?"

She cocked her head again. When she looked at him, she didn't blink, as if she was totally focused on every word. "Aye."

"They've become more frequent."

"It's only natural, Re, for you to dream about the perfect soul mate when your marriage has just dissolved."

"She's real, Claire. And she's here."

"What are you saying?"

He gestured toward the back yard. "It happened yesterday. I was cooking outside there. And right before I put the meat on the grill, she just stepped through the hedges there."

"She just materialized in your own back yard."

"Aye. Right there between'st the gardenias and the patio."

"Re."

"I know it sounds unbelievable—"

"It sounds insane."

"But I swear it's the truth."

"You weren't hallucinating."

"Have you ever known me to hallucinate?"

"No, I haven't."

"There you have it."

"There's a first time for everything."

"My first time to hallucinate hasn't happened yet."

She shifted her weight from one hip to the other, her eyes still focused on his. "And what did you do there, after she materialized in your own back yard?"

"We had dinner."

She raised one brow.

"Right there." He stepped toward the window. "The plates—" He stopped and looked at the table. It was completely bare. The grill top was closed and the cover placed on it. "I am hallucinating."

"No. I'll save you from yourself. I cleaned it up when I arrived. I wondered who your guest was."

"It was her." He looked back at Claire. "I've done something I've never done in my whole life."

"You sure you want to be telling me this?"

"I met this woman. And in less than an hour, I've taken her from the grill to the bedroom. And had the most wildly passionate sex I've ever encountered in my life."

The color rose in her cheeks. "You're having post coital depression, Re?"

"There's more. I'm madly, passionately in love with her."

"But how can that be, Re? You just met her. Are you sure you're not transferring your obsession with your dreams to a woman who happened to show up? And why did she just happen to wander into your back yard?"

"She's a reporter. Working the string of murders here."

"I see."

"She's the woman I've dreamed about, all these years. She even had the dragonfly tattoo on her ankle. Of course, in my dreams, it was always a birthmark, but—"

"Lots of women have dragonfly tattoos on their ankles."

"Do they, Claire?"

"Well, what are you going to do about it now?"

"There's nothing I can do. She's a married woman."

"You made mad, passionate love to another man's wife?" Claire's voice rose in indignation.

"I thought God would strike me dead when I found out."

"Do you think you might've asked her before you took her to your bed, Re?"

"Don't you think I'm fully aware of the wicked irony?"

"Oh, Re."

He combed his hair with his fingers but the locks fell back onto his forehead immediately. "It happened so fast. And it felt so right. I've always had this feeling, like I had a twin in the womb with me. And somehow, coming into the world, that twin was lost. I've always lived with this emptiness, as if someone ought to be there who isn't."

"I know you have, Re. I've always known you have."

"When she was here, when we were together, it—it was as though I'd found my twin. The other part of myself. She made me whole somehow."

"Your twin soul."

"She is my twin soul, Claire. I know we've been together before. I know we have."

"Do you know how insane that sounds?"

He looked away from her in silence.

"Look, Re. I love you. But I must be honest with you."

He ran his hand through his hair again and avoided looking at her.

"This has gone on for far too long, Re. Get help. Get therapy."

"I'm telling you, she's here, she's alive and she's not a figment of my imagination."

"She's a married woman, Re. She belongs to someone else."

"Why would God do that to me? Why would he give me the woman of my dreams and then twist the screws by giving her to someone else first?"

"I can't answer that. But isn't that the way of it sometimes? She can't be yours because she's someone else's. Now get help. The dreams must stop. The infatuation with this perfect woman has to stop. You're only making yourself miserable."

The twins rushed into the room and held out their hands to show Claire how clean they were. Water was spilled down the fronts of their dresses and soap still bubbled along their arms. Claire reached for a pan on the stove. "Get to the table, girls, and we'll have lunch."

As the girls dragged Ryan to the table, one on either side, seated him and placed a napkin in his lap, Claire followed with the pan. "It's Irish stew," she said as she ladled it out. "Your favorite."

Ryan pulled a bread tray toward him, sliced several pieces and buttered them before placing them on the twins' plates. His insides were going numb from the pain and he wanted nothing more than to curl up in bed and sleep away the next ten years. At least he had her in his dreams. And she wasn't married there.

10

There was a meeting in progress when Ryan reached the door to the chief's office. He had just turned to go, thankful for a temporary reprieve, when Chief Johnston called to him. As he turned back around, the chief rose from the conference table.

"We'll finish this later," he said to the others. As they filed past Ryan, he motioned for him to enter. "Close the door."

Ryan complied silently.

"Sit down," Chief Johnston said as he perched on the edge of his desk. He watched Ryan get seated before continuing. "It's obvious you and Mrs. Reilly have some history."

"I—"

"Just listen."

Ryan clamped his mouth shut, glanced at the chief and then averted his eyes. He could feel the tension in his jaw as the chief continued.

"I don't care what happened between you two. But whatever it was, keep it private. You hear me?"

"I do."

"I'll not have you in a shouting match in the police department parking lot—or any other public place—again."

"You've made your point."

"You've been in a very bad mood this past year." He waited for Ryan to respond. When he didn't he said, "And I've been making excuses for you. Too many excuses."

Ryan glanced into his eyes again. He seemed to be looking for an answer but he had none. He felt his face growing hot as his anger began to rise all over again.

"You were once the best detective we ever had."

"Once?" Ryan lifted a brow.

"You've been in a downward spiral ever since you pulled that gun on your wife."

"I didn't pull a gun on her."

"She said you did."

"I pulled it on the man having sex with my wife. There's the difference. How was I to know she'd invited him into our bedroom for a saucy little tryst?" He shifted in his seat. He felt flushed and his jaw ached. He'd expected to be chewed out—and quite deservedly—for his rudeness and unprofessionalism. But he hadn't steeled himself for the memory of coming home from work to find his wife in his own bed with another man. Unable to even consider that it was consensual, he'd assumed the man broke in and was assaulting her. Only after he'd separated them and came close to shooting him, had he realized they'd been having a long-running affair.

It was over. Right then, right there. After throwing the man out, he'd packed his things. And he would have left immediately, had she not called 9-1-1 and reported that he'd pulled a gun on her. It had set in motion a string of meetings, an internal investigation, sessions with the police psychologist, and finally the chief's intervention to keep him on the streets and in his job.

It had taken him the better part of two days to calm himself down enough to pack all his things and not just his clothes, to rent a moving van and park it in his sister's driveway. And it would take another month before he found the rental house and moved in.

No; he hadn't been the same since. That much was true.

"My job," the chief was saying, "is to keep the citizens in this town safe. And we're trying to hold down hysteria while you *should* be apprehending the killer."

At the change in subject, Ryan looked up.

"I have town officials breathing down my neck, wanting to know when we're going to make an arrest. Do you even have a suspect?"

"I'm getting closer."

"That doesn't cut it, Ryan. I asked you in here this morning to find out the particulars of the cases in Atlanta. Have you even spoken to Mrs. Reilly about them?"

"No—I—"

"Put your differences aside, Ryan. Control your emotions. Talk to the woman and find out what she knows."

"I've done better than that, with all due respect."

"I'm all ears."

"I called Atlanta PD. They're emailing everything they've got on the case. And I'm waiting on the lead detective's call now."

"That it? That's all you've got?"

"No. I had a hunch the serial killer wasn't from this area; otherwise, he would have been killing all along. He's passing through here. I started this morning canvassing hotels. But when I spoke to Atlanta PD, I understand their lead detective was following the same course of action—looking at hotel guests— when the murders stopped. Shortly after, they began here."

"What about evidence?"

"No murder weapons were found at any of the scenes. We've got a cast of a footprint from along the Lumber River; there was evidence the woman was running and I knew she had to have been pursued... We also found a few items, perhaps four total from the three crimes combined. I'm waiting on DNA and forensics."

"And the task force I gave you?"

"I have them going door to door in a growing circumference around the crime scenes and the women's homes and offices. There must be a witness somewhere."

"What do we know about the women?"

He pulled his notepad from his pocket. "None of them knew one another. First was a drug addict. Twenty-three years old. Three tykes at home. Coroner thinks she was killed between noon and three o'clock."

"Broad daylight."

"Not a bad part of town but one where there aren't too many residences. Several vacant buildings, though."

"The second one?"

"Nurse. Worked at a doctor's office; went for a walk during her lunch hour and next time anyone saw her, she was dead. Twenty-five years old. Stellar record."

"Similarities?"

"Their ages. Their physical description—long, dark hair. Same body type. Different eye colors."

"What do we know about this last one?"

"College student. Twenty-two. Valedictorian. Wanted to be a lawyer. New to the area."

"Same physical—"

"Aye."

"We beefed up patrols after the first one, as you know," the chief said, moving from his desk to the window. "I'll beef 'em up even further. No vacations, no leave, until we have this guy."

"I think we're looking for a lone wolf. There's been no indication of two or more working together."

"These cases are making national news." It was a simple statement but somehow it sounded accusatory. The chief looked to Ryan as if waiting for a response. When he got none, he continued, "Mrs. Reilly isn't here solely because she works in Atlanta and there was a string of murders there."

At the mention of her name again, Ryan looked at Chief Johnston with what he hoped was a blank expression.

"You know she works for one of the national television stations?"

"I do."

"I won't have you on national news in a shouting match with a reporter."

"I thought we covered this already."

The chief leaned back and crossed his arms. His eyes were narrowed as if he was assessing him. "You're on thin ice, O'Clery."

"It won't happen again, Chief. I can guarantee you that," Ryan said.

"That's what I wanted to hear."

"No offense, but are we done here? I'd like to get back to canvassing the hotels."

"Find somebody to help you. This is the highest priority for this department. I want this guy caught and caught fast."

"Aye."

He waved his hand in dismissal. "You can go."

Ryan was out the door in a flash, his long legs whisking him through the hallway. He could feel eyes upon him and knew after this morning's incident, everyone was aware he'd been called on the carpet. Their tongues would no doubt wag but he was used to it. Rumors had started in earnest when he'd found his wife in bed with another man and it had caused him countless hours of consternation that she had been devious enough to remain in this small town.

He heard someone calling his name as he entered the parking lot and looked up to find a sheriff's deputy approaching him.

"Ryan," the man said. His smile was broad and friendly but there was an uncertainty in his light brown eyes.

Ryan stopped. "How are you doing this fine day, Garrett?" he asked.

"Hot and muggy today," he replied. "And have you heard the latest on Hurricane Irene?"

"Can't say I have. I've been a bit busy of late."

"Yes." Garrett cleared his throat. "So I've heard. The murders, that is," he added hastily. "Well, one of the models shows it coming straight over us. Making landfall just about sixty miles from here."

"Is that so?"

"Yes. Well."

"Is there something I can be doing for you?" Ryan asked.

"Just a few cases to be telling you about," Garrett said, pulling out several subpoenas. He handed one to Ryan. "You were expecting this one, the domestic case where the woman went after her husband with the fireplace poker."

"Aye." He checked the date; it was still three weeks away.

"And this one, the shooting in the parking lot at that bar."

"He's pleading guilty on that one." Ryan took the paperwork.

"Oh," Garrett said as if it was an afterthought, "and this one. Well, I'll be going now."

Ryan accepted the third set. Though he'd been expecting it, his stomach churned as he read it: Sophia Clarke O'Clery v. Ryan Kelly O'Clery. He once thought the names would be linked for all time; it was always Sophie and Ryan, Ryan and Sophie.

He glanced up to find Garrett hurrying toward his car. Ryan began a purposeful stride toward his own vehicle, calling out as he walked, "I won't be shooting the messenger, Garrett. I know you're only doing your job."

Garrett didn't hesitate and didn't turn back around. "Appreciate that!" he called in return as he hopped into his car.

Ryan reached his own vehicle and tossed the paperwork into the front passenger seat. Well, it's done, he thought as he climbed in and started the engine. Three years of marriage dissolved. He wondered if she'd marry her lover now.

For a day that had begun in the blissful arms of a beautiful woman, it had certainly turned foul.

11

The two women behind the check-in counter seemed to be competing for who could be most helpful.

"Here's one who's been here for three days," the manager stated. She was a buxom woman with silver-blue hair and heavy black brows.

"Can't be him," the other said, looking over her shoulder. "He stays here frequently. Went to school here, in fact." She looked at Ryan with big brown eyes as if her statement explained everything.

"No, you're right," the manager answered. "He's here for the twenty-five-year high school reunion. Brought his wife and four children. He wanted a suite so the children could stay in one room with him and his wife."

It had been this way all afternoon and Ryan's patience had long ago given out. "If you could simply print a list," he said in strained professionalism, "that would be most helpful."

They bumped into each other as they scurried to get to the printer first. The younger woman with the big, round eyes and pink hair reached it first but the manager grabbed the papers out of her hand.

"Thank you, darlin's," Ryan said. He glanced over the list. "So you're saying no one has been here all week then? There's been no person traveling alone that might have raised suspicion?"

"The man in 108 asked me out," the younger one said, "but he wasn't my type." She batted her eyes.

"Okay then." Ryan rolled up the papers. "If you think of anything that might be helpful, will you give me a jingle?"

They both giggled as they agreed.

He handed them his card and passed through the lobby toward the parking lot. A woman in a dark suit sipped coffee in the café and another in uniform emptied the wastebaskets. Both looked at him curiously as he passed by. He stopped just outside and glanced around the parking lot. It was largely empty; he'd drive around it before he left, making note of the license plates, as he had every other hotel parking lot in town.

This was the last one and he was no closer to identifying possible suspects than he was before he began. The temperature had steadily risen throughout the day and the humidity was thick enough to cut it with a knife. For one more accustomed to the cold and damp of Ireland, this heat was oppressive.

He was also fighting a deepening depression and a need to escape to his house and spend the evening alone with his thoughts. This day had dragged past like it had been an entire week, all wrapped together.

The door behind him opened. "Detective O'Clery?"

He turned to find the manager standing just outside the door.

"It just occurred to me: have you considered the short-term apartments on the edge of town?"

"No," he said, his senses coming to high alert. "And where might that be?"

She handed him a piece of paper with an address. "It's right down this street," she added. "Just follow it until it dead-ends and turn to the left. You can't miss it. It used to be a motel but it's fallen on hard times. They rent the rooms by the hour but there are some who are more-or-less permanent residents. Maybe they'd know something…"

He was halfway to his car before she finished. "Thank you!" he called back to her as he got in and started the engine.

~~~~~

The structure was one story tall and u-shaped with the office in the middle. On either side of the office were three rooms, followed by an outdoor breezeway before the side rooms began. The exterior of each room consisted of a doorway and a large picture window facing the parking lot, and in front of each window sat a plastic lawn chair. As he drove slowly past one side, he noted some of the curtains appeared to be water-stained. They had a pattern on them in contrast with the crisp white found in most hotels; it was abstract in varying shades of gold and brown. Some were open but the interiors were too dark to see inside. Others were closed, the material billowing out as the individual window air conditioners chugged along noisily beneath them.

He parked in front of the office. As he got out of his car, he noticed a swarthy man sitting in one of the lawn chairs along the side. He wore a sleeveless, stained t-shirt that had difficulty covering his rounded belly. As Ryan caught his eye, the man raised his beer can in greeting.

Ryan entered the office to find a small, wiry fellow behind the counter. "Twenty bucks for the hour," he announced, reaching for a key.

Ryan flashed his police identification. "You get many people in here wanting a room for the hour, do you?"

The man crossed his arms and leaned against the back wall. "Nope. You're the first in months."

"Do I look like I believe that?" The man didn't answer and Ryan continued, "How many rooms you have rented right now?"

He shrugged. "Don't know, off the top of my head."

He looked beside him at the pegboard from which he'd grabbed the key. "Well, I'd say," he said, narrowing his eyes, "out of fourteen rooms, you have eight of them rented." He looked back at the man. "You own this place?"

"Who wants to know?"

"Summon the owner."

"Can't."

"Why?"

"Out of town."

"Well, then. It looks like I'll just have to raid the place and shut it down."

The man's fingers began to fidget. He had needle tracks along both arms and now he crossed them more tightly as if he could hide them from Ryan's prying eyes.

Ryan pointed toward a curtain leading into another room. "Or perhaps the owner is in there." He looked back at the man. "Perhaps you're the owner. It won't take but one call for me to find out."

The man moved to the curtain and parted it just a few inches. "Mama," he said. "We've got company."

Ryan glanced out the window; the man drinking the beer had left the lawn chair and the parking lot was empty, the cracked, uneven asphalt baking in the hot summer sun. He looked back as a heavyset woman made her way to the counter. Her breathing was labored and Ryan noticed one leg was bandaged as though she was having circulatory difficulties.

"You got a warrant?" the woman asked. Her teeth were dingy and the front two were missing.

"I need a list of people who have stayed here this week," Ryan said.

"We don't ask that information."

"You don't ask for identification?"

"Nope." The woman sat down heavily in an upholstered office chair that groaned with her weight. "You want a room, you pay cash up front. No credit. No checks. What you do in there is your business."

"And if I wanted to stay several days, what then? Do I pay for it all up front? Or one day at a time?"

She shrugged. "Don't matter to me. Long as it's paid."

"Who have you had here for several days? Which rooms?" She shrugged.

"You know which rooms. It's how you collect your money."

"You're not from around here, are you?" she asked.

Ryan cut his eyes toward her son, who remained near the curtain. "Get over here and stand beside her," he directed, "so I can keep an eye on you." He waited until they were together. "I have no doubt you've got prostitutes here. And I imagine in any one of these rooms, I can find drugs. Maybe a meth lab. Or two. I can get a couple of marked cars to stay in your parking lot, day and night, and check the identification of anyone coming near. That ought to help your business. And help us close a few cases."

"You INS?"

"No."

"Most folks who stay here are immigrants. We don't ask for ID. We don't ask for proof they're legal, if you know what I mean."

"I don't care about that."

"What are you looking for? Drug dealers? We run a clean business."

"I'm sure you do." He could tell by the look in their eyes that his sarcasm hadn't been lost on them. "And I'll bet you know who the regulars are."

She shrugged again.

"I'm not interested in your regulars—for now. I'm interested in a stranger, somebody who just arrived a few days ago."

"Got a name?"

"I thought you didn't keep names."

"Maybe a description?"

"A stranger," he repeated. "Somebody who just came to town a few days ago."

They exchanged glances but said nothing.

"Well, then," Ryan said. "I'll just radio for a couple of cars. Should take them all of five minutes to get here. They'll stay in your parking lot, checking ID's while I get a warrant. Then we'll go room by room. Of course, if there's anything illegal going on—something I'm not here for to begin with—we'll have to make the arrests." He started toward the door.

"Wait a minute," the woman said just as his hand was reaching for the door knob. "We're reasonable folk here. Who exactly are you looking for?"

Ryan turned back around. "Who arrived in the last few days?"

They exchanged glances again. Just as Ryan was about to turn back around and radio for another officer or two, the woman spoke. "That side over there," she said, gesturing, "they're all immigrant families. It's harvest time for crops, you know." Ryan remained silent and she continued, "They arrived together about three weeks ago."

The last murder had occurred in Atlanta two days before the first murder in town, Ryan reminded himself. "I'm only interested in anybody arriving this week."

"Can't begin to tell you who was here and left. We don't keep records."

A warrant could verify that, he thought, as he continued looking her in the eye.

"But there is one," the woman continued. "He got here maybe four days ago?" She looked at her son and he nodded. "Hadn't never seen him before. Got a strange accent. Kind of like yours. Only different."

"Is he here now?"

She looked at her son.

"Hadn't seen him leave," he answered.

"Which room?"

They looked at each other in silence.

"Which room?" Ryan repeated.

"Ten. In the corner."

"You have a master key?"

They both nodded.

"One of you is coming with me," Ryan directed.

The woman turned to her son and nodded. As he made his way around the counter toward Ryan, she said, "Just remember. We cooperated."

"I'll remember."

As the young man stepped onto the sidewalk with Ryan, he nodded toward the side rooms. "Number ten is that one, by the dogtrot." He walked with a limp. In the sunlight, the needle marks were more visible—and were more plentiful than Ryan first suspected. As he followed, his eyes scanned the other rooms. No one was outside, though one curtain wavered as if someone had been watching from the opposite side.

They were halfway to the room when the door opened and a man stepped outside. He appeared to have been expecting them and as they drew closer, he sat in the lawn chair outside his room and waited for them.

He had white hair cut so short it almost looked like a buzz cut. His face was also pale, his brows so light they appeared almost non-existent. His shoulders were large; they bulged beneath a thin, long-sleeved shirt. His neck was thick and the veins plump. A weight-lifter, Ryan thought. As he leaned back in the lawn chair, his thighs stretched the pants' material taut. He wore work boots.

As he neared, he realized his lashes were also white. His eyes remained fixed on him; they were a strange cross between cornflower blue and lilac; the pupils were so miniscule as to appear almost invisible. Beneath his left eye was a scar the likes of which Ryan had never seen before; it was round and raised like a keloid the size of an ice pick but drooping from the bottom like a teardrop was a long, narrow scar that was also raised and reached partway down his cheek. Both scars had the same lack of color as the rest of his skin. He had both hands tucked into his cargo pants as he watched Ryan's approach.

"Detective O'Clery," he said before Ryan spoke. He had a distinct accent and it was neither American nor Irish.

"Have we met?" Ryan asked.

"Have we?"

Ryan felt his ire growing; he'd never been one to have patience with mind games. "Take your hands out of your pockets, please. Keep them where I can see them."

The man pulled his hands out of his pockets with a forced grin that looked more like a smirk and rested both palms on his thighs.

"Thank you," Ryan said. "How do you know my name?"

"You're all over the news. It's hard to turn on the television without seeing you."

Cathleen Reilly's face flashed before him and he wondered what she was saying about the unsolved murders. "Do you have any identification on you?"

"I don't drive."

"There are other forms of identification."

The man stared back at him with a blank expression.

"What nationality are you?" Ryan asked.

"South African."

"Get your passport."

He hesitated for a moment as if he'd planned on retorting but there might have been something about the way Ryan's face was beginning to redden coupled with his narrowing eyes that convinced him to remain cooperative. Instead he said, "It's in my pocket."

"Get it out. Slowly."

As he reached into his cargo pants, Ryan instinctively placed his hand on the gun he kept holstered on his side. As he handed the card to him, Ryan accepted it by placing his fingers on the edges like a photograph he didn't want mussed.

"Stay here," Ryan said.

"Wasn't planning on going anywhere." His voice turned to ice as he spoke. Ryan had a strange sensation as though a chill was moving up his spine. He felt like he ought to know this man; that the man knew him. But he was certain they'd never met. He'd remember if they had.

He returned to his police car and climbed into the driver's seat. He reached for the roll of tape he kept in his glove compartment and took his time putting tape on the front and back of the passport before pulling it back off and placing them carefully on an index card. He could see the faint outline of a thumbprint on the front and a fingerprint on the back as he reconstructed the tape on the card, and he hoped it would be enough for a positive identification.

Then he entered the name into his computer system. Diallo Delport, he mouthed as he waited for a hit. The passport had been issued in South Africa only a few months earlier. The man was thirty-five years old, six feet four inches and weighed 245 pounds. From the looks of him, Ryan thought as he glanced back at him, it was solid muscle.

He scanned the passport, front and back. The computer was slow and while he waited, he kept his eye on the man. He hadn't moved from the lawn chair and he also had not taken his eyes off Ryan. The proprietor's son had been standing awkwardly beside them and now he approached the car.

"Yeah?" Ryan said as he neared the window.

"I'll be in the office," he responded. "You gonna arrest him?"

"You'll know if I do."

He watched him return to the office and then cut his eyes back at Diallo, who remained perfectly still. He was a patient man, he thought. Other suspects might have been fidgeting. They might have risen from that chair and paced in front of the room. Smoked a cigarette. Gone back inside the room and then he'd have had to get firm or perhaps downright unpleasant as he reminded him to remain where he could see him. And others might have run.

Instead, he remained still and observant. Observant enough, Ryan wondered, to stalk his victims? Patient enough to bide his time and strike when the time was right?

If ever there was a man who projected an air of evil intent, it was Diallo Delport. But he couldn't arrest him based on that.

On a hunch, Ryan retrieved a couple of evidence bags from the glove compartment and tucked them into his shirt pocket, along with a set of plastic tweezers.

Finally, the system returned a message that there were no outstanding warrants. There was no criminal record on file, either. The system would only contain domestic information, however. And if he'd arrived in America only recently, he might have committed a string of crimes—including a series of murders in Atlanta and now here—but had remained wily or lucky enough to avoid being caught.

He'd have to get back to the office to have access to INTERPOL.

Ryan climbed out of the car and took his time returning to Diallo. Handing the card back to him, he said, "Where's your stamped passport?"

"You asked only for identification."

"Aye. And now I'm wanting to see the stamp of entry."

His eyes didn't waver from Ryan's. "It's in the room."

"Get it."

The man rose. He was about two inches taller than Ryan and though Ryan was not a lean man and could hold his own with weight-lifting, Diallo was bulkier. He found himself strategizing if he had to arrest him and if the man resisted.

"Keep the door open," Ryan said as he entered the hotel room.

He watched Diallo as he crossed the room toward a dresser. It was dark inside; the carpet was filthy and old and mostly threadbare. The furniture looked as if it was a good fifty years old and none of it matched. The bed was made and as Ryan peered toward the back of the room at a sink and counter, it appeared empty of personal possessions, even a toothbrush.

Ryan cut his eyes toward the lawn chair. He thought he detected a hair and he pulled the tweezers and a bag out of his pocket and leaned in to take it.

"There are plenty of hairs in my brush."

Ryan turned around to find Diallo watching him.

"If you're offering them, I'll take them," Ryan answered.

He handed him the stamped passport. "Why would I do that?"

Ryan looked at the passport. "When did you enter the country?"

"Last month. Just as it says there."

"What brings you here, to this town?"

"Visiting old acquaintances."

"Who?"

"You're wanting names?"

Ryan returned the man's stare without answering.

"Am I under arrest?" Diallo asked.

"Right now, Mr. Delport, you are a person of interest."

"In what case?"

Ryan didn't respond.

"In your unsolved murders, no doubt," Diallo answered himself. "I have concrete alibis for every day I've been here."

"I'm listening."

They stared at each other almost as if waiting for the other man to blink. The wind picked up, sending the trees into a disorganized dance.

"Where were you last night and this morning?" Ryan asked.

"Right here."

"Anybody with you?"

"No."

"Did anybody see you?"

Diallo shrugged. "Don't know."

"Make any phone calls?"

"No."

"Did you go to breakfast this morning?"

"Matter of fact, I did." He pointed across the street. "Walked over there."

"What time?"

"Around six o'clock."

"What about your acquaintances in town? When did you see them?"

"I'd rather not drag them into anything."

"What might you be dragging them into, Mr. Delport?"

"I think in America, I have the right to remain silent."

"That's if you're arrested."

"Are you telling me, Detective, that the law requires me to answer your questions if I have not been placed under arrest?" His voice was smooth and even.

"The law allows me to bring you into the police station for questioning."

"And it allows me to have a lawyer present."

"Are you saying you want a lawyer, Mr. Delport?"

"Storm's coming," Diallo said. His voice was barely over a whisper and he said the words as if he relished them.

"Mr. Delport," Ryan said as he handed the passport back to him, "I'd like for you to come down to the police department and answer a few questions."

"Are you placing me under arrest?"

"No."

"Prudent decision, since you have no evidence."

The wind whistled as it came through the breezeway. He could bring him in now, Ryan thought. He could hold him in the interrogation room while he checked INTERPOL. There was a voice inside him, urging him to take him in. Diallo licked his lips.

He's ready for a fight, he thought. Maybe he wants a fight. And his mood had been so black all day that just maybe he could get out a bit of his own aggression in the process.

Another voice was more logical. There was no evidence. The man was shrewd enough to know he could request a lawyer. And once he did, Ryan could not ask any questions until his legal representation arrived.

The chief said no more shouting matches in public parking lots. Wonder if that included beating a suspect resisting arrest?

Diallo was watching him. His eyes appeared nearly translucent and as he narrowed them, Ryan could swear he was trying to read his mind.

"Tomorrow morning," Ryan said. "Eight o'clock. Do you know where the police station is located?"

"I'm not from around here. And I don't drive."

"I'll pick you up myself," Ryan answered.

"You know I'll want my lawyer present. I'm putting you on notice of that."

"Then I'd arrange for him to meet us there. Or drive you there, whichever you prefer."

Diallo's lips curled in a slight smile. "Looking forward to it. Am I free to go now?"

"We're done for now, if that's what you're asking. But don't leave town. I'll be back for you in the morning. We'll just go to the station for a little chat."

Diallo chuckled. "A chat, you say." He slipped the passport into his pants pocket along with the other one. "Sleep sound," he said as he returned to his door, "and I shall see you in the morning."

Ryan waited until the door had closed before returning to his car. Once there, he radioed dispatch for two cruisers to meet him in the parking lot across the street. Then he started the engine and repositioned the car so he had a clear view of Diallo's room.

The cruisers arrived within five minutes. As he stepped out of his vehicle and met them in between the police cars, he could see the staff of the fast food restaurant watching intently. Several patrons also turned to observe any drama about to unfold.

"I need surveillance on Room 10," Ryan said, motioning toward the motel. "The room in the far right corner by the breezeway. He's a suspect in my murder investigations."

"You're not bringing him in?" Officer Zuker asked. He was a tall, lanky officer with an easy-going disposition. He was slightly older than Ryan and had been on the force longer but for one reason or another had spent his entire career on the streets and in uniform. Ryan suspected he could have moved up in rank and sometimes wondered why he hadn't.

"I have nothing to hold him on. We've got no evidence. And he's wanting his lawyer present."

"Why would he want a lawyer if he's got nothing to hide?"

"Precisely." Ryan took a deep breath. "I'll be back at eight o'clock tomorrow morning to take him down to the station for questioning. He'll presumably have his lawyer meet us there. For tonight, I want to know if he leaves the room and where he goes. If nothing else, we can prevent another murder if he's under surveillance. And I don't care if he knows you're here."

"There an exit on the back side?" the other officer asked.

"I glanced inside the hotel room and I don't believe there's a window at the rear. But just to be safe, I'd like someone to remain here, in this lot, overnight. The other can take the back side. Just make sure if he leaves, we know it."

"We both get off work in an hour," Zuker said. "I'll call this in and arrange replacements for the next shift and again in the morning."

"That'll do nicely. Make certain I'm notified if he leaves." He waited as the second officer returned to her car and repositioned it across the street behind the motel.

"No windows on this side," she radioed. "But I've got a clear view if he tries to slip out the front and around the corner."

"He won't leave without me seeing him," Zuker said. He moved his car so he was pointed directly at Diallo's door. He rolled down his window and called back to Ryan, "You said you don't care if he sees us?"

"Not at all."

"Then he'll see us. All night long."

Ryan took one last look at the run-down motel. A group of Hispanic children began to play in the parking lot, streaming out from several rooms.

Then he headed for the police station. He needed evidence; something to hold him on. He could feel that he had his suspect. He could feel it in his bones.

12

Ryan placed the evidence bag and the taped index card on the tech's desk.

"What's in there?" The technician was shorter than Ryan by several inches and much leaner; he had the chiseled face one normally saw on Roman statues and he kept his hair very short, though it wasn't quite a crew cut. Arlo Bartolomeo was displayed on his name tag.

"I'm hoping it's a hair that matches any DNA found at the murder scenes."

Arlo slid a piece of paper across the desk. "Fill this out," he instructed as he held up the bag to the light. "And this?" he said, putting down the bag and retrieving the taped card.

Ryan explained what he had done with the passport as he filled out the necessary paperwork for forensics.

"Detective O'Clery."

The voice was unmistakable and as Ryan glanced up, he saw Arlo visibly stiffen.

"Chief Johnston," he said, turning around. "I was just on my way to see you."

~~~~~

The chief leaned back in his chair and listened to Ryan as he described the only suspect he had. When he was finished, he rubbed his chin for a moment in silence. Then he said, "Tell me again why you don't believe it can be a local resident."

"We're dealing with a serial killer," Ryan answered. "Of that I'm sure. The method was identical; it couldn't even be a copycat crime."

"But you can have serial killers living in your midst. Happens more often than we'd like to admit."

"Aye," Ryan said. "But someone who kills this many people so close together has killed before. We have no open murder investigations other than these three I'm working on. That means the killer has been somewhere else. Most likely he arrived in town recently."

"Just to cover all bases, get a list of all murders taking place here in the last few years. Get a run-down on each of the killers; they ought to be in prison but if anyone has been let out recently, I want to know about it. Find out where they are and talk to them."

"Will do."

"Why didn't you question the migrant workers?"

"They're traveling with their families. Those blokes are never alone. They go to work with other men in their group; they come home with them. They live in tight enclaves. They even shop together, dine together..."

"Question them. Find out if any of them were missing for any length of time. Check with their employers, if you need to."

"I'll need a Spanish interpreter."

"Try Rodriguez. I'll reassign him to you."

"Fine."

"Go back through the hotel list. Just because a man is traveling with his family or has business here, doesn't mean he isn't a killer. Don't get tunnel vision and breeze right past a possible suspect because he's not fitting your narrow profile."

Ryan nodded slightly but didn't respond.

"This suspect you've got—why not bring him in here tonight?"

"I don't have the results from evidence found at any of the scenes. I have nothing to hold him on. I have Arlo working on some fingerprints I gathered this afternoon; he's checking with the feds just to make sure this bloke isn't wanted by any of their agencies. I need something more substantial; otherwise, we're just having a chat and he could tell me anything. I'd feel better if I have something I can hold him on even for a few days, while we try to put together a case against him."

Chief Johnston nodded thoughtfully. "And you've got surveillance on him?"

"Aye. One car at the front and one behind. There's only one door to the room and that's in plain sight. I especially wanted to know if he tries to leave right after my visit—and where he goes, who he speaks to. And I know he'll be there in the morning when I pick him up and transport him here." He took a deep breath. "He's requested an attorney be present."

"Already?"

"He's a smart one. Wily. He knows I can't question him after he's asked for a lawyer."

"Any priors?"

"None in America. I'll be checking with INTERPOL and Arlo is double-checking with the feds, as I mentioned."

"Interesting that he'd ask for a lawyer but he has no prior arrests."

"Isn't it."

The chief nodded and fell silent as Ryan waited for further instructions. Finally, he leaned forward. "O'Clery, do not leave any stone unturned. You got it?"

"Aye, sir," Ryan answered immediately. "And I will catch the killer. I can promise you that. I've got good instincts; you've said so yourself. It's in my blood. And I know I'm on the scent of a good trail."

13

The house was as silent as a tomb. Ryan made his way into the den where he turned on the television. Hurricane Irene was still on course to hit the Carolina shores; possible landfall was anywhere from Myrtle Beach on the southern end to Virginia Beach to the north. It was a given that heavy rainfall and high winds were expected in town even if it remained offshore until it was well north of them. It would make for one big mess and possibly massive power outages. He knew the police department was putting their disaster plan in place, which also meant he had the use of the men on his task force for another day or two at the most before they'd have to be reassigned. It could delay catching the killer and closing the cases, something he certainly did not want to see happen.

He emptied his pockets at the kitchen island. He removed his police belt with his weapon and paraphernalia and placed it atop of the refrigerator where the twins couldn't yet reach. Then he poured a glass of whiskey and carried both the bottle and the glass to the couch. He sat for all of five minutes before removing his shoes and stretching out on the soft leather. His eyes burned like he'd been awake for two days, assaulted by drying winds and unforgiving pollen. He placed his fingers at the bridge of his nose and closed his eyes. Soon his breathing took on a deeper tone, the sound eventually drowning out the voices on the television set.

He knew, in those first few moments, that he was still at rest on a leather couch in North Carolina but he felt whisked away to another place, another time...

~~~~~

He became aware that he had leaned back and closed his eyes but another body was pressed against his. And as Rían stirred and opened his eyes, he found himself reclining in a large bath filled with bubbles. Leaning against him with her back against his chest was the woman he loved more than life itself.

She ran her hands along his legs as they rested on either side of her, sending a surge of emotion through him. "If we stay here much longer," she was saying, "we're likely to look like two dried plums." She lifted one shapely leg out of the water as if to prove her point and he found himself staring at a birthmark that looked like a dainty dragonfly had landed on her ankle.

"Don't make us move yet, Cait," he answered. "It feels too good. I want this moment to last forever."

She turned her face toward him and smiled. Her hair was pulled on top of her head in a loose, quickly arranged bun and he considered grabbing the pin that held it in place and allowing it to cascade over his body. But he knew the length of the brunette tresses would reach the water and she'd made it clear in a gentle way that she wanted to keep it dry. He knew once they climbed out of the bath, she would allow her hair to escape from its confines and it would surround them as it had just an hour ago during their passionate lovemaking.

She tilted her head now and looked back at him. The candlelight danced on her features and highlighted eyes the color of the Irish Sea. They made his heart quicken as they always did and he reached through the bubbles to wrap his hands around her and press her ever closer to him.

She responded by turning her head further toward him until he leaned into her and gently traced her mouth with his lips. Her lips were hot and moist and she parted them provocatively, teasing him with her tongue.

He lifted one hand out of the water and placed it against the side of her neck, allowing his fingers to trace her jawline. He never grew tired of feeling her skin, so silken and warm. His other hand embraced her waist before moving to her breasts, gently caressing them until she moaned softly.

The sounds she made always exhilarated him. And her kisses invigorated him. He had never been one to play the field but he'd kissed a few women in his time. It was always a pleasing feeling but hers were different. Cait could open her mouth and allow her breath to escape a little; and when he felt her soft, sweet air, it was as though she was breathing life into him. And when he did the same to her, she always responded by pressing closer, opening wider, her movements growing faster and more urgent.

Now she responded by turning her whole body toward him, nestling into his arms. Her legs were intertwined with his; the chilliness of water that has stood for too long warming under the heat of their bodies. The bubbles grew sensuous as she allowed them to fill her palms before she moved them over his body, the combination of the effervescence and her fingers arousing him once more.

She opened her eyes and pulled back slightly as she ran her fingers through his dark hair, coaxing his locks onto his forehead. He didn't care that her hands were wet or that she left tiny bubbles in the hair that fell against his neck. When she looked at him as she was doing now, he felt as if he could lose his soul in the depths of her stormy eyes like a ship lost at sea. He didn't care if he never returned; he could live there forever in the knowledge that she loved him and he loved her and the rest of the world could cease to exist.

When their ardor grew too intense for the bath's confines, she reluctantly pulled back from him, her fingers lingering even as she rose to her feet. Now he had an unencumbered view of a body that might not have been perfect but it was perfect for him. The candlelight danced over skin that was taut and ivory as most Irish skin can be; the small of her back gently sloping to a full derriere that he couldn't resist leaning forward and kissing as his arms wrapped around her thighs. He was gentle enough not to cause her to lose her balance and when she turned toward him in a flirtatious, playful manner, his kisses swept around her body.

As he glanced upward, her breasts enticed him and her hands moved from his hair to her own. She pulled the pin, releasing her tresses so they cascaded across her shoulders and down her back. Her hair always threatened to send him over the edge; it was carnal this hold she had on him, and he felt himself a willing prisoner.

At the sight of her locks tempting him from above, he came to his feet and pulled her to him, wrapping his arms around her even as he intertwined his fingers with her hair. She smelled of fresh flowers and as he ran his lips over her skin, she tasted sweet and clean. He wished he could fuse them together, just like this, for all eternity.

She shivered as the chilly air reached her moist skin and he reluctantly released her. They both grabbed for the linens at the same time and wrapped each other in the soft, dry cloth as their kisses lingered on each other's lips.

When they opened their eyes a few minutes later, her pupils were large and dark, her eyes almost glowing with golden specks that outshone the gray-blue storminess of her irises.

He lifted her into his arms and cradled her against him for a long moment as she drew his head closer to hers and their lips found each other once again. He knew what he wanted to do; he wanted to carry her into his bed chambers, drop her gently onto a bed still rumpled from their previous exertions, and make love to her as gently and passionately, with measured purpose and reckless abandon, as he possibly could.

But he could not force himself to break the hold she had on his lips and his mouth until a sudden rapping at the front door interrupted them.

"It's Finn," she breathed softly.

Reluctantly, he set her down just outside the bath and then hastily joined her, pulling the cloth around his waist as he made his way to the door. The knocking grew so insistent that he heard himself shouting, "Coming, Finn!"

"It's another murder!" Finn yelled through the door.

Now his steps grew faster and more urgent. He forgot the cloth around his waist, forgot his ardor and his plans for the evening. As he reached the door, he half-turned to find Cait standing in the doorway at the end of the hall, the linen gathered around her, her face pale and her eyes wide.

"Hurry!" Finn shouted as the door opened. "A young woman has been found in the lough!"

It was a nightmare, this constant string of bodies—and not just any bodies but those of people he knew, women who sat near in church pews, whom he passed on the roads, from whom he bought cakes and pies and vegetables and fruits. They were his neighbors, his friends, his friends' wives…

~~~~~

Ryan heard himself groan and with the sound of his own voice, he became aware that he was still lying down. And someone was standing over him.

His eyes flew open as his hands balled into fists. He was ready to come off the couch fighting but he found himself staring into four curious faces.

"Did you forget it's date night, Re?" Claire said quietly. Her brows were furrowed and her mouth was pursed.

"No," he said, sitting up. "Of course not." He ran his hand through his hair as he glanced at his sister again. She was looking at him intently with those eyes that always seemed to know what was going on in the private recesses of his mind. "Yes. I did. But it's okay."

"Can we have cheesy rabbit for supper?" Emma said boldly, placing her tiny hands on one of his shoulders.

"Oh, I just love cheesy rabbit," Erin said, moving his hands out of the way so she could sit in his lap.

He looked up again, his eyes falling on his brother-in-law. "Tommy," he said, nodding in greeting. Tommy was a large man with red hair that curled in every direction at once and a light red mustache on a big, round face. He wore a short-sleeved shirt from which freckled arms emerged.

"You're sure you have no other plans?" Tommy asked. His blue-green eyes implored him *not* to have other plans. And with these two precocious girls, Ryan understood his need to be alone with Claire, even if it was only for a few short hours.

"Of course not," Ryan said. "Go. Have a good time. And I'll have a special date with my two favorite lasses."

14

Ryan finished stirring the pot of macaroni until the cheese was completely melted. Then he opened the cabinet and retrieved a cake pan shaped like the head of a rabbit. It was the little things he appreciated, he realized as he placed it on the counter. A year ago, he would have been rummaging through the cabinets, moving pots and pans and cookie sheets to find it. The divorce took care of excess possessions. He had two pots and two skillets, one cookie sheet and the rabbit cake pan. And that was fine. At least he'd saved the rabbit pan.

He poured the macaroni into the pan and leveled it. Then he opened another cabinet where a dozen boxes and cans were stored, neatly arranged because there was plenty of space in which to arrange them. He retrieved a canister of bread crumbs and placed it on the counter before pulling a package of ham slices from the refrigerator. He got a small cutting board and a paring knife and went about creating his masterpiece.

He supposed it had been two years ago when he found the cake pan. Easter was approaching and he wanted to do something special with the twins so he'd bought it with no clear plans in place. Somehow he'd come up with the idea of making them macaroni in it. Once the cooked pasta and cheese was in the pan, he used the bread crumbs to outline the big ears and add shading to the face. Then he cut the ham into various shapes and used it to finish off the ears and create the cheeks and whiskers. The finishing touch was supposed to be olives for the eyes and nose but he didn't have any so he improvised with more ham.

Sometimes dinner was a piece of art. More often, it came out looking like anything except the rabbit he'd set out to make. But the girls liked it and that was all that mattered.

Tonight, he felt as if he wasn't even seeing what he was creating. His hands moved as they always did but his mind was reeling from a bath that felt more real than a nap on the couch and a declaration of murder that felt more like a premonition.

He placed the pan in the oven and set the timer. Before he turned back around, he realized the house was silent.

He stepped to the island and peered into the other room. The television was on, the sound turned down. Oversized coloring books and a variety of crayons were scattered across the low, wide coffee table. But the girls were nowhere in sight.

He placed both palms on the counter. He could see the back door from this vantage point; it was locked, the chain across the door.

"Ladies!" he shouted.

He waited for the pitter patter of little feet coming down the hallway but heard none.

"Emma Lucy!" he bellowed. "Erin Leigh! Get your buns in here this very instant!" He used the most stern, no-nonsense tone he could muster. It was one that could have adults cowering or scattering to avoid him but he knew from experience that nothing intimidated the twins.

In seconds, he heard two little voices talking non-stop as they hurried down the hall toward him. It was a wonder either one could listen to the other, he thought; they were both too busy talking.

As they rounded the corner, his jaw dropped.

They had removed all their clothing except their panties, and had body paint smeared all over themselves. They looked, he thought, like a Jackson Pollock painting had come alive.

"What the devil!"

"We found our paint set," Emma said, rushing toward the bar stools.

He raised his hand as if to stop her but the counter was between them. "Don't touch anything. Stop right where you are."

She stopped as a smile spread across her face. At least, he thought it was her face but it was difficult to find her eyes in the middle of all that paint.

"It washes off," Erin said, joining her.

"And we took our clothes off."

"Except our panties. Because you're a man."

"Well, thank you for that," he said. "The only thing is, dear darlin's, now you've painted your panties and have none other to wear."

"Oh, yeah." Emma and Erin looked at each other in stunned silence.

Ryan turned around and shut off the oven. He pointed down the hall. "Into the bath, ladies." As they both hurried back down the hall giggling, he shouted after them, "And don't touch anything else! Get in the bath, panties and all!"

When the doorbell rang, it startled him. He hadn't realized he was standing next to the front door as he followed the girls down the hallway and now, with the words fresh out of his mouth, he knew whoever was on the other side had heard him.

The twins had already disappeared into the bathroom.

He opened the door a few inches, expecting to see a Girl Scout or salesperson on his stoop that he could dismiss in short order. Instead, he found himself looking directly into Cathleen Reilly's surprised face.

He couldn't imagine what expression his own face held. He was staring into the same stormy eyes he'd seen in his dream; the same long brunette tresses framed the same facial features. He was so stunned that he thought in some bizarre twist, he was still dreaming.

She held out a DVD to him. "I took the liberty of putting together my news reports from the Atlanta murders," she said. Her face was flushed and her eyes wide as she looked at him. Her eyes were also ringed in red, as if she had been crying.

As she continued holding out the disk to him, her gray-blue eyes imploring him to accept it, he came out of his stupor long enough to take it from her. "That wasn't necessary," he heard himself saying.

Her downturned mouth and clouded eyes told him he had sounded rude and he silently berated himself. In an attempt to veil the myriad of emotions that were surging upward without warning, he had come across as a complete oaf.

She didn't want to leave; that much was clear. She'd come to give him the disk and he'd accepted it. And now she remained at his door, looking up at him with those same eyes he felt he could get lost within. Locks on either side of her face were still in the braids she'd sported this morning, the same braids he saw in his sleep, that he'd always seen in his dreams... And he had nothing to say. Nothing could right the wrong they had done to themselves and each other. And he wouldn't allow himself to become a man he deplored; a man who took other men's wives.

The silence dragged on. Finally, he said, "It's not a good time." He didn't tell her it would never be a good time. He couldn't bring himself to close that door completely.

"I know. I heard." She said it evenly, without malice. But it sounded empty to him and he didn't want to hurt her like she'd hurt him.

The door was wrenched out of his hands and he looked down to see two little girls standing beside him, staring at Cathleen.

"I thought I told you two to get in the bath," he said.

"It's rude to keep company standing outside, Uncle Re," Emma chided.

"Won't you be introducing us?" Erin added. "It's rude not to introduce us."

"Cat got your tongue, Uncle Re?" Emma stepped forward, extending a paint-covered hand. "My name is Emma."

Ryan expected Cathleen to take a step back, politely refuse the paint-covered hand and take her leave but she surprised him by stepping forward and shaking her hand as if there was no paint on it at all.

"And I am Erin," her sister said, moving alongside Emma and offering her hand as well.

"Uncle Re has forgotten his manners," Emma said in a voice that made her seem thirty years old. "Won't you come in and join us?"

"We were just about to have supper. Uncle Re has cooked up his homemade cheesy rabbit. It's the best you've ever had."

Cathleen's expression was a mixture of astonishment and amusement. As the girls opened the door wider, she held her palm toward Ryan. It was covered in six colors of paint. "I guess I'll have to," she said, a slow, shy smile crossing her face. "I can't get back in my car until I've washed this hand."

~~~~~

Ryan bent to his knees on the bathroom floor. As he started running water into the tub, he dumped a hefty portion of baby shampoo into the water. It immediately began to foam and bubble, threatening to spill over the side of the tub.

He'd done it without thinking. He'd babysat the girls from the time they were one week old and he'd long ago discovered liquid soap or shampoo in the water was necessary, as the girls were always more intent on playing than cleaning themselves. But now he stared at the bubbles as they mounted, remembering the feel of the woman against his chest, the way the candlelight played across her features and the way she massaged him with the soft, clean bubbles.

"Oh, Uncle Re," Emma said from behind him, "that is simply delightful."

He didn't try to stifle a smile as he turned to look at her. She was standing on a footstool in front of the sink, trying to wash Cathleen's hand. Cathleen caught his eye and winked. The simple act caused the heat to rise in his cheeks.

"Your shirt is getting soaked," Erin pointed. "You mustn't do that, Uncle Re."

He looked back as the bubbles mounded against his shirt. Shutting off the water, he unbuttoned his shirt and slipped it off. He could feel Cathleen's eyes on him but he didn't turn around.

"And what might your name be? We told you our names," Erin was saying.

"It's Cathleen but my friends call me Cait."

At the mention of her name, he felt his knees go weak and the room seemed to swim in front of him. He'd misunderstood her, he thought. He kept his eyes focused on the bath, though the water was off and there was no reason for him to remain there.

"Just like Kate Middleton," Emma breathed to Erin. "She's a princess now."

"Yes, it's pronounced the same but it's spelled differently." She spelled it for them.

Ryan pretended to focus his attention on the temperature of the water as he listened to the twins conversing with Cait. Ironic, he thought; how he'd been so intimate with her and hadn't known what her friends called her. And though the name had never been spelled in his dream, he somehow knew it was Cait and not Kate. He was losing his mind, he thought as he tried to push the dream into the recesses.

"In the tub, girls," he said, coming to his feet and lifting them one by one into the water, panties and all. "Make sure every bit of paint is removed."

"But now our panties are all wet," Erin said.

"We'll toss them in the dryer once you've got them clean." He turned around and then realized during the act of lifting them into the tub, he'd gotten paint all over his hands and forearms.

"Let me help you," Cait laughed, pulling him toward the sink. As she turned on the water and soaped up his hands, he felt as if a jolt of electricity had surged through him. He was fully capable of washing his own hands; he knew that and he was certain she knew it as well. And yet he felt powerless against her as she massaged the paint off him.

"You're very good with them," Cait said finally, shutting off the water and reaching for a hand towel.

"I've known them their whole lives," he said, taking the towel from her after she'd dried her own hands. His mouth felt dry. "When my sister was expecting them, we made a pact."

"Oh? And what was that?"

"I promised her that once a week I would babysit them so she and her husband Tommy could have a date night."

"And what do you get in return?"

"Besides the pleasure of their company? When—*if*—I have children of my own, she will do the same for me."

"You like children." It was said as a statement and not a question.

"I wouldn't have minded if I had a whole house full of them." His voice sounded wistful, even to himself, and he averted his eyes.

"Your wife—she enjoyed them too, I'd imagine."

"Actually…" He hesitated. Emma and Erin were busy dunking their heads under the water to see what bubble shapes they emerged with. Content that they weren't paying any attention to him, he continued, "She discovered she didn't have the patience. So once a week, she went out with 'the girls' while I babysat. Little did I know 'the girls' turned out to be another man."

"I'm sorry."

He turned to look at her and immediately regretted it. She was watching him intently, her eyes a turbulent gray-blue, her lashes thick and long. It was there again; the look she'd given him just last night as if she longed for him to pull her into his arms. And when he didn't make a move toward her, they seemed rimmed with sadness and he didn't know what to say or do to make things right.

"Don't be," he heard himself saying dryly. "Had I known I couldn't trust her, I'd never have married her." He realized as soon as he'd said it that it applied to her as well and for some reason, it pained him more with Cait than it ever had with Sophie.

~~~~~

"I've never had rabbit before," Cait confessed as she settled into a chair.

Ryan pulled the pan out of the oven and carried it to the table, where he deposited it on a trivet. "I hope you're not disappointed but we won't be having it tonight, either." He tilted the pan so she could see it. "And I'm afraid the ham is a bit overdone."

She laughed then; it was so light and melodious that he found a small smile tugging at the corners of his mouth. She didn't seem to be the type to cheat on a husband, he thought. But then, what type would that be?

He cleared his throat. "I hope you don't mind but each of the girls gets a rabbit ear. It's tradition, you know."

When he scooped some food onto her plate, he said, "It's not much of a dinner, come to think of it. Had I known you were coming…" He didn't know quite what to say so his voice trailed off as he sat down. Emma immediately instructed them to join hands for a supper prayer, recited aloud by both twins, and he found himself grateful for the interruption.

~~~~~

"They really are adorable," Cait said as she helped to dry the dishes.

Ryan glanced behind them at the twins. They were putting away the coloring books and crayons from the coffee table. Both were talking non-stop as if the other was being perfectly silent. They'd talked like that their entire lives and yet it still amazed him.

"You like children?" he asked. It might have been an innocent question but now for some reason he felt as if he'd crossed a line.

She didn't seem to notice his discomfort. "I love them. I come from a big family and I guess I always wanted one, too."

He thought of mentioning her husband and how that was probably possible for her, but thought better of it. The mere thought of another man holding her and making love to her sickened him.

"Listen, Ryan," she said, her voice low and serious, "we need to talk."

"Do we?" His voice sounded loud and rude, even to himself.

She hesitated, the plate still held in her hand. She dropped her chin a bit and peered upward at him, her head slightly cocked. He'd seen that same tilt in every one of his dreams. But not the expression. The expression she had in his dreams was one of pure love and trust. Perhaps those were emotions that didn't exist in reality, he thought. And perhaps the woman of his dreams didn't look like her at all; perhaps he'd only convinced himself they looked to be one and the same.

"You don't think we should talk things out?" she said. Her voice wavered a bit and he busied himself with the dishes in the sink. When he didn't answer, she continued, "I mean last night was magical. But this morning—tonight—you seem to be a completely different person. It's like two people residing inside one body."

"Look," he said as he washed a plate that was already clean, "what happened last night—it shouldn't have happened. End of story."

"It shouldn't have happened?" Her voice sounded incredulous. "Look me in the eye and tell me it should not have happened."

He pretended not to hear her but his ears felt red and hot.

"Look me in the eye and tell me you don't feel something for me," she insisted. Her voice wavered and he wondered if she was fighting tears. Refusing to look at her, he plunged his hands into the dishwater and pretended to be engrossed in what he was doing.

"I don't understand you, Ryan O'Clery," she said at last.

Out of the corner of his eye, he saw her put the drying cloth on the counter and turn toward the den. He glanced at her, catching her profile as a tear escaped and raced down her cheek. He wanted to take her in his arms, to pull her close to him and tell her he was sorry for hurting her. He wanted to beg her to leave her husband, to move in with him, to allow him to love her completely and without restraint. But he wouldn't be that man. He couldn't be that man.

She made her way to the twins and knelt down. He could hear their voices murmuring but couldn't make out the words. Both the girls hugged and kissed her.

Then without another word, she rose and left the room. When the front door opened and closed, he felt as if the air had been sucked out of the house. She hadn't even looked in his direction. And for some reason, that made him feel as if he'd been kicked in the gut.

15

Emma didn't awaken when Ryan lifted her into his arms and carried her to the waiting car. She never did and it never ceased to amaze him that she felt so utterly safe and secure.

There was a storm brewing in the distance and the sky felt lower than normal, as if he could reach up and touch it. It was also darker, the stars and the moon obscured by foreboding black clouds.

Claire opened both back doors to her minivan and as Ryan gently deposited Emma into her seat and buckled her up, Tommy repeated the procedure on the other side with Erin. The twins both listed toward the center, their sleeping heads meeting as if by design.

"The hurricane," Claire said, nodding toward the sky.

"No," Ryan said, "it's too early to be the hurricane. It's just a summer storm, 'tis all."

He had always felt a close bond to Claire and she with him. Now as he watched the twins touching even in sleep, he remembered nights when he remained awake as she fell asleep against his shoulder. Sometimes it was while leaving someone's home, as the twins were doing now. Other times, it had been while watching television or during a late-night conversation.

It was just the two of them. When their mother passed away of cancer at an early age, they had relied on each other—she, to work through the pain and he, to work through the anger. It was always anger with him, he realized, as if any emotion could morph into that. Their father had been heartbroken and he thought it literal as well as figuratively speaking. Though healthy at the time of their mother's passing, he died in his sleep from a massive heart attack just a few months later.

Then one day Claire announced to him that she wanted to leave Ireland and move to America. And when he couldn't talk her out of it, he felt he had no choice but to follow. He missed Ireland at times but all in all, it had worked out well; though he had to admit, she had fared better than he.

Now Claire looked at him with concern in her eyes. "Are you alright, Re?"

"Of course I am," he answered automatically.

"You wouldn't be lying to me now, would you, Re?" Her voice was gentle and loving, as it always was, and as always, he felt as though she saw straight through him. Sometimes he wondered if she knew what he was thinking before he knew himself.

"Did you enjoy your date night?" he asked.

"It's not over yet," Tommy said, winking at Ryan over the roof of the car. "We had a wonderful buffet and probably ate too much. Then went to see a play."

Ryan thought of asking which play and which buffet but he remained quiet. He didn't feel like talking anymore. Tommy climbed in behind the steering wheel and Claire looked up at him through the open window.

"You're sure you're okay?" she asked.

"You may as well know we had an unexpected guest for dinner," he heard himself saying.

"Oh?" Her brows knit. "You don't look happy about it, Re."

He looked down at his feet. Why did he feel like such a heel?

"It was her, wasn't it, Re? The married woman."

Tommy jerked his head in their direction. "You're not—"

"Don't look at me like that. It's not as if anything happened. The girls are always my first priority, you know that."

Claire chewed her lip and Tommy continued staring at him. He was behind the wheel now, clearly caught between wanting to leave and wanting to hear the gossip.

"She was good to them, Claire," Ryan said at last. "And they liked her."

"It's not right, Re."

He suddenly felt his ire seething just beneath the surface; so close he felt it could burst through at any moment. She'd only vocalized what he'd been feeling himself but somehow it was different, hearing it from someone else's mouth, hearing the words spoken out loud.

She put her hand through the window to touch his arm. Her hand was gentle and soothing, as it always had been. "Call me if you need anything."

"You do the same." He patted the hood of the car and then stepped back as they drove off. He didn't usually watch them but tonight he felt rooted to the end of the sidewalk. After they drove out of sight, he continued standing there, looking at the sky and the neighborhood without really seeing it.

Finally, he returned to the house. Just the simple act of walking into the house, knowing the laughter and voices of the twins were gone, knowing that *she* was gone, was enough to send him over the edge. He stood in the doorway, listening to the silence that enveloped him. Then closing the door behind him, he leaned his forearm on the back of the door and placed his forehead against it. Feck me for the horse's arse I am, he thought.

The only decent thing to do was apologize. He hadn't just been rude; he'd been hurtful and no matter, Cait hadn't deserved his scorn. He'd jump in his car and go straight-away to her hotel and apologize in person.

He had already grabbed his keys and was on his way out the door when he realized that he had no idea which hotel she was staying in. He thought of pulling out the phone book and calling each one until he found her and then going there unannounced. For some reason, he didn't want her to know he was coming; he was too afraid she would tell him not to bother.

After calling a dozen hotels and being told at each one that she was not registered, he was more depressed than ever. It appeared that even when he wanted to do the noble thing, the right thing, Fate always stepped in to stop him.

He still had her business card from the previous evening and he pulled it out now and studied it. It didn't say "Mrs." in front of her name but then it was a business card and it wouldn't. It also listed the name by which she'd introduced herself—Cathleen—and not by the nickname she'd given the girls.

It seemed like the two images began to fuse themselves together in his mind as he stared at the card. There was the image of her in the bath with him, though it felt as if it was a world away and a century earlier. Then there was the image of her in his arms just the night before. She'd looked at him with the same trusting eyes, the same beauty, the same grace. And every time he saw her with her hair braided, whether it was in his dreams or reality, he wanted to run his hands through her tresses and smooth them out.

He dialed her cell phone number. His heart quickened as it began to ring and his breath grew shallower. On the sixth ring, her voice mail answered.

He thought of hanging up. But as he listened to her voice and her outgoing message, he knew he couldn't.

When the beep sounded, he realized he hadn't rehearsed anything and suddenly his mouth was moving. "Cathleen—Cait—this is Ryan. Ryan O'Clery. I called to apologize for my inexcusable behavior. I had my head so far up my own arse that I couldn't see how rude I was acting. How rude I was talking. And I apologize. You deserve better than that. I hope you'll forgive me but I won't blame you at'all if you don't." He hesitated. He should say more but he didn't quite know what to add. Then the beep sounded again and cut him off.

He leaned over the island separating the den from the kitchen and stared at his cell phone. That was the most idiotic message I ever could have left her, he thought. He wished he could take it back. As he stared at the tiny screen, the digital clock stared back at him. It was nearly midnight. How did it get so late?

Oh, that was beautiful. He probably had awakened her with the stupid phone ringing and then he'd left her a stupid message. And now she knew he was awake at stupid midnight, pining after her. What an arse he was.

He put the phone down and ran both hands through his hair. What a blasted idiot.

Abruptly, he straightened and whirled around to head to the bedroom when he ran straight into the boxes Claire had delivered earlier. With the force of his shoe ramming into the bottom box, the stack began to teeter dangerously. He struggled to grab the boxes before they toppled to the floor, but the uppermost one slid right over his forearm, crashing to the floor like a heavy piece of furniture. He righted the remaining three and then turned to survey the damage. The bottom of the box had ripped open and before he could make a move to stop it, papers were flying all over the floor.

A string of oaths escaped his lips. Was there nothing that would go right this evening? He started to pick up the box but the rest of the papers inside it hurtled out the bottom like they had come alive. I am not believing this, he thought as he stared at the mess. How could someone across the pond put this much paper in a box and tape it shut with one fecking piece of tape? How did they expect it to arrive in America in one piece?

As he bent to his knees to begin pulling the papers together into one pile, he thought it was a miracle it hadn't busted open in the post. He could imagine all these loose papers all over the back of a truck, the middle of a postal center or spread out over the ocean.

Perhaps the gods were with him after all. At least his entire family's history wasn't scattered across the Atlantic. What kind of an irresponsible waster puts one piece of tape on a box?

As he tried to pull the papers back together in the order in which they'd spilled out to keep them somewhat in sequence if they ever had been, a leather book drew his attention. Even as he reached for it, he knew it was very old; the leather was handmade, the binding meticulously sewn by hand. It was oversized but not thick and now his fingers seized it like it was meant for him and him alone.

He leaned back on his haunches and opened it. The odor of aged musty papers tickled his nose. The pages were yellowed, the edges frayed, but the text was readable; the handwriting was elaborate and precise in perfectly straight lines.

The first line on the first page read "Rían Kelly" and the second line began "December Thirty-first, the Year of Our Lord Eighteen Hundred and Thirty-Eight." There was a dash after it as though an ending date should have been entered but it was blank.

Rían Kelly was a name as familiar as his own. He was his mother's uncle, five generations back and the man for whom he was named. It was a family tradition to name the next generation after relatives admired in the current or previous one and for six generations, there had been many named for him. He'd been a constable in an Irish village and known for his honesty, his loyalty and his fairness. He, like generations before him, had sworn to uphold the law of the land and his doggedness at pursuing those inflicting injustice was legendary.

Somewhere along the way, the name Rían was Anglicized to Ryan, though it was pronounced the same. It was that connection to Rían Kelly that caused Ryan's determination that it be pronounced in the Celtic manner. Otherwise, it was just a name.

He turned the page. The first entry had been written on January 1, 1839 though it was concerning the previous night. He carried the book to the armchair and turned on a lamp so he could decipher the stilted writing under better light. It read in part:

It is unfathomable that on the eve of the new year as I was destined to ask my great love to join my hand in marriage, that a terrible murder took place nary more than a few arm lengths away. We had been at the home of the Honorable Judge Rankin, as were nearly all the peoples of the village, welcoming in the New Year with optimism.

When, as the hour approached, I stole my love away from the others. Making our way down a long hallway, I spied an unoccupied room and hastily

encouraged her inside, where I closed the door behind us.
As the merriment continued with laughter and song
and dance, I had but one thought that even: to ask her
hand in marriage.
I dropped to one knee and held her hand in mine.

Ryan stared at the page for a long moment before raising his head. He caught his reflection in the television screen on the other side of the room, which was now blank and silent. His eyes gazed back at him and for a moment, he felt as though he was looking into the eyes of Rían Kelly. He didn't know quite what to make of reading a passage so similar to the dream he'd had just two nights ago.

After a time, he returned to the journal.

I had but uttered the words when she immediately
responded and to my delight and utter relief she accepted
my proposal. But at the exact moment those blessed
words escaped her lips, a scream was heard to rise above
the gaiety. Then my name was called in a chorus of
terror, the cries growing louder.

I had no choice but to open the door and call out to
those who called to me. Then afore I knew it, I was
whisked away from my dear love, now my betrothed, as
a woman had been found in the courtyard just outside
the windows of the room I had just left, the room in
which I proposed.

It was Brighid Beklea. Having only arrived a
fortnight ago, she was a member of a traveling group
that had been performing at the theatre in the village.
Twenty-three years old, there were those in the village
who would not look upon her for she was a member of
the Gypsies and beneath ourselves.

But as I turned her body over to determine if she
was indeed alive or deceased, I could not but notice the
similarities between her and my beloved. Fair of skin,
not olive complexioned like many of the others with
whom she traveled. High cheekbones and dainty hands.

> *Her eyes haunt me still; they were open and staring as
> if she still looked upon her murderer even in death.
> Wide eyes, filled with terror, but brown eyes. Had they
> been the color of my betrothed, the color of the sea, it
> might have driven my imagination to the edge.*
>
>   *Her hair was long and brown and straight and a
> single braid was partly undone. There is something about
> a braid in my beloved's hair that always teases me and
> taunts me and I cannot rest until it is undone…*

Again, Ryan stopped and looked up from the page. The room
was beginning to take on a surreal quality. Perhaps it's genetics,
he thought, this total fascination with braids in a woman's hair…

He glanced at his watch. Logic dictated that he head to the
bedroom and at least attempt to get a good night's sleep but he
was too wound up. After another long pause, he rubbed his eyes
and with a resigned groan, he came to his feet.

The papers were still strewn across the floor but they would
have to wait until morning. He was too tired to attempt to gather
them in the same order in which they'd tumbled out; he most
likely would have to look at each and every paper for a date or
clue as to its sequence and he was too spent to attempt it now.

Instead, he walked past the mess with Rían Kelly's journal
in hand as he made his way down the hall toward the bedroom.
He dropped the book on the foot of the bed and wandered into
the bathroom, where he turned on the shower. He took his time
removing his clothes as he remembered that just twenty-four
hours earlier, he was passionately engaged with Cait Reilly in
this very room. When he drew back the shower curtain, his
thoughts centered on their shower together and the way he'd
washed her hair. He found himself wondering whether Rían Kelly
had also washed his lover's hair. Just as quickly, he wondered
what had happened to his betrothed; it was well known that
Rían Kelly had never married but had spent his adult life married
to none other than the law. He'd purportedly lived a lonely
existence.

He leaned into the warmth of the water, allowing it to
massage his shoulders and loosen muscles that seemed too tightly

wound. But when he closed his eyes, he saw the image from his dream as if it was playing out before him in slow motion; the image of him leading his love down the hallway into a vacant room, closing the door behind him and dropping to one knee in front of her. But when he looked up, he saw not the face of some nameless woman from a century earlier but the face of Cait Reilly, her stormy eyes looking down on him with love and trust and respect.

And then he saw himself rising, his hands moving toward her hair ready to undo those braids and draw her to him when the cries rang out and he was drawn away.

He remained in the shower longer than he needed to, far longer than he desired; but he couldn't shake the memory—the image, he reminded himself, for it could not possibly be a memory—of that long ago night.

And when he finally turned off the water and toweled off, he made his way straight to the journal. It called to him now as though the spirit of Rían Kelly himself still resided within those yellowed pages and he was powerless to turn away from it. So he climbed into bed with the aged, hand-bound book, and resumed his reading.

> *Some in the village profess to have seen Brighid imbibing in opium and say she was reliant upon it. But since they have supposedly only seen her on the theatre stage and have not invited her into their homes nor they into hers, I cannot deem that information reliable.*
>
> *It is known, however, that she is the mother of three children. The oldest is purported to be six years of age; the middle, three years and the youngest, still an infant. They are rumored to be of three different fathers. I do not know. But I knew as I stared into her face that I must locate her husband and inform him of the grisly news.*
>
> *As I continued looking at her lifeless body, I knew an investigation into the cause of death would not be necessary for the cause was apparent to anyone and everyone. Her neck was sliced in one place, not clean*

across; but that one spot, less than one inch wide, was directly over a major artery.

The only question I had as I moved to close her terror-stricken eyes, was whether she would have died instantly or if she would have lain there, bleeding out and unable to gather a voice to cry out. I shuddered when I thought of being just there, on the other side of the window from her, on my knee and proposing to my great love, whilst poor Brighid lay there drowning in a pool of her own blood...

The entry stopped there but Ryan continued staring at the page. The wall clock in the hallway sounded almost deafening and invasive as the second hand ticked by, as if his senses had become hypersensitive. He felt as though everything that had occurred since he'd walked back into the house had been a dream. Perhaps he was dreaming even now, he thought. He hadn't really telephoned Cait and left an embarrassing message on her voice mail. He hadn't toppled the packages, leaving an entire box of his family's history strewn across his den. Rían Kelly's personal journal had not slipped away from the other documents and called to him like a lighthouse in a storm. He had not just finished reading a scene out of Rían Kelly's life that he had dreamed. And he could not be investigating a string of murders identical to the killing of Brighid Beklea.

But as the book slipped out of his fingers and his eyes closed with the weight of a long, frustrating day coaxing him into slumber, he knew it hadn't been a dream. It wasn't possible for a killer to remain on the loose for more than one hundred and seventy years; human life spans prevented it from becoming even remotely possible.

But as his head sank into the pillow and his own breathing lulled him to sleep, he knew a murder that had occurred six generations earlier had somehow placed his own fate into motion.

16

It was dark outside when he awakened. But then, it was always dark in Ireland at this time of year. In the summer, short as it was, nighttime could last a mere six hours. But in January, the darkness set in for eighteen hours a day; and even during the daylight hours, the sun seemed to have disappeared from the skies.

Rián lay on his side and watched the rain hit the bedroom window. It had a more solid sound to it than usual and he realized it was sleeting. It came down in sheets that obscured the view outside his cottage in a swirling ashen freeze that seemed to come alive. It clawed at the glass in a sadistic attempt to get in and Rián wanted nothing more than to sink deeper under the covers. It was warm there and the tip of his nose told him there was wintriness just outside the wool blankets.

He rose onto one elbow and tried to gather the will to rise and stoke the fire that had collapsed into dying embers during the night. Without the warmth radiating in the chimney, it allowed the cold and the damp access into his bed chambers. He knew once he rose, one of the blankets would come with him to prevent his teeth from chattering as he tried to bring warmth into his small space.

Finally, he stretched his long legs out; as the cold had descended during the night, he must have curled his body into a ball to keep warm and now his spine and his legs ached. As he extended his body, he felt something soft against his foot. It was cold as ice and he ran his foot along it for a moment before turning over.

Cait lay on her side with her back toward him. Her long dark hair spread across her pillow and onto his and he stroked it gently as he moved in behind her. She was nude and her body was frigid. He wrapped one arm around her and caressed her in an attempt to warm her. She didn't stir but remained on her side. He parted her hair away from her ear and whispered his love to her in a gentle attempt to awaken her but she remained motionless.

It was just as well, he thought as he cuddled her against his chest and thighs. It gave him an excuse not to rise just yet; his work could wait just a few more minutes. He tried to slip one leg between hers but her knees remained locked. It was so unlike her to be so cold, he thought. She was always commenting about how hot she felt and he could attest to it after the countless times she had warmed his body with her own.

"Cait, darlin'," he whispered, shaking her gently. "Time to awaken." He ran his hand along her side, feeling his way to the small of her back and the tender slope to her rounded derriere. "Cait," he whispered a little louder.

The side of his face felt clammy and he wondered how he could be perspiring when it was obviously so frosty. He tried to reposition it on the pillow but it seemed the closer he got to Cait, the wetter the pillow became. Had she been crying? But he had done nothing to cause her pain; he would rather hurt himself a thousand times over than wound her gentle heart.

He rose onto one forearm and with his other arm, he tried again to nudge her awake. Her name became insistent on his lips and still she did not respond. As he rose higher to peer over her side, he realized the pillow was dark and sodden. Her hair was damp and growing more soaked with every second. And as he stared at it in horror, he realized the darkened spot was growing wider.

He forced her onto her back and as her rigid body turned under his hand her knees remained bent in the same position. Her skin was blue and nearly glowed in the darkness. Her large eyes remained fixed on him, unblinking and unseeing, but widened in a final terror—a terror that seized his own mind and soul as he realized she was lying in a pool of blood.

~~~~~

Ryan gasped as he flailed at the bedcovers in a panicked attempt to escape the bed. His own voice awakened him and he realized he had somehow managed to ensnare himself in a knotted mass of sheets. His hair was soaking wet, the locks spilling onto his forehead and against the back of his neck in stubborn curls. He managed to free one hand, which he used to wipe the perspiration from his forehead. Instinctively, he looked at his palm afterward, breathing a sigh of relief that it was not red with blood.

A wicked clap of thunder rolled through the darkness simultaneous with a flash of lightning. As he lay back on the damp bed, it trembled with the force of the storm.

He turned to stare at the spot next to him but it was empty. And as much as he would have preferred to have spent the night with Cait in his arms, he was glad now that she wasn't there, that she wasn't lying on her side with her back to him, and he didn't have to roll her over to make certain she was alive.

He extricated himself from the sheets, marveling at how entangled he had become. He must have been tossing and turning, fighting some unknown horror. No, he corrected himself; it was not unknown. For the brief time in which he'd drifted into slumber, he had become Rían Kelly; he could taste the winter air on his tongue, could feel the lumpy mattress beneath him, could hear the sound of the sleet against the windowpane. He could see Cait lying next to him, could feel the coldness of her back against his chest and he felt his heart break with the pain of losing her.

He struggled to force himself into the present. He reminded himself he wasn't in Ireland; he was in America. It wasn't 1839; it was 2011. It wasn't January; it was August.

And Cait wasn't lying in bed next to him in a pool of blood.

He stuffed the pillows against the headboard and leaned against them as the storm raged on. His heart was still beating so strongly and so rapidly that his chest was beginning to hurt. His breath came in short, shallow spurts and he felt haunted by the shadows that crept across the room. He stared at the windowpane, watching the drops form rivulets that raced down the glass in a frenzied dance.

It wasn't quite dawn and he knew he had another hour in which to sleep but he didn't want to close his eyes for fear he would see her staring at him with lifeless eyes. The logical part of himself reminded him that he was a grown man and nightmares were for children. But his soul retorted in a furor of emotion that had his insides in knots.

Finally, he dropped his legs over the side of the bed and reached for the remains of the whiskey left in his glass. The liquid burned as it went down but it helped to steady his nerves. He sat there, with the now empty glass in his hand, watching the storm and wondering what Cait was doing at that very moment.

He was still sitting there an hour later when the phone interrupted his thoughts.

"This can't be good," he said aloud as he stepped to the dresser and picked up his cell phone. The caller ID showed the police department. "Aye?" he answered.

"It's Wanda with PD."

"Aye?" he repeated.

"You've got another murder."

17

The outer band of Hurricane Irene was approaching the coast, bringing with it a torrent of rain. The roads were slick, the shoulders filling up with water that the drains couldn't handle quickly enough. Rain was always a problem in this corner of North Carolina; the storms came on fast and heavy, flooding the streets and low-lying areas. Sometimes the sandy soil absorbed it rapidly and when luck was with them, the sun came out quickly and dried the rest. But as Ryan struggled to see through a windshield nearly obscured with thick sheets of water, he knew today wouldn't be one of those lucky times. The storm was just beginning. The eye was still hundreds of miles offshore and while there was no doubt it was bearing down on them all predictions indicated it could take another two days before it would turn inland.

He spotted the flashing lights as he neared the edge of town. Unable to see the shoulder, he pulled in between two police cars and hoped for the best. He could feel the soft dirt under the tires and once he was confident the tail end of the car wasn't poking into the roadway, he stopped and turned off the engine.

An officer was already making his way over to the car when Ryan opened the door. The rain hit him with a vengeance and he held onto his hat to prevent it from blowing away.

"Over here!" Officer Yeldon was a tall man with a deep brown complexion. He walked with a slight limp from a football injury sustained in college that permanently derailed a potential career in sports; today, perhaps from the dampness, his limp seemed more pronounced.

Ryan followed him as they slipped and slid beside a drainage ditch that was perhaps four feet wide and six feet deep. He wasn't a fisherman but he'd picked up some waders after another particularly vicious rainstorm and now he was glad he had. His long black raincoat was buffeted by the wind. No way was he going to wear his nice trousers on a day like this.

It appeared that the woman had been killed on the opposite side of the ditch, perhaps falling with her feet pointed toward it. He could clearly see a wide imprint in the mud where her body had descended bit by bit as the rains pelted it. Now she laid suspended half in and half out of the ditch. The lower half of her body was coated with a mixture of water, mud and blood and as the rain pummeled her, she bobbed almost as if she was still alive. Her arms were splayed to each side and as she sank lower, he knew she would soon be submerged.

"Forensics on their way?" He shouted to be heard above the storm.

"Should be here any minute," Officer Yeldon answered, turning his back to the driving rain.

He bent down to be more at eye level with her. His hat kept the rain out of his eyes but created a waterfall as it flowed off the brim onto the ground so he felt as he looked through it that he was looking at a watercolor painting. She had long, straight brown hair that cascaded over her shoulders; the long tresses were soaked through and hung in massive folds. Even from this distance, he knew she was petite; her frame was small and her skin was ivory.

He took a deep breath. There was no way around it; he'd have to jump that ditch or wade through it. He rose slowly as his eyes searched the terrain for a narrower place to cross. A group of people gathered as two officers held them at bay some thirty feet away.

"Who are they?" Ryan asked.

Officer Yeldon turned his back to the group so he was facing Ryan. "The media." His downturned mouth showed his displeasure. "You see the big black umbrella?"

"Aye."

"That's the TV reporter you had it out with yesterday."

"Lovely." As his eyes moved beyond the umbrella, he realized a cameraman was standing on the other side of her, the camera angled so he was focused on her and getting a shot of the crime scene at the same time. With his luck, he'd fall into the ditch and end up on the six o'clock news.

A fire truck pulled onto the shoulder and before it had completely stopped, he was at the door.

"Can you use the ladder to lift me across that ditch?" he asked.

A few minutes later, he was stepping off the ladder onto the soft dirt on the other side. The forensics team had also arrived, and they were following Ryan's lead on the ladder. The rain hadn't begun to let up at all and as he bent down to more closely inspect the body, he knew any evidence could be washing into that ditch and away from him.

Her face was unlined, her brows perfectly arched. Her eyes were open and staring straight ahead with the same look of terror he had seen in his dream. The eyes were blue and against the gloom of the storm, they appeared vivid and bright, the white surrounding them making them look even larger. Her mouth was partially open; the lips were full and he watched the rainwater tumble off them for a brief moment before turning to her clothing.

She wore a sleeveless t-shirt, under which he could clearly see the outline of a sports bra. Her arms were toned, her nails short. There was no sign of a struggle; no broken nails or blood or skin immediately apparent beneath them.

Seeing Arlo Bartolomeo a few feet away, he gestured for him to join him. "Get your pictures," he directed, "and then assist me with pulling her out of this ditch." He pointed to the swath of mud her body had made as it was sucked ever deeper into the ditch. "She didn't die there."

As he waited for Arlo to take photographs from every angle, he peered toward Cathleen Reilly's umbrella. She turned toward him, motioning; it was clear she was reporting. He was unhappy with his unsolved string of murders making national news, as any self-respecting detective would be. But in an odd sort of way, he was glad it had brought her into his life. He hoped the brim of the hat shielded his eyes and he tried to keep his expression blank.

Finally, Arlo gave the word and joined Ryan behind the body. Reaching into the ditch where she still hung suspended on the side, he grabbed her beneath one arm while the other man did the same on the other side. On Ryan's command, they hauled the body upward, clearing the ditch and depositing her on her back about five feet away.

Ryan stood above her for a long moment as his eyes moved over her body. Below the t-shirt was a pair of skimpy jogging shorts and at the end of some of the longest legs he'd ever seen were muddy running shoes. The t-shirt was without pockets but two pockets on the shorts were both empty.

Then on a hunch, he checked her socks. He found a driver's license tucked inside and he studied it for a moment. So he had a name and an address; she was around the same age as the other victims and fit the same profile. After a moment, he handed it to Arlo to catalog and he went back to the body.

There were no scratch marks on her arms or legs and he had a feeling that she had not been sexually molested. His eyes moved back to her face. Her hair was spilled around her, crisscrossing her neck, and now he knelt as he gently pulled the strands away from her skin.

The wound was identical to the others: it was clean and neat and precisely over the jugular. As he stared into her unseeing eyes, he wondered how four women could have such clean knife wounds. They were more in keeping with what one would expect on an operating table, the patient under anesthesia and unable to move. How could it happen to four women who were awake and presumably able to fight back? The wound wasn't even jagged but completely precise.

He kept the hair away from the wound and moved back a few inches so photographs could be taken. As his eyes swept over her again, he realized now that she lay flat on her back, her bra was even more visible under the thin t-shirt. Her breasts were rounded but between them was something else, something obviously out of place.

He moved close enough for the brim of his hat to shelter her breasts from the storm and then pulled back the top of her t-shirt so he could peer inside. Out of the corner of his eye, he saw the cameraman step slightly away from Cathleen and adjust the camera toward him. He berated himself for not moving to the other side of her, where his broad back could have obscured his movements.

It wasn't to be helped now, he thought as he leaned closer. Stuck into the middle of the sports bra was a piece of paper inside a clear plastic bag. He slipped his hand inside and retrieved it, holding it by the corner. The evidence gloves he wore were beginning to feel hot and sticky and now as he stood and prepared to open the bag, the gloves felt clumsy.

He spotted one of the technicians holding an umbrella strategically over the camera so pictures could be taken and he motioned for them. "I need that umbrella," he said as they neared. "Hold it over me while I open this."

He reached his right hand under his raincoat and rubbed it against his thighs in an attempt to dry it somewhat. The technician offered him a pair of polypropylene tweezers. Ryan pulled apart the bag and used the tweezers to extract the piece of paper. He held it under the umbrella while he carefully opened it.

The words were printed in a black, heavy marker. Then pieces of clear packing tape had been carefully laid atop the words. He didn't have time to marvel at the objective of the tape and whether the killer had the forethought to keep the note from getting soaked or if it had been intended to obscure any prints.

His heart felt as though it had stopped beating as he stared at the words.

It read simply, "Déjà vu."

18

Ryan climbed into his car and slammed the door shut behind him. Water poured off the brim of his hat and he tossed it into the floorboard and then ran his hands through his hair. He caught a glimpse of his eyes in the rearview mirror; they were so green, so wide and so disbelieving.

He radioed the dispatcher, asking who was assigned to the surveillance at the motel. Two shift changes had occurred but no sooner had the dispatcher reported the police numbers than they were radioing him as well.

"I'm leaving this scene," he said, "and heading to the motel now. Should be there straight-away." He hesitated before adding, "Forensics will be here for a bit longer. The body should be transferred to the morgue within the hour."

He started the engine and backed into the roadway. But as he prepared to drive toward the motel, he found himself pulling in just a few yards down the road in front of the crowd of people. Rolling down the passenger side window, he caught Cathleen's eye and motioned her toward the vehicle.

She didn't hesitate but hurried toward him, one hand holding up the umbrella while the other held onto a microphone. On her heels was the cameraman but Ryan noticed the camera was pointing toward the ground as he approached. When she reached the passenger window and leaned in, the cameraman raised his equipment and prepared to shoot.

"May I speak with you alone, Cait?" he asked, pointedly nodding toward the cameraman.

"Off camera? Or off the record?"

"It's personal so I'd say both."

She hesitated.

"Please."

She turned around and said something to her cameraman before turning back to the car. As she opened the door and climbed inside, he noticed the man's crestfallen face. Obviously, they thought they were getting an exclusive.

He rolled up her window and pulled a few yards past the crowd before stopping again.

"Terrible weather," he commented.

She waited for him to continue. When he didn't, she said, "I'm sure you didn't ask me in your car just to talk about the weather."

He slipped the car in park before turning to her. The windows were fogging up and he was thankful it kept them from prying eyes.

"That your cameraman?" he asked.

"The guy carrying the camera? *That* guy?" She cocked her head.

He didn't answer. He felt the sting of her sarcasm and wished he'd said something more intelligent.

She sighed. "His name's David. And yes, he's my cameraman."

"I phoned you last night."

"I got your message."

"I hope I didn't wake you. I didn't realize the time until after I'd called."

"I was still up."

He thought of asking why she didn't answer the phone if she was still awake. Or why she didn't telephone him back. Instead, he sat in silence for a long moment.

"Look, if—" she started to say.

"I'm sorry," he blurted. "I'm a horse's arse. You know it. I know it. The world knows it."

Her lips curled up slightly and she looked away.

"I'm a complete idiot," he said for good measure.

She turned back to him. "Is that so?"

"I don't know why I've been so rude to you. The fact is—" he stopped himself.

"The fact is—what?" she said after an awkward silence.

"I know this sounds crazy," he started, trying not to stumble over his words, "but I don't see as how I've got anything to lose by telling you. I'm attracted to you. I think that's pretty obvious."

"Are you saying you're always rude to people you're attracted to?"

His face felt hot and he turned the air conditioning fan up higher. "No. I don't think so. At least, I hope not."

She made a sound that he couldn't quite decipher.

"Will you see me again?" he asked.

She looked at him out of the corner of her eyes with what looked to him like a dubious expression.

"Have dinner with me tonight. Just you and me." He tried to keep his voice from sounding as if he was begging.

"We've had dinner the last two nights."

"I want to show you that I am capable of being decent."

"Decent meaning, keeping your clothes on? Or decent meaning, you'll be nice to me?"

He hesitated. He wanted to reach for her hand, to lean across the car and kiss her, pulling her toward him so she was nestled against him. Then just as quickly, he realized he didn't want to make out in front of a murder scene; he didn't quite know how he could explain that to the chief.

"I've got work to do," she said finally, reaching for the door handle.

"Please," he said, grasping her arm.

She stopped and looked pointedly at his hand on her before looking into his eyes.

"Please. Hear me out."

She dropped her hold on the door handle and crossed her arms in front of her. "I'm listening."

"You were right last night. We do need to talk," he said. "I can't explain what's been happening to me lately. Not even to myself. But I am a decent man—a good man—and I'd like to make it up to you for my inexcusable rudeness."

She looked away from him at the rain pelting the car. "How?"

He wasn't prepared for that question and he didn't know quite how to answer. Then the words tumbled out of him and he hoped as he spoke that he didn't sound nonsensical. "Steak. I make the best steak you've ever had. Wine. A nice relaxing evening."

She began to shake her head.

"I want to get to know you," he added.

She remained silent.

"I want to know you," he emphasized. "Please."

"Why should I?" she asked.

A conflicting jumble of thoughts rolled through his mind, none of which sounded sane or convincing. After a moment, she rolled her eyes and chewed on her bottom lip.

"The chief wants me to look at the evidence from Atlanta," he said finally.

She sighed. "I gave you the DVD. You don't need me to hold your hand while you watch it."

"I may have questions."

"So call me." She reached for the door handle again.

"I've got to see you," he blurted, "because I've been dreaming of you my whole life."

She raised a brow. "So, has that line really worked for you before?"

"It's the first time I've ever used it. Honestly."

"Well, I wouldn't use it again. It's pathetic." Despite her words, her lips began to curl upward.

"I can assure you it is not a pick-up line."

She raised one brow.

"Tell me," he said as he reached his hand to her neck and stroked it lightly. She sighed, her face instinctively tilting downward to his hand so he ended up racing his fingers over her cheek.

"Tell you what?" she whispered.

"Tell me," he said, swallowing, "you didn't feel anything. Tell me that night wasn't enchanting. Tell me you didn't feel an instant connection deep in your soul."

She leaned her head against the seat back. Ryan watched her intently, noting her eyes as they stared through the windshield at the rain still stubbornly coming down, at the way her mouth moved like she was chewing the inside of her lip, and the way she folded her arms in front of her body again, rubbing her arms as if she was cold. She wasn't leaving, he told himself. That was a good sign in itself.

Finally, she looked out the passenger side window as she answered. "I don't know."

"You don't know if you want to see me again? Or you don't know if you felt anything for me?"

When she looked at him again, her eyes were moist. He leaned in but she looked away and he was left wondering if he'd imagined it. "Yes," she said. Her voice was soft. "I feel something when you kiss me. I felt it even before you kissed me."

He felt his heart quicken and he leaned in further.

"But you've left me totally and maddeningly confused ever since."

"I apologize," he said immediately. "I've been under a bit of a strain lately and I haven't been myself."

"Everybody says you're always rude."

"Everybody?" She didn't answer and he frowned. "Well," he added, "that's something I'll have to work on, isn't it?"

"Well, when you've got it worked out, give me a call."

"Please," he said, "please let me make it up to you."

She looked out the passenger window again. The crowd showed no sign of dissipating. She turned back to him. "Give me an exclusive."

"What?"

"You heard me. I have questions about these cases you're working."

He leaned away from her.

Cathleen opened the door and began to open her umbrella. As she turned around to close the door behind her, he called out to her. "It's a deal."

"Seven o'clock," she said. "I'll be there."

"Wait—" he raised his palm toward her as if to stop her.

"What?" she said.

"Your cameraman—is he staying at the same hotel?"

Her jaw dropped. "What business is that of yours?"

"Hear me out," he insisted. "Don't be out by yourself. You fit the profile of every victim. And I'm concerned about you."

She hesitated briefly. Without responding, she closed the door and he found himself staring at the back of her umbrella as she walked away.

19

Ryan pulled the car in front of Diallo Delport's room. He'd radioed as he neared the motel and now the two officers conducting the surveillance met him on the sidewalk.

He was relieved it had stopped raining though the skies continued to appear ominous. "Any word on the hurricane?" he asked as he approached the officers.

"Saturday landfall," Officer Zuker answered. "They're saying it will hit the North Carolina coastline but they don't yet know where."

"Lovely," he said grimly. He nodded toward Diallo's door. "What's the story?"

"No story. He never left."

"At all?"

"At all."

"He didn't leave for dinner last evening? Breakfast this morning?"

"Nope."

"So I suppose his lawyer didn't show up, either."

"If there had been any activity at all, we would have notified you immediately," chimed in Officer Blake. She was petite but Ryan had seen her in action and knew she was not to be trifled with. "I've been on the back side all morning. But there's no exit from the rooms back there—not even a window."

"So the only way in and out of that room is through this window and this door." He frowned.

"Anything wrong?" Zuker asked.

"Another murder," Ryan answered.

"Yeah. We've been listening on the radio. Couldn't have been him, if the time of death was after surveillance started."

Ryan nodded. Though he hated to admit it, even to himself, this did pose a problem. The road on which the fourth victim was found was a major artery. He was certain she was killed sometime after dusk the previous night; otherwise, she would have been spotted long before this morning. The grass near the ditch was short and well maintained by the city; there was no underbrush or obstacles to prevent anyone driving past from seeing her. It was, he thought, as if the killer wanted her to be found quickly.

He tried not to think of the note left in her sports bra. It was meant to provoke him; he was certain the killer was intentionally mocking his efforts.

"Well," he said finally, "I plan to ask Mr. Delport here down to the station for a bit of questioning."

"Want us to stick around?" Blake asked.

"May as well in case he's a dodgy bloke."

Zuker eyed Ryan with a sly smile. "If he breaks bad, you're well suited to stopping him."

As Ryan approached the door, he had to admit he was right. He had taken down his share of suspects; had chased them through back alleys and over fences, been shot at but never struck; and he'd even wrecked two police cars, one as he intentionally drove through a tobacco field and hit the fleeing suspect because he didn't feel like getting out of his car.

But he had a bad feeling about this guy. And like it or not, he was coming downtown with him and if there was any way for him to hold him, he would. He hoped forensics had something from one of the crime scenes they could compare against the fingerprint and hair sample he'd brought in. That would go a long way toward making a credible arrest.

He stood beside the door and banged on it. "Mr. Delport," he yelled, "Police. Open the door."

Zuker and Blake positioned themselves on the other side. There was no sound of movement inside and the curtains beside the door didn't part with the telltale sign of someone peering out.

"Diallo Delport," he shouted louder, followed by a more urgent banging, "Police! Open the door!"

He caught a glimpse of the proprietor heading his way, nervously fingering a keychain from which dozens of keys jangled. Ryan didn't wait. He nodded his intent to Zuker and Blake and then drew his leg back. He had massive legs; he supposed it was genetics, as all the men in his family were tall and large boned and strong. And when his foot hit the door beside the deadbolt, the metal instantly bent and the door began to shake loose. One more rock-solid kick and the door swung open, leaving both the door and the doorframe twisted.

The three of them were inside in seconds, their guns drawn.

The room was empty.

Adrenaline was pumping through his veins now and in a split second, his brain had registered the perfectly made bed, as if no one had ever slept there; the built-in night stands and dresser, all perfectly clear; the carpeting with straight, horizontal lines left by the wheels of a vacuum cleaner. He glanced behind him at the path the police had taken and noted their feet made heavy indentations in the carpeting. But in front of him there was nothing.

He took long, quick strides toward the back of the room. The closet did not have a door; not even an empty coat hanger was left. The bathroom sink and vanity were clearly visible through a wide entryway; it was old, the surface cracked and permanently stained but no hair in the sink and no signs of soap residue or toothpaste. He stepped into the bathroom and pulled the shower curtain back so forcefully that it ripped away from the rod. The bath was so stained with rusty water that he wouldn't have put his own naked feet inside it, but a bar of soap was still wrapped and the towels and wash cloths, though threadbare, were still perfectly folded.

Officer Blake had been correct; there were no windows on this side of the motel. The only way in or out was through the door or the window at the front of the room.

He returned to the bedroom and holstered his gun. Zuker was standing up after looking under the bed and Blake was looking through the drawers. Upon seeing him, she shook her head. They were all empty.

The proprietor had joined them. He stood in the doorway, looking at the damaged doorframe and then at his keys as if his mind was operating in slow motion. As Ryan approached, he noticed his pupils were nearly as large as his irises and his hands trembled.

"Has this room been cleaned today?" Ryan asked. His voice sounded loud and exasperated, even to himself.

The young man looked at him as if seeing him for the first time and Ryan repeated his question with even less patience.

"I can answer that," Officer Zuker said when the man looked like he didn't understand their language, "nobody has been in or out of this room since I came on early this morning."

"You got drugs on you?" Ryan asked the proprietor. He mumbled something indecipherable. Ryan stared pointedly at the pocket on the front of the man's t-shirt. Then shaking his head, he reached into the pocket and extracted a plastic bag with a white substance inside. "Want to tell me about this?"

The man stared back at him with eyes that were clearly unfocused and a brain obviously out of gear. Ryan turned to Zuker and Blake. "Either of you want to bust him for coke?"

"I'll do it," Blake said, stepping forward. Ryan handed her the bag.

As she made the arrest, Ryan took one last glance around the room. How could he have escaped? With police officers watching the only entrance the entire time, it seemed surreal that he could have simply vanished.

His eyes landed on the nightstand. Frowning, he stepped to the edge of the bed and stared. There was mud on the nightstand and it wasn't random. It was in a perfect pattern resembling a running shoe.

As his eyes moved upward, he swore.

"What is it?" Zuker asked, moving back into the room.

"Drop ceiling." Ryan climbed atop the bed and moved a section of the ceiling to the side. He stuck his head into the opening and then quickly looked back at Officer Zuker. "You got a flashlight on you?"

"Yeah." He handed it up to him.

Ryan again poked his head into the opening. This time he shone the flashlight in both directions. It was tight; there were plumbing pipes and electrical wires strewn so haphazardly that he had to wonder what the contractors were thinking. But it was possible, he deduced, for a man to get into this space, though one the size of Diallo Delport could have run the risk of crashing right through it. Further, there was an intricate network of cobwebs crisscrossing the space, but they were torn away from an area about three feet wide. There also appeared to be mouse droppings on most of the tiles but the few closest to him and stretching toward the back of the building were clear or the droppings smashed against them as if by a heavy weight. He had the sudden urge to go home and take a shower.

He turned the light off and allowed his eyes to adjust to the darkness. He peered in both directions and then ducked his head back into the room. Handing the flashlight back to Zuker, he said, "Come with me."

With a purposeful stride, he left the room and walked through the breezeway, past a decrepit soft drink machine and a candy machine whose coin return had been jimmied open. Arriving at the end of the breezeway, he stepped away from the building and allowed his eyes to roam over it.

"There," he said, pointing.

One piece of the drop ceiling was missing. As he stared back down the breezeway, it was in direct line with Delport's room. He looked down the length of the building in both directions and then pointed. "If you follow this side of the building to the end there," he said to Officer Zuker, "I bet you'll find some shoe prints matching the one in the room." He looked in the opposite direction. On the other side of that wing, Officer Blake would have been sitting all morning, watching for someone who never appeared. Instead, he had dropped to the sidewalk, followed it in the opposite direction until it ended, and escaped behind Officer Zuker's back as he watched the door to his room.

Ryan returned to his car, swearing under his breath. He slipped into the driver's seat as he called Dispatch. "I need to put out an alert," he said. He pulled up Diallo's scanned image from the previous day and read his name. "Thirty-five. Six feet, four inches. Two hundred and forty-five pounds. Hair white. Eyes blue. Scar beneath the left eye. Presumed armed and dangerous. Wanted in connection with four homicides."

A few seconds later, Chief Johnston's voice came over the radio. "Detective O'Clery. Meet me in my office. *Now.*"

20

I don't know what it means," Ryan said, removing his raincoat and draping it over a chair. As he turned back around, he caught Chief Johnston eyeing the coat as it dripped rainwater all over the upholstered chair but he made no attempt to move it.

"Fourth homicide in a week. And she's wearing a note that says 'Déjà vu' and you don't know what it means?" the chief said.

Ryan sat in the other chair and wiped his forehead. It was hot, sticky and muggy, even inside the air conditioned building. "Obviously, he's taunting me."

"Why?"

He shrugged. "Obviously, he's a perverted son of a— Obviously," he started again, "he gets his kicks out of playing games with law enforcement."

"Four murdered women go beyond game playing."

"I agree. But I don't think we're dealing with a typical killer, if there is such a thing. I think he chose this place and this time to mock us."

"To mock us or mock you?"

"Excuse me?"

"Has it ever occurred to you that the killer might know you?"

Ryan leaned back in his chair. The chief remained in front of his desk, leaning back but not quite sitting on the edge of it. His arms were folded in front of him just as Cathleen's had been less than an hour before. "What in God's name would give you the impression that he knows me or that I know him?"

Chief Johnston shrugged but his eyes didn't waver. "Just a question."

After a moment of silence, Ryan said, "I'd bet my career this Diallo Delport is involved. His passport shows his nationality as South African. I've never been to South Africa and as far as I know, I never met anyone from there—either in Ireland or in America."

"So why don't you tell me how Diallo Delport managed to leave his motel room after you left him yesterday?"

He knew this was coming; he could feel it the instant he'd heard the chief's voice over the radio. He explained the positions of both officers and how the suspect had managed to climb through the ceiling and escape behind them.

When he was finished, the chief looked at him a long moment without speaking, his eyes narrowed as if he was deep in thought. Finally, he said, "Why don't you tell me again why you didn't question him at the station last evening?"

"I questioned him at the motel. But I had nothing to hold him on. I was hoping something would break with the forensics overnight and I'd have some evidence to confront him with this morning."

"Do you have any evidence?"

Ryan shook his head. "Not yet."

"But you issued an APB on him."

"Aye. I did. As a person of interest. But he is my number one suspect."

"Number one?" Chief Johnston cocked his head.

"My only suspect," Ryan acknowledged. "I'd say he's wanted on *something* or he wouldn't have escaped as he did."

Major Johansen poked his head in the door. "Dr. Gravestone is here."

"Send him in."

Ryan started to rise. "Are you finished with me, then?"

Chief Johnston waved him back down. "This is about your case."

Puzzled, Ryan remained standing as Major Johansen introduced them. When the four men were seated, the chief said, "Dr. Gravestone is a profiler with the FBI."

"FBI." Ryan peered questioningly at the man. He'd been in law enforcement long enough to know when the FBI became involved, local law enforcement was likely to take a back seat in the investigation.

"Have you studied the cases in Atlanta yet?" Dr. Gravestone asked. He appeared to be in his early 40's. His face was chiseled, his nose was patrician and his jaw squared. His dark blond hair was cut short and he wore a dark blue suit, a white shirt and a conservative burgundy tie. Anyone spotting him from a mile away would have known he worked for the feds.

"I've requested information from the detective on the case," Ryan answered. "I've been working this latest homicide and haven't checked my email yet this morning." Sensing that this sounded more like a flimsy excuse for not properly doing his job, he added, "I also have a meeting scheduled later today regarding the Atlanta murders and any possible connections."

"The murders occurred over a one-week period," Dr. Gravestone said. His eyes were small and seemed to be gauging Ryan's reaction. "Five women. Then they stopped abruptly. A few days later, they began here."

"Jugular cut?"

He nodded. "In every instance."

"The young women," Ryan continued, "all had long brown hair, in their 20's?"

He nodded again. "You could have placed them in a line-up and they would've looked like sisters."

Ryan's mind immediately pictured Cathleen with her long brown hair and petite figure. She hadn't answered him when he'd warned her and now he felt a chill race down his spine.

"We have a profile of the killer," Dr. Gravestone continued.

"Do you now?" Ryan knew his voice sounded skeptical but he made no attempt to soften it.

"Contrary to popular belief," Dr. Gravestone continued undaunted, "serial killers are not monsters. They don't look any differently from you or I. They may attend the same church, may work in the same professions, and may even be model citizens."

Ryan's eyes moved to Chief Johnston. The chief's face was expressionless and as Ryan returned his attention to Dr. Gravestone, he noticed the doctor's eyes had been following Ryan.

"We believe this killer is Caucasian. He has ties to both the Atlanta area and this area. He most likely has family in both places. We believe he may have grown up here, still has parents here, but moved to the Atlanta area at some point. His age is most likely between forty and fifty—"

"Pardon me," Ryan interrupted. "Did you perhaps also profile the DC Sniper?"

Dr. Gravestone's mouth snapped shut.

"Meaning no disrespect," Ryan continued, "but wasn't it FBI profilers who determined the DC Sniper acted alone and was Caucasian?" Receiving no response, he added, "And based on that information, which was widely disseminated to law enforcement, on at least one occasion the *two* snipers were stopped at roadblocks but allowed to pass through because they were African-Americans."

"I've worked in the Behavioral Analysis Unit for many years," Dr. Gravestone said. "I believe I have much more experience than you at working serial murder cases."

"I have a suspect. He's thirty-five years old. He's from South Africa though he does happen to be Caucasian. He is not from here and I have no evidence at the present time on any ties to Atlanta, though my case against him is just beginning to build. I'd wager you won't find him in church. He won't be working side by side with upstanding citizens in either Atlanta or here. And I'd guarantee he wouldn't be mistaken for a model citizen." Ryan turned to the chief. "May I leave now? I have a few murder investigations I am still working on and I can't do my job sitting in here. No disrespect intended."

"I've asked the FBI for assistance," Chief Johnston said.

Ryan raised one brow pointedly.

"There are too many similarities between these murders and those in Atlanta."

"Where does that leave my investigation?"

"For now, continue running down leads on your suspect." As Ryan stood, the chief continued, "But know that most likely before the end of today, we'll have a federal task force in place. And you'll be working with them."

"May I go?" Ryan asked icily.

The chief nodded and half-waved toward the door. Ryan shook hands with Dr. Gravestone, nodded in parting to Major Johansen and politely left the room.

On his way down the hall, he could feel his anger beginning to boil over. What a crock. He was working this case, he was close to solving it, and he knew who the killer was. He could feel it in his gut, in his bones, in his soul. How dare a bunch of academics waltz in and try to take over. And the chief had invited them! Had he lost total faith in his abilities? Hadn't he even said himself that he was their best detective?

No, he answered himself. He said he *once* was one of their best. Past tense.

He reached the end of the hall as Charlie was entering the building. He held the door open for her, peering over her head at the parking lot as he calculated his next move.

As she walked in, she glanced up at him provocatively. "Good morning, Ryan."

"Charlie," he said.

"There's a play showing in town. *Pirates of Penzance.*" She looked at him expectantly.

"Well, I think you should go," he said. Glancing down at her, he realized his voice had been curt. "Seeing as how you enjoy plays," he added. "I'm not one for them, myself."

As she turned away from him she half-nodded, disappointment on her face.

He started through the door and then abruptly turned around. "Charlie?"

She stopped and looked back at him.

"Which theatre?"

21

The front doors to the theatre were closed and locked and the sign listed their hours as 6:00 PM to 10:00 PM. A billboard advertised *The Pirates of Penzance* showing this evening, as it had every night this past week.

Ryan glanced at his watch. It was only mid-morning, though it felt much later than that. He stepped away from the theatre door and studied the building. He didn't know much if anything about live productions but he assumed they needed to rehearse.

On a whim, he walked around the red brick building until he found a side door. It was closed but unlocked, and he wandered inside.

He found himself in a small alcove. There was a door to one side and a stairway directly ahead. He decided to take the stairs, which ended two floors up at the management office. As he walked in, a bell chimed. There was no one in the front office and as he started through to an adjoining office, a gentleman stepped out.

"May I help you?"

Ryan displayed his identification. "Detective Ryan O'Clery," he said. "Are you the manager here?"

"Yes. Kevin Huntington."

"I'm working a series of murder investigations—"

"I've been hearing about them." He looked at Ryan with a curious expression.

He pulled a photograph out of his pocket and handed it to him. "This was the first victim. I was wondering if you'd ever seen her before?"

The manager took the photograph to a broad window, where he stared at it under the light. When he turned around, he handed it back to Ryan. "Yes. She came in with the theatre group downstairs."

"The group performing *The Pirates of Penzance?*"

"Yes."

"They're here now?"

"Come with me." Kevin led him through the outer office and down the hall to a set of double doors. As soon as he opened them, Ryan heard the voices. He found himself in a darkened theatre balcony and as he and the manager ventured toward the center, he looked down at the stage below.

"You see that woman standing there, just off-center?" Kevin asked.

Ryan nodded. "Aye."

"She's playing the role of Mabel." Glancing at Ryan out of the corner of his eye, he added, "It's the main female role. You see, Frederick falls in love with her and—oh, never mind. The young lady who was killed, the lady in your picture, was her understudy."

"Is there a chance I could have a word with her?"

"I'll walk you down there myself."

~~~~~

"Yes, of course I know her," Madeleine Grady said. "We've had this production on the road for close to four months now. She's been my understudy."

"Meaning?"

"If something happened to me, she's ready to step into the role at a moment's notice. Was ready," she corrected herself. She nodded toward another young woman standing in the wings. "She's been hired to replace her."

Ryan reached into his jacket's inner pocket and pulled out photographs of the other victims and the scanned passport for Diallo Delport. He handed the suspect's photograph to Madeleine. "Is he with your production?"

"No," she said immediately. "I've never seen him before."

"Are you certain?"

She handed the photograph back to him. "I'd know if I'd ever seen him before. He looks spooky."

Ryan half-smiled. "I suppose he does." He waved his hand toward the others, who had stopped their rehearsal and were watching them. "If he isn't an actor, could he be part of the production in some other capacity? Helping to put up the set perhaps?"

She shook her head again. "No. You can ask anybody here. It's a small group and we all know each other pretty well. We'd have to, traveling from one place to another like we do. We're not on Broadway, you know. Each of us has to help in ways other than acting the parts."

Ryan thought of saying no, he didn't know; he hadn't a clue what was involved. But as he studied each of the people gathered on and around the stage, he knew it didn't matter.

"But your understudy," he said, "she was from around here."

"Yes. She was very excited about the possibility of appearing in her hometown." Her voice grew softer. "We'd been rehearsing earlier, just like we're doing now. Acoustics tend to be different in every theatre." She looked at him curiously. "We'd just broken for lunch and Sara said she wanted to take a walk. She'd seen some interesting architecture a few blocks from here… She never came back."

Ryan felt the skin at the base of his neck grow cold and prickly. "Is it possible he wandered in," he said, tapping the photograph of Delport, "and watched a rehearsal?"

"Not him. We would have seen anybody watching us. I would have remembered him."

Reluctantly, Ryan returned the photograph to his pocket. "How long will you be performing here?"

"Tomorrow's our last night."

He nodded. "Thank you for your time." He started to take a step away when he stopped and turned back. She was still standing in the same position and had obviously been watching him. She had long brown hair that spilled over her shoulders. She might have been in her early twenties, Ryan thought. "Ms. Grady, I'd advise the members of your troupe here to stay together. Don't go wandering off alone."

Her face paled.

"Just a precaution. No need for alarm. But it's always a good practice, especially in a strange town." Before she could respond further, he made his way toward the stairwell and the side door. The manager followed him onto the sidewalk.

"You don't think the killer is associated with this production, do you?"

"Apparently not," Ryan answered. Though the sky was filled with ominous looking clouds, the air was very still and there was a strange sensation to it. The calm before the storm, he thought. It was going to be a bad storm; he could feel it. "I'm just exploring all the possibilities."

"You know," he called after him as Ryan started to walk away, "we have closed circuit cameras. Would you like to review the tapes?"

22

The air was filled with the sounds of voices and ringing phones. But as Ryan sat at his desk, his eyes riveted to the computer screen, the phones sounded no louder than insects buzzing and the voices seemed to fade into the distance. He was vaguely aware that police officers and staff had created a constant stream past his desk and a variety of citizens and suspects were lined up in chairs along the wall, waiting to be interviewed on various cases. But they were nameless and faceless and created no more of an impression upon him than wisps of air.

He occasionally glanced up to view the row of television screens suspended from the ceiling a few yards away. Each was set to a different 24-hour news station. But when he looked back at his computer, he couldn't remember what he'd just viewed on the TV sets; the images had become just a hodge-podge of different colors moving around on flat screens.

He had opened every attachment the Atlanta homicide detective had emailed him and reviewed every case. The murders were eerily similar and the victims' profiles nearly identical. He had looked at all the autopsy photographs as well as pictures of the victims when they were alive, provided by their families to the media and police. When he placed them side-by-side with his own cases, the faces blended together in one constant stream of long brown hair and pale faces, of young women whose lives had been cut suddenly short, of victims who had not been sexually molested or robbed but their throats cleanly sliced.

The Atlanta task force was pursuing a medical connection, believing only a doctor, coroner or someone else intimately familiar with the human body could manage to slice each woman's throat in precisely the same location. But they had no evidence.

There had been no fingerprints or DNA left at any of the crime scenes. The killer had to have worn gloves, he thought, such as latex gloves worn by surgeons or others in the medical profession. But they hadn't found even one fiber or a single hair that could link anyone to any of the crimes.

Then suddenly, they stopped. Days later, Ryan had responded to the first of the string of homicides.

Atlanta was surrounded by a network of interstates. This town straddled a major artery in the southeastern corner of North Carolina. To get here from Atlanta, the fastest route was Interstate 20 to Florence, South Carolina, where the killer would have picked up Interstate 95 and ridden it straight into town. That left dozens of cities and towns between them virtually untouched.

Then why here and why now?

As he continued staring at the photographs, he wondered at the killer's choices. The victims were not random in age, sex, race or physical characteristics. He wasn't like the DC Sniper who killed a man or a woman, young or old, black or white. He didn't kill from a distance. He carefully selected his victims based on very specific physical characteristics. And then he killed them up close—close enough to feel their blood on him when the jugular was sliced. Close enough to look into their eyes and see their terror as they lay dying.

He wore an earpiece so he could listen to each of the news reports presented by Cathleen Reilly. She had carefully placed each one in chronological order for him on the DVD delivered the previous night. He found himself going through each one at least twice. It was inevitable that the first time through, he focused more on the woman doing the reporting than the report itself; so after the first time through, he repeated the segment, sometimes closing his eyes so he could hear the report and allow the words to sink in.

None of the victims knew one another. Atlanta police, like Ryan's own task force, had interviewed each family and turned over each stone. They looked for someone who wanted that specific woman dead—a jilted lover, an estranged spouse, a disgruntled coworker, a disagreeable neighbor. But in each instance, they came up empty-handed.

There was only one difference between the two sets of cases: the killer had not taunted Atlanta police. There had been no message left on any of the victims, no cryptic note to provoke the lead investigator.

Ryan turned back to the copies of the theatre videos. He began when the doors opened and watched as patrons filed past the front doors. In each instance where he spotted a flash of white hair, he quickly found it to be an elderly man or woman and usually accompanied by what appeared to be a spouse or friend. He watched the side door as the play's members or production crew filtered in; none of them remotely resembled Delport. As the ticker time counted toward 7:00 pm, the crowds dwindled. Ryan presumed it was because they were already seated and awaiting the start of the play.

After that, there were occasional passersby on the sidewalk in front of the theatre and one of the staff members stepped outside to catch a smoke.

He was just about to stop wasting his time when he saw a flash of white at the edge of the screen. He leaned in closer to the computer screen as he watched Diallo Delport walk toward the theatre entrance, his hands in the pockets of his casual slacks. The employee held the door open for him before snuffing out the cigarette on the sidewalk and following him into the lobby.

Ryan marked the time stamp and location and then switched to the theatre audience. He fast-forwarded the video until after the time Delport had entered the lobby. He didn't wait long before the back door to the room opened; it was hard to miss, as the theatre was dimmed but a swath of light peeked in as the door was opened. He followed the white hair and pale skin to a seat in the middle, toward the front.

Delport sat nearly motionless throughout the play. He did not appear to give anyone in the audience more than a passing glance but kept his eyes straight ahead on the stage.

The understudy never took the stage and as far as Ryan could ascertain, she was never visible. So had his intended target been Madeleine Grady? She had been on the stage quite a bit and she also fit the profile of the victims.

He leaned back in his chair and steepled his hands in front of him.

So he could place Delport in the theatre the night before the understudy was killed. What did that prove?

Absolutely nothing.

Just as he couldn't charge anyone else at the theatre that evening with the murder, it wasn't sufficient evidence to charge Delport. In fact, he reasoned, it wasn't evidence at all. It wasn't even circumstantial.

He fast-forwarded toward the end of the play to determine whether Delport had made his way backstage afterward. Perhaps he'd engaged in conversation or had stood by and observed the understudy. But before he could reach the end, Delport stood up abruptly and left.

So he'd arrived late and left early. And as far as he could tell, he had never come in direct contact with anyone in the production.

Next, Ryan logged into INTERPOL and searched for information on Delport but came up empty-handed. He uploaded Delport's photograph from his passport and requested a facial recognition check. He received an instant notification that results would be sent to him via email. He typed in his email address and other requested information.

He glanced at his watch. It was approaching one o'clock. He hadn't eaten all day and his stomach was beginning to growl. He pulled out the case information on the second murder. He would be paying the doctor's office a visit next. Maybe he could grab a bite to eat on the way.

He'd just stood up and begun tidying his desk when Officer Zuker said, "There's your girl."

He looked up to see Cathleen Reilly at the scene of the latest murder. It was raining heavily and she had to turn to the side so the cameraman could pan past the umbrella. He zoomed in on the victim's body as Ryan knelt down to look for pockets and possible identification. The camera caught him peering down the front of her t-shirt but thank heaven it showed him with the evidence tweezers pulling the plastic bag out; otherwise, he might have looked like a pervert.

"Turn it up," Ryan said. The officer rolled to the next desk and retrieved the remote. He turned it up just as Diallo Delport's photograph was plastered across the screen. Cathleen's voice could be heard in the background, describing Delport and stressing the fact that he was wanted for questioning in the case.

When the screen returned to Cathleen, Ryan found himself staring at her high heels and the way her slim ankles angled upward, providing a distant view of her dragonfly tattoo. Her raincoat fell just above the knee and as he stared at her legs, he couldn't believe they had made love moments after meeting. It felt surreal. His dreams felt surreal as well and he found them beginning to fuse with reality. Had he washed her hair in the shower? Or had they taken a long bubble bath together?

He shook his head and finished tidying his desk. Then without a word, he left the station. He had work to do.

23

Ryan sat in an exam room and looked over his notes. After arriving at the doctor's office unannounced, the office manager provided the room so he could interview the staff in private. It was relatively quiet there; each time the door was opened, he could hear a myriad of voices and patients and staff shuffling along the hallway. He was grateful for the silence now. It gave him an opportunity to think and hopefully connect the dots.

He'd interviewed two nurses who had worked with the second victim, a registered nurse by the name of Jade Leigh. He'd also interviewed the office manager and now he was waiting for the receptionist to join him. He wanted to interview the doctor but unlike most professions in which he could derail someone else's well-planned schedule, doctors were often a different breed. He'd already been advised that he would be sandwiched in between patients and he was debating whether to wait.

He'd determined from everyone he'd interviewed, both today and on the day of her murder, that she was an exemplary employee and citizen. Involved in several civic organizations and charities, she rarely missed work, was seldom late, knew her job and did it well.

The door opened and the receptionist walked in. Ryan rose and shook her hand. He'd given her his business card when he'd first walked in and he noticed she still held it in her hand.

"I just want to ask you a few questions about Jade," he said. The receptionist appeared to be nervously eyeing his notepad and he tried to make his voice casual without sounding flippant. "I'm just trying to reconstruct her last day."

She nodded and sat on a stool across from him.

"Your name is—"

"Shelley Mae Pera."

"Ms. Pera," he said, writing down the name, "you're the receptionist here?"

"Yes."

"And you were working the day Jade disappeared."

"That's right."

"Do you remember what her morning was like?"

"It was like every other morning. We unlocked the front doors at eight o'clock and we already had several patients waiting. Jade started bringing them back, checking their vitals, before the doctor saw them…" She dabbed at the corner of her eye.

"And did she work with the patients all morning?"

Shelley nodded.

"Did she get any phone calls? Anything out of the ordinary?"

"We try not to interrupt the nurses or the doctor while they're seeing patients. So I take messages and they usually return them after lunch."

"And were there any messages for her that morning?"

"Usual stuff. Mrs. Landon called about her prescription needing to be refilled. Mr. Grey was experiencing heart palpitations and thought his medicine needed to be adjusted…"

"Can you get me a list of messages she received that morning?"

"I guess so. It's patient information; I'll have to check with the doctor."

"I understand." Ryan scribbled a few notes. "Did Jade leave at any time that morning? Run an errand or anything?"

Shelley shook her head. "Just when she left at lunch."

"Tell me about that. Do you remember what time she left?"

"Of course I do. She always left at twelve o'clock. We close the office at twelve and reopen at one thirty. Sometimes we still have patients finishing up… But on that day, we were done by noon."

"So she left at noon. Did she tell anyone where she was going?"

"She didn't have to. We all knew her routine. It never varied. We tried to get her to go to lunch with us sometimes, but she never wanted to." She hastily added, "It wasn't like she didn't like us or anything. She just had her routine."

"And what was that routine, precisely?"

"What country are you from?"

"Ireland. How does that factor into her routine?"

Shelley smiled sheepishly. "I guess it doesn't."

"She left at noon. Where did she go?"

"She has—had—a circuit she walked. Three miles. She'd lost close to fifty pounds and wanted to lose another ten. She did a circle out of the office park and into the residential neighborhood next door."

"Which way did she start off? Left or right?"

"Right. Always right."

Ryan nodded. Her information was identical to what he had received from the other two coworkers. A creature of habit, she left each day at precisely twelve o'clock, walked three miles through the adjoining residential area, and then drank a smoothie at her desk while she answered emails.

"So on this day, she went on her walk as usual."

"Yes, sir."

"Did you happen to notice anyone about? Someone you didn't often see hanging around?"

"No."

"When did you become alarmed that she hadn't returned?"

"I got back from my lunch at a quarter till one. I thought it was unusual that she wasn't at her desk. She always had a milkshake thing she concocted. Part of her diet."

He looked through his notes. "And at a quarter after one, you decided to call the police."

"We all decided. But Dr. Bridges made the call."

Ryan knew the rest of the story. Shelley was obviously on the verge of tears and he knew there was no point in discussing what happened after that.

Just two blocks from the doctor's office was a cemetery and by early afternoon, a family and friends of a recently deceased individual were beginning to gather for the funeral when someone spotted Jade's body propped up against a headstone. He determined that shortly after she left for her daily walk, she was killed on the sidewalk as she passed the cemetery; the amount of blood on the sidewalk and the adjacent brick wall was enough to show that the jugular had sprayed heavily. Her body had been dragged through a break in the wall and propped against the headstone—in full view of a plot that had been dug just that morning.

It was as if the killer wanted the body found promptly.

He watched Shelley dab at her eyes for a moment. "Thank you," he said. He could make his voice soft when it needed to be and he hoped he sounded comforting. "I know this has been difficult for you. I appreciate your time."

She rose but made no move to open the door. "I don't understand it," she said. "Jade was nice to everybody. And everybody liked her. She always went the extra mile for every patient, no matter how much extra work it meant for her. Even the guy who showed up that morning without an appointment—"

Ryan jerked his head up from his notepad. "What guy?"

"He wasn't even our patient. He was from out of town, just passing through, and he said he'd had blood pressure problems and asked if she could just take his blood pressure."

"You get that sort of thing often?"

"Almost never."

"Do you remember what this man looked like?"

"I don't know if I'll ever forget him. He was albino or something."

Ryan pulled the photograph of Diallo Delport from his pocket. He'd shown it to the nurses during their interviews but they hadn't recognized him. Handing it to the receptionist, he knew immediately that she'd seen him before. Her face became very pale and beads of perspiration broke out.

"That's him."

"You said he just stopped in for a blood pressure check?"

"Yes. We hadn't even called back the first patient yet. Jade was in the front office when he came in. We had a cuff right there so she did it right then and there. He asked how much he owed and she said it was free. It just took a couple of minutes…"

"Did you get a name? Did he fill out paperwork?"

Shelley shook her head. "If there had been something wrong, we'd have asked him to stay and see the doctor. Then we would have needed him to do a medical form, insurance form—"

"But nothing was amiss?"

She shook her head. "His blood pressure was perfect."

Ryan felt like he was seeing Shelley for the first time. He studied her blond hair, cut short and curling around her face. She was slightly overweight but not obese. And she appeared to be young. "May I ask your age?"

She blushed and he immediately wondered if she'd misunderstood his intent. "Twenty."

He nodded. Still, the blond hair cut short and the weight… She didn't fit the victims' profiles. But obviously, Jade had.

Had it been simple luck that Diallo had chosen that particular medical office? Or fate?

"Do you have an alarm system here?" he asked.

"Of course. I think all doctors do. The medicines we keep here—"

"Do you have cameras?"

~~~~~

A few minutes later, Ryan was standing in the parking lot, his eyes roaming from one closed circuit camera to the next. They were positioned at each corner and if luck was with him, there were no blind spots. In his hand, he held a DVD on which all the videos had been copied, beginning on the day before Jade's murder.

24

It was beginning to rain again as Ryan left the coffee shop and crossed the parking lot to his car. The sky to the southeast was growing ominously black, the clouds tumbling as if in a battle of the gods. He had just slipped inside when the torrent began. It hit the windshield with a vengeance; the rain seemed more gray than clear and in a matter of seconds, he was barely able to see. In front of him, a narrow strip of grass separated the parking lot from the roadway. Though he was just yards from a major intersection, he could no longer view the stoplight or see anything more than the colors of a few bright cars like watercolor paintings being washed away. Everything else was obliterated by the sheets of rain.

He set his coffee in the cup holder and turned the computer toward him. Slipping in the DVD, he fast-forwarded through the footage, pausing or slowing it down as individuals appeared near the medical building. His eyes were tired and the phone call he'd received early this morning felt as if it had occurred days before.

His mind wandered. He still had to go by the supermarket and buy steaks for tonight's dinner. And he needed to redeem himself in Cathleen's eyes. He was as confused by his invitation as he was delighted in her acceptance. When he thought of her in his arms, it felt right and it felt eternal. It also felt wrong and shameful when he thought of a husband, possibly at home in Atlanta, waiting for her return. Tonight he would have the talk with her that he should have had that first night.

There had been no movement in front of the medical building in quite a while and he sped up the video and sipped his coffee. The rain was slowing now, leaving as quickly as it had appeared, but leaving behind strong winds that buffeted his car. A few small branches snapped off a tree across the street and tumbled along the ground.

He turned back to the computer as the door was just beginning to close. Stopping it, he rewound until he saw the receptionist unlocking the door and opening it for a few patients who had been waiting outside. There was a young mother with a small boy held in her arms, his head across her shoulder. Then an older man in worn overalls followed by one of the largest women Ryan had ever seen.

As the door began to close, it was gripped by a muscular arm.

Ryan sat up a little straighter as he watched Diallo Delport walk inside. He stopped the film and made a note of the date and time stamp. Five minutes later, he exited. He looked directly at the camera and Ryan could have sworn he smiled.

He wants to be caught, Ryan thought.

He stared straight ahead. Though the wind and the remnants of rain continued to whip around him, his mind was elsewhere. He could now place Delport at the scenes of two victims' employment. It was circumstantial at best. And certainly not enough to convict him. He needed more.

If he wanted to be caught, why hadn't there been any evidence left at the crime scenes? He had no murder weapon, no fingerprints, no DNA.

Unless...

Ryan squirmed a bit in his seat. Unless he planned to continue killing, mocking him with each new murder, perhaps leaving a little more each time...

He thought of the chief's remark—could he have met
Delport at some time in his past? He shook his head. It wasn't
possible. The man was so physically unique that he would
certainly have remembered him. But he found himself tracing
his memories through the years he'd been in America and then
backward through Ireland. He knew he'd never met him. Could
he have been related to someone he'd busted and sent to prison?

That was a possibility, he acknowledged. But who? He'd
worked in Ireland for three years before leaving for America. He
might have arrested hundreds of people there. Then hundreds
more, certainly, in America. It would be a daunting task to go
through each of his cases on the off chance that Delport was
somehow related to one of them.

Or he could be related to a victim, he thought. Perhaps a
victim in which the courts did not convict the defendant. Maybe
he was now seeking revenge for a wronged family member. But
why go after the cop? Why not go after the judge, the prosecutor
or the jurists?

His windows were fogging up and he started the car and
turned on the air conditioner. It was muggy and sticky and he'd
need to shower before Cathleen came over. He glanced at his
watch. It was only mid-afternoon. This had to be the slowest
day of his life.

The coffee was tepid now but he continued to sip it. He
ejected the DVD and labeled it, then recorded the evidence in
his notepad. His eyes fell to the journal Rían Kelly had maintained;
he'd carried it with him this morning, unable to leave it behind
as if it beckoned to him somehow. He needed a short break and
this would get his mind off the cases for just a few minutes, he
reasoned. When he came back to them, he'd be fresher.

He picked up where he'd left off the night before, on January
1, 1839.

> *As luck would have it, Doctor MacGowen arrived
> in the village this morn. Had he not come about, we
> might have been compelled to transport the body to
> Dublin for a death certificate or I suppose we could*

have kept poor Brighid at the undertakers until Doctor MacGowen's next visit.

We have not had the fortune of a resident doctor in quite some time since Doctor O'Brien died suddenly of consumption at the age of 59. And it took more than a bit of cajoling to persuade Doctor MacGowen to visit our little village once a month. Even at that, he often didn't call as expected and the ill have been obliged to make the trip to Dublin.

But Providence was with us for he rode into the village just this morn. Accompanying him was his medical assistant, Miss Aislin Murphy. I accompanied them to the undertakers forthwith and in a matter of minutes, he had prepared the death certificate and was on his way to the home of the judge, where he was to set up his medical practice for the day.

Ryan rubbed his eyes and finished off the coffee. He thought of going back inside the coffee shop for another cup but didn't feel like getting out of the car. After a moment, he turned the page to the next entry.

January 1, 1839

Same day as the first entry, he thought.

Providence is not with us but surely Satan Himself has descended upon our little village. For this eve as I was locking my office in preparation for a much-needed and much-anticipated visit with my darling betrothed, two of my neighbors, Aengus McGee and Crevan Gallagher, did converge upon me, begging my presence at the church.

Though they endeavored to prepare me for what I would witness as we rode there posthaste, no amount of explanation could have removed the horror.

For when I arrived, I found Doctor MacGowen's medical assistant, Aislin Murphy, murdered in the

*cemetery adjacent to the church. She had been so beautiful
and was still beautiful in death, though I cannot fathom
how anyone could be so evil as to cut short her life in
such a vicious and vile manner.*

*Her throat had been sliced in precisely the same
location as Brighid's and she was left to bleed out. In a
further violation of the dear soul, she had been dragged
through the cemetery, as evidenced by a path of blood
splattered grotesquely upon leaves that had been flattened
by the weight of her, and made to sit against a tombstone.*

*So it was when Aengus and Crevan visited Father
Fitzpatrick as was their habit, that they found Miss
Murphy, her legs spread like that of a doll's and her
beautiful long brunette hair undone and spilling into
her own blood. Her eyes remained open when I saw her
and she carried the same look of terror as had Brighid.
It was quite enough to make the four of us—for Father
Fitzpatrick was present as well—nearly collapse into
tears. Though now I must admit the tears would not be
entirely of sorrow but anger as well and now my heart
has hardened against the killer and I shall see him hang.*

Ryan paused as his mind began to race. It wasn't possible, he thought. He turned back to the beginning and reread the passage. But when he was finished, he was more perplexed than ever before.

On the night of December 31, the first woman—who had come to town with a theatre group—was found murdered, her throat cut across the jugular, just as the understudy had been earlier in the week.

Less than twenty-four hours later, the second woman was killed; and she, like the second victim in his case, had been a nurse—or medical assistant. He honestly didn't know the difference between the titles but it didn't matter. The similarities were too striking.

How could it be possible for two murders to have occurred nearly two hundred years apart on two different continents with such conspicuous parallels?

The air conditioner had done an excellent job of defogging his windows and now he shivered as much from the two sets of murders as from the chill that was enveloping him. The storm had slowed to a steady rain that might have been welcomed had it not heralded a hurricane on its heels. The wind was still fierce, causing the trees to bend and sway against a threatening sky.

Unless…

He turned back to the journal. Unless his string of murders was a series of copycat crimes.

He reached for his cell phone. He was calling Claire right now, right this minute, and find out who had access to these records before she turned them over to him.

He stared out the windshield as he hit the speed dial. He barely saw the cars as they came to a stop at the intersection; there were two lanes of vehicles, bumper to bumper, waiting for the light to change. As he listened to Claire's phone ringing, he stared directly into the car in front of him.

It was a medium blue Mustang GT Convertible. His own vehicle was pulled into the parking space so it faced the road and now he stared at the driver's profile inside the sports car. White hair. Pale skin. Bulky shoulders and a chest so substantial that the seat looked to be positioned all the way back.

He heard Claire's voice but he lowered the phone and leaned forward.

The light changed and the cars began to move. Then Diallo Delport, his hand casually stroking the top of the steering wheel, turned and met his eyes.

And smiled.

25

Ryan had the car in gear and his foot on the gas pedal so hastily that the car jumped the curb and landed in the roadway, clipping another vehicle. He didn't hesitate but continued his pursuit through the stoplight, careening to the left on the rain-slick road as he hit his blue lights and siren.

His car was unmarked but with the assortment of antennae and the lights flashing in the grille, vehicles were maneuvering to scurry out of his way.

"926," he radioed his badge number, "in pursuit of murder suspect Diallo Delport. Heading west on Roberts Avenue. Blue Mustang GT Convertible. Late model. No license plate. Approaching Interstate 95."

"926," the dispatcher radioed back, "switch to channel five. All cars joining pursuit, switch to channel five and report."

Once he switched over, he heard the dispatcher repeat the description of the suspect's vehicle. Three uniformed officers also radioed in, joining the pursuit.

"Crossing over Interstate 95," Ryan broke in, "remaining on Roberts Avenue."

He'd felt this same rush of adrenaline many times before. It was like a jolt directly to the heart, causing his blood to rush to his head and his fingers to tingle. His eyes remained glued to the Mustang, which was pulling further ahead and putting more ground between them. His own foot was approaching the floorboard and as they left the city for a long stretch of county road, he pressed down further and leaned into the steering wheel.

Delport had the vehicle lights off and with the gloom of the approaching storm it was growing more difficult to see the blue car. Ryan wondered why he hadn't pulled onto the interstate; he could have traveled much faster and if he'd headed south, he could have crossed the state line in a matter of minutes.

A lumbering piece of farm equipment pulled out of a side road directly in Ryan's path and he swerved around it, crossing the double yellow line and narrowly missing another vehicle traveling in the opposite direction. The police car crisscrossed the roadway before sliding sideways as he tried to set it right. The streets were too wet and the tires too worn. He caught a glimpse of the passengers in another vehicle as they lurched out of his way before he managed to get the car back in the correct lane and facing west once more.

Out of the corner of his eye, he could see the blue lights of a marked police car as it sped along a parallel road. It was separated by a broad tobacco field that was already flooding with the heavy rains.

Delport had managed to put more distance between them and now he made a 90-degree turn onto another road. As Ryan neared a closer intersection, he also turned right; now he was driving parallel to the road Delport was on. In his rearview mirror, he could see the other police car turning right as well and gaining speed. The roads would converge in a five-way intersection and as Ryan glanced ahead, he realized there were stopped cars at each corner.

He punched the gas pedal as the car approached a hundred miles an hour. He was gaining on Delport; he began to realize they would converge at the intersection at the same time. He heard the officer behind him radioing their location and now across another section of tobacco field, he saw another car, this one a county officer, joining the pursuit.

He reached the intersection in seconds. He saw it in slow motion: the stoplights, the cars with drivers and passengers, all seeming to wear the same expression with mouths open and eyes wide; the blue car swerving from its current road onto the intersecting road; and Ryan reaching the middle of the intersection and trying to turn the car to the left.

Delport was less than one car length away as he entered the intersection but again the tires slipped on the wet road, causing the police car to fishtail. It slammed into one of the stopped vehicles, jerking Ryan to the left with such violence that his head hit the driver's side window with a resounding crack. He struggled with the steering wheel as he tried to reposition the vehicle and he swore as the blue car again gained ground.

As he righted the vehicle and made it through the intersection, he glanced into the rearview mirror. The county vehicle was stopping at the car he'd spun into as a plume of steam rose from their hood. He didn't have the time to wonder if anyone had been injured or about the amount of damage he'd caused as he leaned into the gas pedal in an attempt to overtake Delport.

He could hear the radio traffic increasing as other law enforcement joined in the pursuit. A small voice inside him warned that he was in unfamiliar territory; he was well acquainted with city streets as they were his jurisdiction. But though he'd traveled the main roads in the county, he was ignorant of any of the side streets and lesser used roadways. They were approaching an area in which he couldn't see ahead. The low-lying fields were being replaced now with businesses and small shopping centers, areas in which other vehicles were rapidly increasing.

Another police car was approaching from the opposite direction but events were unfolding too rapidly for there to be time to stop and toss road spikes in Delport's path. In seconds, the Mustang would be even with the approaching police and Ryan wondered what course of action to expect.

At the last second, the car turned 180 degrees in front of the Mustang and Delport careened onto an adjacent roadway.

This one was a forty-five degree angle heading back in the direction they'd just come. And as Ryan approached it, he tried to calculate the benefits of slowing down to make the turn or risk losing more ground. His foot seemed to have a mind of its own as it plunged even deeper onto the gas pedal and he took the turn at eighty miles an hour. The other police car was now turning around once more to join again in the pursuit and they entered the road at the same time. He was forced into the oncoming lane and now he stared directly into the grille of a pickup truck that was growing closer by the millisecond.

At the last second, both the truck and the other police car veered onto separate shoulders and Ryan took the center of the road, the car fishtailing on the wet roadway, as he tried to gain ground on Delport.

They had entered a technology corridor and now they both raced past multi-story buildings and parking lots filled with pedestrians as well as vehicles. And beyond the Mustang, barricades in bright yellow became visible through the rain; the road was ending.

The Mustang veered off and as Ryan fell in behind it, he realized they were in a restaurant parking lot. Behind him, he heard a growing chorus of police sirens and a glance in his rearview mirror showed several cruisers gaining on them.

Delport whipped around the edge of the building and Ryan followed suit; now they were racing through the lot parallel to the other officers. The rain was coming down in another fierce wave and he leaned forward, trying to see beyond the rapid strokes of the windshield wipers. At the edge of the parking lot, Delport veered sharply to the left.

Ryan followed, rounding the corner as a group of pedestrians were stepping into the crosswalk. He jerked the wheel abruptly as he fought to avoid striking them. The police car went airborne and now neither his foot on the pedals nor his hands on the steering wheel could change what fate might have in store.

He could feel the tires leaving the hard, rough ground surface; he could sense the car flying through the air as though the wind had picked it up and was tossing it forward. As he looked out the driver's window, he caught a glimpse of the pedestrians; they all had upturned faces filled with horror as they watched the vehicle gain momentum.

He sailed past the edge of the parking lot and to his complete dismay he realized he was over water. A feeling of dread washed over him and he knew there was absolutely nothing he could do to change his course.

Then the car ceased its upward momentum and seemed to stop in mid-air for the slightest moment before tilting forward. Now he was on the downturn, the nose angling sharply forward like a roller coaster gliding over a crest. In the middle of a storm with rainfall flooding the area, it felt totally surreal to see a fountain emerge before him with a half dozen streams of water bursting in the air.

The journal, the DVDs, his paperwork—they had all become airborne inside the car and were sailing all around him as he stared into the cast iron fountain. He reached for the door handle and the seat belt at precisely the same time. But before he could open the door or release the belt, the car slammed into the fountain.

The impact instantly released the air bag and he found his face buried in fabric that felt as if it contained a hundred tiny razors. White powder was spraying the vehicle with a film so thick, he might have thought he'd struck a tractor-trailer loaded with talcum. He could hear the air whoosh out of his body so violently that his lungs burned. His spine felt like a steel rod, unyielding and inflexible, as pain shot through him.

His knees hit something solid and his thighs felt sandwiched between a force on his spine and another on his knees. He cried out, the sound of his own voice sending his anxiety rocketing. Then at last, the vehicle seemed to settle.

He tried to push the bag out of his way, expecting the vehicle to quickly fill up with water. But as the bag deflated, he realized the car's nose had speared the fountain and he was pointed almost straight down. The top of the fountain was protruding into the dashboard but whether from the force of the impact or someone's quick action, the water was no longer spraying.

He could still hear the radio traffic; between the cars still in pursuit of Delport and those who had stopped to lend assistance to him, the voices seemed to be climbing over one another.

And now, as he stared straight down into the man-made pond, his car skewered like a kebob on a grill, he glimpsed a stream of reporters converging on the scene amidst flashbulbs popping and cameras rolling.

26

Every muscle in his body throbbed and no matter how he tried to reposition himself in his chair, he could not make the pain go away. It was after six o'clock and all he could think of was getting to the grocery and buying those steaks for his dinner with Cathleen.

"Tell me again what the hell you thought you were doing?" the chief demanded.

"I saw Diallo Delport," he repeated for the umpteenth time. "I was in pursuit."

"Why?"

"Because he's wanted for murder."

"No; he's not wanted for murder. He's wanted for questioning."

"I've placed him at the workplaces of the first two victims." His head hurt.

"You know our policy on high speed chases. You know it!" Chief Johnston jabbed his finger in Ryan's direction.

"He was leaving. In a matter of moments, he might have been on his way across the country."

"In a matter of moments, he was outside your jurisdiction! And he still might be headed out of this area."

Ryan sighed and rubbed the area between his brows. He needed an ice cold shower to take the sweat off him followed by a hot shower to ease the pain. "So they didn't catch him."

"No. They didn't." Now it was the chief's turn to sigh but unlike Ryan's, his was filled with total exasperation. "Do you have any idea how much trouble you caused me? We're trying to prepare for a Category 5 hurricane and we've got car accidents strewn from the center of town to the far corner of the county—all on account of you. Do you have any idea how much this is costing? How many men are writing up accident reports?"

Ryan moved his hand from his brow long enough to glance at the chief. Surely, he didn't expect a response.

"Not to mention we'll be on every major news report this evening. I'm told witnesses have already uploaded videos to the Internet."

Ryan groaned. Anybody else could have a bad day at the office and only four walls would know it. He has a bad day and he ends up on YouTube.

"I've got an FBI task force out there—" he waved toward his closed office door "—calling you a complete idiot."

Ryan squeezed the bridge of his nose and wished the pain would stop.

"You're better than this, O'Clery," the chief added.

"May I go, sir? I'm not feeling quite like myself."

"Are you even listening to me?"

"Aye. Though I wish I weren't."

Chief Johnston swore as he made his way behind his desk. Ryan could hear his chair groaning as he sat down. He continued rubbing his brow. The lights in the office seemed much harsher than usual and he closed his eyes.

"Here's what's going to happen," the chief said after an awkward silence. "The FBI is taking over this investigation." At Ryan's protests, he raised his hand. "No discussion. I'll let you know tomorrow morning whether you'll be assigned to work with them."

"But I'm—"

"I said no discussion. When you get into work tomorrow—provided you can drag yourself in—you'll spend the morning filling out reports on every accident you caused this afternoon."

"Unbelievable."

"What's unbelievable is the fact that you managed to wreck more cars in less than thirty minutes than we've had wrecked in the past fifteen years combined."

Ryan tried to reposition himself in the chair but his back was beginning to hammer with the pain.

"You're on desk duty—"

"Desk duty!"

"—unless you can provide a medical clearance. I understand you were brought to the hospital."

"I told them I was fine."

"Yeah. I can see just how fine you are." He eyed him critically. "They do x-rays?"

"Aye."

"They find anything?"

"No broken bones. I'm just sore, is all."

"I was told they wanted to keep you overnight for observation."

"It wasn't necessary."

"Can your sister stay with you tonight?"

"Sir?"

"As angry as I am with you right now," the chief said, fixing him with a no-nonsense glare, "I have an obligation to make sure you didn't injure yourself more than you're letting on. At the least, I would've thought you'd suffered a concussion. I don't want you alone overnight. That's an order. Find somebody to stay with you or I'm ordering an officer to take you back to the hospital. You look like—"

"Fine. My sister will babysit me. May I go now?"

Chief Johnston stared at him for so long that Ryan contemplated just getting up and walking out. The only thing that kept him in his chair was the realization that he didn't have a ride home.

Finally, the chief pushed a button on his intercom. When Charlie responded, he said, "Get someone to take Detective O'Clery home."

Ryan started to rise but the pain in his spine was enough to keep him seated a moment longer. When he finally did get up, he tried to avoid looking at the chief. Though he attempted to keep his face expressionless, he knew he couldn't avoid the grimace that insisted on betraying him.

"O'Clery," Chief Johnston said as Ryan opened the door.

Ryan kept his hand on the door knob but didn't turn around; he was concerned if he turned his body once more, his spine would split in two.

"Take care of yourself tonight. Get a good night's rest. And if you don't feel like coming in tomorrow, don't."

27

It was a quarter past seven when the police cruiser turned the corner to Ryan's neighborhood and he knew that despite his best intentions, he'd probably lost Cathleen forever. Not that he ever had her to begin with, he reminded himself.

But when his house came into view, he was surprised to see her white compact with the station's call letters emblazoned on the side parked in front of his house.

"You want me to go around the block?" Officer Zuker asked.

"No," Ryan answered. "I invited her." He glanced at Zuker's surprised face. "It's personal."

"Okay," Zuker said slowly as he pulled in front of Cathleen's vehicle.

As they came to a stop, Ryan opened the passenger door and tried to step out as if nothing was amiss. But he found himself moving as slowly as a turtle crossing the road.

"You need help getting out?" Zuker asked.

"I'll be fine." Ryan glanced in the side mirror and watched Cathleen as she exited her car. She reached back inside and pulled out a large plastic bag and her pocketbook before turning toward them. Ryan tried to come to his feet before she could watch how painful the slight movement was but she was halfway to his door and he still hadn't managed to do more than put his feet on the curb.

He was accustomed to helping others. He was the one with broad shoulders on which to cry, muscular arms for support, a strong back and robust countenance. Now he found himself sitting on the edge of the car seat looking up at Cathleen as she hesitated in front of him.

"I'm sorry I'm late," he managed to say. "I had a bit of a delay at the office."

Behind him, he heard Officer Zuker's door opening and closing. A voice inside urged him to get up now while he could still maintain a semblance of self-respect, but his back and legs were obstinately disobedient.

At Cathleen's silence, he looked up and found himself staring into wide blue-gray eyes that appeared positively stunned. Her mouth was slightly open as if she was trying to form words but none would come. Her face looked as though the blood had drained from it completely.

As Officer Zuker rounded the front of the car, Ryan tried to come to his feet. The grimace was back, no matter how desperate he was to conceal it and Cathleen rushed toward him, sliding her shoulder under one arm. "Lean on me," she urged.

Zuker reached around the door for his other arm and despite his objections, they walked him to the door. He clutched the journal and DVD's in his hands; at least, no matter how terrible his day had turned out, the journal had not been submerged and the writing was still intact.

~~~~~

"I figured you wouldn't be in any shape to cook dinner," Cathleen said as she set the plastic bag on the kitchen counter. "So I picked up something from a local restaurant. I hope you like Italian."

Ryan rested one palm on the countertop. But as Cathleen came within arm's length, he found himself grasping her and pulling her to him. As she settled against his chest, he rested his cheek against her hair and closed his eyes. After a long moment of silence, he asked, "How did you know?"

"You're kidding me, right?" When he didn't respond, she continued, "It was all over the police scanners. The only reason I wasn't there was because I didn't know the area. By the time I found it, you were gone." She hesitated. "The car was still there."

Ryan closed his eyes tighter and tried not to think about the fire truck they'd called in and how they'd extended the crane while an embarrassingly large audience watched two firemen cut him out of the front seat while he dangled face down. He wondered what was involved in getting a video removed from YouTube.

"They said you'd been taken to the hospital," she continued. Her voice was soft but her arms were strong as they squeezed him tighter. "By the time I got there, you'd left there, too." She tried to laugh but it sounded forced. "I guess I need to work on my timing."

"Your timing is perfect."

She pulled gently away, though he continued to keep his hands on either side of her waist. "Do you want me to leave?"

"No," he answered immediately. "I want this pain to leave. But you—you, I want to stay."

"Okay," she said, her voice changing as she clearly took command. "Tell me about the pain. And don't sugarcoat it."

"It's nothing—"

"I said," she emphasized, "don't sugarcoat it."

"Right about now," he answered, "a morphine drip would do nicely."

She reached for a small paper bag on top of the journal. "What's in here?"

"Something they gave me at the hospital. Whatever it is, I'll take two."

While he continued to hold onto her as much to keep himself vertical as anything else, she leaned around him and emptied the bag. She read the label and then reached for a glass in the dish drainer. When she turned on the faucet, he said, "I'll take it with whiskey."

She peered at him for a moment before filling the glass with water. "I don't think so." She gave him two pills and the glass and watched him down them before speaking again. "I'm pretty good at taking care of the injured," she said, eyeing him. "And I'm going to call the shots tonight."

God was punishing him for what he'd wanted to do with her, Ryan thought. And now he had rendered him helpless as a young boy.

"First," she said, "While I heat up dinner, you're going to soak in a hot tub."

He let out a sigh. "You're an angel."

She smiled. "I know."

~~~~~

Ryan sank his head into the pillow and sighed. He had to admit, if he was going to need a nursemaid Cathleen made a fine one. She seemed to know everything to do; first, she'd escorted him straight to the master bath where she'd drawn a hot Jacuzzi. Not only did her giant plastic bag contain dinner but she'd also brought a box of Epsom salts and he suspected there were more surprises in store.

She'd wrapped a bed pillow in several plastic grocery bags and propped it at the head of the tub, helped him disrobe and into the water where he reclined as the jets massaged his sore muscles. He heard her banging around inside cabinets but the pain killers had begun to take effect and he didn't care what she was doing.

He didn't know how much time had passed before she slid a bath tray in front of him. He opened his eyes to find a glass of whiskey on it and as she ducked out, he smiled and raised the glass in a toast to himself. Things were definitely looking up.

His cell phone had just begun to ring as she returned with another tray.

"Claire Erickson?" Cathleen read.

"My sister." He held out his hand. "If I don't answer, she'll come right over."

She handed the phone to him. "Then you'd better answer."

"Claire," he said.

"Where are you?" Claire demanded.

He eyed Cathleen as she arranged the tray on the bathroom counter. The aroma of garlic bread and Italian pasta tickled his nose and he wondered if she planned to have him eat in the bedroom. The Jacuzzi felt so relaxing that coupled with the whiskey and the painkillers, he realized he was perfectly content to remain just where he was until morning.

"I'm in the bath," he said.

"At home?"

"Aye."

"I'll be right over."

"No." His voice sounded abrupt and Cathleen turned to look at him quizzically.

"Don't tell me 'no'," Claire admonished. "I just finished watching you on the nightly news being extricated from a vehicle you'd just impaled. And after I make certain you're alright, I'm going to thrash your arse for not phoning me straight-away."

"But—"

Cathleen stepped to the side of the tub and Ryan realized Claire's voice was loud enough to be heard by the both of them.

"Don't talk back to me," Claire interrupted. "You think Mum hurt you when you were a tyke. I fashion to wallop your hide when I get over there. You've just taken ten years off my life."

"Run for the hills, Uncle Re!" Emma shouted in the background.

"She means it, Uncle Re!" Erin added. "Mummy's taking you to the woodshed!"

"Don't get cheeky with me, girls," he said loudly. Ryan rolled his eyes and whispered to Cathleen, "You can't argue with her."

"Don't backtalk me under your breath," Claire said. "I'm heading out the door now. I'll be there in ten minutes."

Cathleen snatched the phone out of Ryan's hand. "He's not alone," she said abruptly.

"Who the hell are you?" Claire's voice rose an octave and despite his injuries, Ryan felt a slow smile forming.

"My name's Cait. I've got your brother in a nice hot bath and I've just prepared him dinner. I have no intention of leaving him alone. You can whip his 'arse' some other time."

"Have we met?"

"I'm certain we have not."

There was a moment of silence on the other end of the phone. Then Claire's voice sounded a bit quieter. "Your voice sounds very familiar."

"No disrespect but yours does not."

"You had dinner with my girls last evening, didn't you?"

Cathleen's eyes widened and she smiled. "Yes. Yes, I did. And they are delightful."

"They enjoyed you very much."

Ryan groaned. "Get off the phone, Claire!" he shouted.

Cathleen frowned at Ryan but Claire said, "Well, then. If you're sure I'm not needed…"

"Thank you, but no. I have everything under control."

"If you mean you have Ryan under control, good luck with that."

Cathleen giggled. "Yeah. I know what you mean."

"Get off the phone, Claire!" Ryan shouted again.

"Call me if you need anything," Claire said.

"Thanks. Will do." Cathleen clicked off the phone. "That was incredibly rude of you."

"So. You brought me supper?"

~~~~~

Ryan was seated in the Jacuzzi finishing an oversized slice of tiramisu and feeling like he'd died and gone to heaven. Not only had he eaten a fabulous Italian dinner while reclining in a hot bath but he'd done it with a nude woman on the other side of the bath tray. Shaming himself in front of the world was worth it for this outcome.

He topped off her glass of wine and then poured a bit more whiskey in his glass.

Cathleen leaned back until her breasts threatened to float along the water's surface. Sipping her wine, she asked, "How are you feeling?"

He thought of giving her a snappy comeback but said, "A thousand times better."

She studied him for a moment. "You scared me this afternoon."

"I scared myself this afternoon."

"This kind of thing happen often to you?"

"First time. Hopefully, the last time." He carefully removed the bath tray, set it beside the tub and leaned back. His long legs stretched the length of the Jacuzzi, ending with his feet pressed flat against the opposite side, on either side of Cathleen's shoulders. Her hair was gathered into a bun that now threatened to come undone and he longed to reach for the hair clip and help it on its way. But there was something guarded in her eyes, even though she'd disrobed and joined him without so much as an invitation. Not that she'd needed one, he thought. She was welcome to his bath any time.

"This isn't exactly how I thought our evening would turn out," he said apologetically.

She set down her wine glass. "What are you doing to me?" Her voice was so soft that he had to lean forward to hear her.

He hesitated. There were times when a woman asked an open question and the man had better give a lot of thought to the correct answer. Otherwise, things could head south in a hurry. After a moment, he said, "I don't understand."

She adjusted her legs and he found one foot angling up the side of his leg. He reached under the water and ran his fingers gently along her foot and then held it.

"You do something to me," she said finally. "I don't know how you do it but you do. I didn't come here—to this town—to meet anyone. I came to do a job."

He squeezed her foot as he listened.

"But when I saw you in your back yard, the day we met—I had the strangest feeling that you'd met me before. And I should have remembered it."

He let his eyes drop away from hers. Silence ensued as if she was waiting for him to respond.

After a moment, she continued. "And when you kissed me, it was as if I'd felt you before." She wiggled her foot against his side, stroking his skin with her toes. "Like I'd felt your lips on mine before. Like the most natural thing in the world was for me to be in your arms."

His answer was automatic. "You do belong in my arms." He set his whiskey glass beside the tub.

A myriad of emotions flickered across her face. He thought she might lean toward him; perhaps move into his arms. But a second later, her eyes appeared sad and a veil seemed to shift over her face. "Then you treated me so badly," she said. He could feel the pain in her voice. "I came here last evening to fulfill my obligation, to give you the DVD about the Atlanta murders. And you sucked me in again. Then I watched you being so gentle, so caring and so loving, with those little girls…" Her voice faded and she swallowed before continuing, "Then you cut me off again. Then this morning… It's a roller coaster, this thing with you."

"I need you, Cait."

She chewed on her lip for a moment. He started to shift forward, to find her hands under the water and pull her to him, when she spoke again. "You're going to break my heart. I can see it coming. And I know I ought to be keeping my distance from you." She tried to chuckle but it sounded forced. "And yet, here I am." Now she sat up and grasped both of his hands. "And I am begging you not to hurt me."

He pulled her toward him and she came willingly. He nestled her against him, letting her sink her back against his chest. He reached for a lock of hair that had escaped her bun and had tumbled across her forehead. Brushing it back, relishing the feel of her silk tresses against his hand, he said, "I won't hurt you again. You might leave my heart in shattered pieces but I won't knowingly or intentionally hurt you again."

She turned her face toward his. Her brows were knit together. "Why would I shatter your heart?"

He allowed his gaze to drop to her mouth. Her lips were downturned and her bottom lip trembled slightly. He couldn't bring up the topic of her husband; not here, not in these circumstances. Not with her leaning into him like it was the most natural thing in the world. It *was* the most natural thing, he realized. She married someone else because she didn't know at the time that he existed. Now, through whatever twist of fate had bound them together, they were here and they were together.

He closed his eyes and leaned his face against hers. He could picture a jealous husband appearing in the doorway of the bathroom, a gun in his hand, and both of them disentangling themselves, naked and vulnerable, begging or shouting at him to put down the gun.

It was almost the way his own marriage had disintegrated. Only they had been in his house and in his bed. And they'd been fully engaged. The man had tried to cover himself with one hand while splaying his other hand toward him, as if his palm could deflect a bullet from his body. His voice had been conciliatory, even pleading. Sophie had been upset with Ryan for coming home early; she'd been shrill, accusatory and angry.

He didn't think he could ever forgive her. He'd heard through the grapevine that the affair was on again, off again and she'd tried to reunite with him afterward but he turned a deaf ear. It was easier to feel the inner rage than the pain and humiliation.

And if someone had told him even three days earlier that he would be that other man, he wouldn't have believed it. He couldn't have believed it.

She placed her hand against his cheek and allowed her thumb to stroke his dimple. Her fingers were soft and sensual and when he closed his eyes as he did now, he remembered somewhere deep within his soul, another bath and another woman.

Yet when he opened his eyes, he found himself looking into the same stormy eyes beneath the same long brown hair. Everything was the same: the petite nose with just a smattering of freckles, the jawline, the angled chin. He placed his hand against her face now and she leaned into his palm, closing her eyes in a small display of abandonment. He'd seen that look before; he'd observed her in slumber and had lightly run his fingers over her fine dark brows. He remembered her breasts intimately, the curve of her spine, the way her ribs showed a bit more on one side than they did the other. The birthmark on her ankle shaped like a dragonfly…

He remembered.

He remembered the candlelight and the way the shadows played across the wall as it stormed outside. He remembered her standing as she started to do now; remembered his hands falling away from her, his eyes roaming over her as she unclipped her hair and allowed the tresses to cascade down an ivory back still wet and inviting. He remembered her turning slightly toward him, knowing how she excited him, knowing how he would risk anything and everything to have her, and he remembered her speaking to him in a soft Irish accent.

He remembered.

28

Rían drifted in and out of a troubled sleep. The bedcovers smelled different and the sheets did not feel the same. But that's the way it had been for quite some time.

He had arrived home to find that his home no longer existed. The village had not survived the great flood and massive winds; in a matter of hours, the waters had rushed in, consuming everything in its path.

No one seemed to know where all the water had come from. Most survivors said the entire ocean had swept over Ireland. By the time the storm reached Dublin and Rían was fleeing the city, it had already marched across the countryside and Cait was already gone.

During the days that followed, Rían tried to remain busy and it wasn't difficult to find more than enough to do. Everything was in ruins and many thought it to be the end of the world. There were bodies emerging as the waters receded; bodies that needed proper wakes and burials. Some of the cemeteries had been washed away and now they found themselves reconstructing what had once been. Moving through the rubble left in the storm's wake, they found three hundred year old tombstones miles from where they once stood; cattle and sheep, caught unawares, had perished by the hundreds; homes, shops and offices—they were all gone.

He felt like he was sleepwalking through life. He rose from a stranger's bed who'd given him refuge for the night, whether it was hay in a barn or a mattress in a home. And he walked for miles on end, gathering refuse with the others. Sometimes the items they found could be washed and used, as so many were without any possessions at all. And sometimes they began huge bonfires and watched their pasts and their futures go up in smoke.

He was an empty vessel; he'd long ago lost the desire to eat and with the water polluted with debris, days passed where he couldn't remember anything touching his lips at all. His insides felt ripped from him while his legs moved forward without thought or emotion.

And when the darkness of night settled in, it was sheer torture.

He buried his face in a pillow that felt foreign to him and bawled like a baby and he no longer cared who overheard. He'd long ago lost the shame of crying along with pride, anger, happiness... and love.

All that was left was a growing desire to end this life.

For with Cait gone, he felt as if his very soul had been split in two. She had made every day worth living; every moment with her had been joyous, sensuous, filled with laughter and smiles and kisses and love. Their entire lives had been laid out before them; their hopes, their desires, their plans for a future together; a future in which they would grow old and gray as man and wife, as lovers, as two halves of a whole.

As twin souls.

And with her absence, he knew in the depths of his soul there could never be another. No other woman could ever measure up to Cait's inner beauty, her compassion, her love for life, her love for him.

There were those who turned to the church for answers, those who sought solace within the walls of the chapel and those who sought answers within the pages of the Bible.

But Rían knew, as his shoulders shook with sobs wrenched from the pit of his being, that God had forsaken him. For some unknown but massive sin, he had taken from him the only thing he had ever truly wanted, ever truly loved. He had left him broken, shattered, destroyed.

He had loved Cait with every breath in his body, every ounce of flesh, every thought and every desire. And now he would curse himself every day for the rest of his miserable existence for leaving her alone.

His trip to Dublin should have taken only a day. A few hours on horseback to reach the city, an hour at most to meet with officers there, and a few hours' travel back home. He should have arrived before nightfall in plenty of time for supper with Cait and another night of passionate love.

He'd replayed the events time after time. Even when he tried to forget them, they ridiculed him in his sleep. In the wee hours of the morning when the sky was blackest, he could still see her waving good-bye to him from the village. He'd wanted to return to her then and yet he allowed duty to call him away. If he could only bring back that moment...

Had he been there, could he have saved her? When the air grew completely still, so still that survivors said voices traveled for miles, would he have known something catastrophic was about to occur? Would he have whisked Cait to higher ground? Could he have saved her life?

And the lives of the two heartbeats that grew within her belly?

~~~~~

Ryan buried his face in the pillow and allowed the sobs to be wrenched from his soul. "Cait," he cried over and over again, "Cait! Cait!"

His face was wet with his tears and still he thrashed about, tossing bedcovers off his miserable body, running his hands through hair soaked from tears and sweat. He felt his soul being slashed in two, just as it had every night since that fateful, horrific day.

Then a light appeared and he turned to see a figure standing in the doorway, surrounded by a yellowish glow. He knew the moment he laid eyes on the silhouette that it was his beloved Cait.

Her hair was long and streamed out and around her body; and yet her locks could not obscure the shape of her breasts, of her waist, her hips.

He held his hand out to her as he cried out her name again and again and to his astonishment, she rushed toward him, her graceful body seeming to fly onto the bed as she gathered him into her arms.

If this was a dream, he hoped he would never awaken. For he could feel the softness of her skin, inhale the perfume that was uniquely hers and the souls that had been so viciously severed seemed to mend miraculously as they blended into one.

His arms wrapped themselves around her and held her tighter than he ever had before. His hands wanted to feel every inch of her body to ensure him that she was indeed there, she was living and breathing and she was his once more.

He cried like a baby, his tears soaking her hair and her skin as he continued to call her name over and over again. He pressed his head to her breast to hear the beat of her heart, a sound he thought gone forever. He tried to hear the heartbeats of the twin babies within her belly but his own heavy, wracked breathing and his own heart thudding against his chest made it impossible to hear anything else.

He held her against him, rolling her onto her back in the soft mattress, and smothered her with kisses; he pressed his body close to hers so they could fuse together for all time.

She spoke and her voice was muffled and low and urgent. He turned his head so his ear was against her lips but he heard not the voice of his beloved Cait but the voice of a stranger.

He pulled slightly back, afraid to let go, afraid he would find he'd held an apparition. Her features were the same; he knew that long, brown hair. He knew those stormy eyes. He knew those features. He knew that body held within his hands better than he knew his own.

"Ryan," she gasped, pushing her hands against him, "you're smothering me. I can't breathe!"

Her words didn't register. They were not of the Gaelic tongue but some other and he pulled back further and stared into her wide, almost panicked eyes.

He became acutely aware of his heavy, labored breathing and the strong, almost frenzied beat of his heart. His knees were not pressing into hay in a barn or a soft but strange bed; they were pressing into the mattress he'd purchased after his divorce. The aroma of fresh coffee tickled his nostrils as soft music wafted from the sound system near his bed.

Yet he continued to stare into Cait's eyes until slowly it registered that he was still crying and his tears were dripping onto her face. And she was pressing her hands vainly against his chest.

"I can't breathe," she said again, her brows furrowed and her face growing pale.

He pulled back until his weight was borne by his knees; knees that felt bruised and battered.

"You were having a bad dream," she said as she caught her breath. Her brows knitted further, and her hard gaze into his eyes showed deep concern.

He continued staring. No words formed on his tongue and he felt suddenly as if he could neither speak English nor Gaelic. All he could grasp were images and all his images blended into her face beneath him.

"Are you awake now?" She reached to his cheek and ran her fingers along his tears. Her skin against his felt like fine silk and yet her touch was electric. "You were crushing me," she added almost apologetically.

Without a word, he rolled off her and onto his side. Then with a hand that felt as large as her waist, he pulled her with him until he was flat on his back and she straddled him from above. He kept both hands on her waist in his anxiousness to assure himself that she was still there. She had not been a dream.

She leaned back so she was seated atop him. Her hair billowed about her face and dropped to his naked waist. Her eyes didn't waver from his. She placed her hand against his cheek once more and slid her fingers over his skin. "I was in the shower," she said, her voice soft, "and I heard you crying out."

He could see the doorway in his peripheral vision; the light that had shone around her silhouette like the aura of an angel had in fact been cast from the light bulbs over the vanity.

"Are you okay?" she asked.

He stared at her, the words barely registering.

"Say something," she said, frowning. "You're scaring me, Ryan."

He could only imagine how he must have looked to her; unshaven, covered in perspiration and his own tears, his black hair soaked into waves that fell across his forehead and against the back of his neck.

She opened her mouth to say something else but he found his own voice, husky and thick with sleep. He held her in a vise-like grip as he blurted, "I love you."

Her eyes widened. He watched as a mixture of emotions sailed across them: disbelief, relief, astonishment, devotion... love.

She opened her mouth, but he pulled her down until her lips brushed against his own, silencing her. "I love you," he repeated. "And I don't want to spend one minute out of a single day without you by my side." He was insistent as his lips found hers and he wasted not a single moment before he forced her mouth open. He felt as though he was inhaling her; inhaling her like she was the breath of life itself. Her body relaxed into his. She moaned softly, the sound causing his heart and his soul to quiver. As he wrapped his arms around her, he knew he could never get her too close, he could never hold her too tightly; he could never feel her too completely.

They rolled over as one until she lay with her legs intertwined around him and her back gently arched. And now her passions grew against him as her hands combed through his hair and her mouth sucked against his bottom lip. And he knew they would make pure, soft, passionate, wild, exhilarating love until neither of them had the strength to move.

As his lips traveled over her cheek and her jaw, she whispered, "I love you, Ryan O'Clery. I believe I always have."

29

Ryan was pouring a cup of coffee when the front door opened and closed. He glanced at the wall clock as he returned the pot to the coffee maker. Cathleen had left just ten minutes earlier. And if she was returning now, it would ensure that neither one of them would be able to walk again for a week.

"Can I come in?" The voice came from the foyer.

Ryan pulled another cup out of the cupboard. "In the kitchen, Claire," he answered as he poured her coffee.

He was getting the cream from the refrigerator when she settled onto a stool at the island between the kitchen and the den.

"I ought to thrash you," she said.

"Good morning to you, too." He set her coffee in front of her and added cream.

"Do you have any idea how it feels to turn on the telly and see your brother hanging in mid-air above a fountain?"

"Can't say I do."

"It's beyond awful. And what was worse was you didn't even phone me up. How was I to know whether you were fighting for your life?"

"You're my next of kin. Had I been fighting for my life, the police department would have fetched you."

"Before or after you died?"

He looked at her without answering.

"How are you feeling?" she asked.

"Sore."

"You're covered in bruises."

Ryan glanced at his reflection in the side of the toaster. He wasn't sure how he'd managed to bang up his face so badly.

"Look at your legs," Claire said, leaning over the counter to stare at his knees.

He lifted up each leg in turn and inspected them. His knees looked twice their normal size and were turning a rainbow of colors.

Claire sipped her coffee. "So you phoned your lady friend but not me."

"I didn't call her, either, if it makes you feel any better."

"In an odd sort of way, it does."

"She heard the news and was waiting for me when I arrived home."

"She stay all night?"

"Aye."

"Is this the married woman?"

"You would bring that up, wouldn't you now?"

"Oh, Re."

He returned the cream to the refrigerator.

"I hope you know what you're doing," she added.

"Claire, I have some questions for you," he said, grabbing his coffee cup and settling in beside her. "I was moving the family records to the spare bedroom and I happened across Rían Kelly's journal."

"Did you now?"

"I did. And I was just wondering, is all, how it was that he never married."

She sipped her coffee for a moment before replying. "Well, the official story handed down through the generations was simply that he was married to his job. Dedicated to law enforcement, as it were."

She seemed to be studying his face before continuing. "But there's also a tale that might be more myth than reality."

"Oh?" He tried to appear casual. "And what might that be?"

"I know you too well," Claire said. "You're wanting the story of Caitlín O'Conor, aren't you?"

"Who?"

She smiled. "Her name was Caitlín O'Conor. She was supposedly the great love of Rían Kelly's life. It was a star-crossed love story. Her father was a prominent man in the village and Rían was a 'lowly county inspector' and though they were deeply in love, her father would not permit Rían to ask for her hand in marriage."

He felt his chest tighten and he sipped his coffee to avoid Claire's piercing eyes.

"The tale is that they sneaked around for years; everybody knew it. Everybody except Caitlín's father, that is. They were madly in love." She sighed wistfully.

"What happened?" He kept his eyes on his coffee. "Did she marry someone else?"

"Her father died. Quite unexpectedly. Heart simply stopped. And without him in the way, they were clear to be married."

As if it was a memory that he held of himself, he could see the hallway on New Year's Eve, whisking Cait to an unused room and going down on bended knee. "So they married then," Ryan said quietly.

"No. You said yourself he'd never married." She brushed non-existent crumbs from the countertop before continuing. "He asked for her hand in marriage on New Year's Eve. Let's see, I believe it was 1838. Yes, that's right. December 31, 1838."

"How can you be so certain of the date?"

"Because seven days later, Caitlín was dead."

His head jerked up and he stared into Claire's eyes. They were as green as the fields of Ireland and now she cocked her head and eyed him curiously.

"He'd gone to Dublin, so the story goes," she continued slowly.

"Rían Kelly."

"Aye. He'd been called away on business. And as Fate would have it, the great flood came while he was gone and Caitlín was swept away."

"The great flood."

"Don't you remember any of your schooling, Re?"

"I suppose I don't."

"Aye, surely you do. It was Oíche na Gaoithe Moire."

"Oíche na Gaoithe Moire," he repeated the Gaelic name. "Night of the Big Wind."

"Aye; that's it. History says that just a couple of days prior, they had a huge snowstorm that blanketed Ireland. With it came a cold front. But the next day, they had warm temperatures the likes of which they hadn't experienced in years. It caused all the snow to melt and melt rapidly."

"So the great flood was caused by melting snow."

"You really don't remember your schooling now, do you, Re? It wasn't that at all. It's just that the warm front settled in over Ireland as another cold front came across the Atlantic. It was January 6, 1839—Epiphany." Her voice took on a whispered note as though she was telling a ghost story. "There were those in the faith who had forecast the end of the world would occur on January 6, 1839—the day of Epiphany. So when the air grew completely still, so still they could hear the voices of neighbors miles apart, there were some who thought the end was near."

He waited for her to continue. His cheeks were growing flush and he could feel beads of sweat beginning to pop out across his brow. "What happened then?"

"By nightfall, there were gale force winds. They moved from the western coast of Ireland all the way to Dublin, where Rián Kelly had traveled. Some said the winds were accompanied by an eerie moan, a rumbling of sorts. But not thunder; it was a sound never heard before nor since. It increased as the winds grew. And then the northern sky turned a shade of red that had never been seen before." She sipped her coffee while she watched him. "We know now it was the aurora borealis. But there was widespread panic amongst the people. And when the sky darkened once again, it darkened to the color of pitch."

He reached for a napkin and mopped his brow.

"Are you feeling alright, Re? Would you care to lie down?"

He shook his head. "I want to hear the rest of the story."

"Well, so the myth goes, Rián Kelly left Dublin immediately. It was a miracle he made it back to the village at all. He traveled through the night, in the rain and the hail, with the winds all about him. Bridges had been washed away; the wind had been so strong—stronger than anything Ireland had experienced in more than three hundred years—so strong that it whipped the Atlantic into a fury and pushed it all the way across the island. Streams and creeks became raging rivers. Whole villages were wiped out. Even some of the castles were beyond repair."

He rested his elbows on the counter and put his head in his hands.

"You're sure you don't want to lie down, Re? You look as if you might faint."

"I'm fine," he said. "What happened when Rián Kelly reached his village?"

"It was gone. Oh, there were a few buildings still intact. The church, for one. But Caitlín O'Conor's home had been washed away. There was no sign of Caitlín."

"So that's where the story ends, does it?"

"Oh, no. I suppose it's where it just begins."

He turned and looked at her, but she was staring into her coffee.

"He looked far and wide for her, he did. Folks said he could be heard for miles around, wandering the countryside, calling her name. His own home was washed away as well, but he never rebuilt. He lived out his days staying a few nights with friends here or there. He was always restless, always searching, always pining for the great love of his life."

"I need a glass of water."

"I'll get it. You stay put." Claire rose and grabbed a glass from the dish drainer, popped some ice cubes in it and filled it with tap water. After handing it to Ryan, she watched him down the whole thing. Then she poured more water into the glass and set it in front of him.

"Why didn't I know any of this?" Ryan asked quietly.

She shrugged. "You were a young boy. You were busy with dreams of becoming a knight. Remember how you used to practice jousting with the broom handle?"

He stared at the ice cubes as they melted.

"I, on the other hand, was infatuated with the story of Rían Kelly and Caitlín O'Conor. It was the greatest love story I'd ever heard. And for a time, every time it rained, I would pretend to be Caitlín waiting on my Rían to come and rescue me." She reached for a lock of his hair that had fallen across his forehead and pushed it back. "Remember how I would walk around with a pillow under my dress?"

"Mum always threatened to thrash you when you did that."

"She was always worried about what the neighbors would think." She chuckled.

He looked up, watching her intently. He felt as though his cheeks had grown both hot and cold at the same time and the room began to swim in front of him. He narrowed his eyes so he could focus on Claire's face. "Why *did* you do that?" he asked.

When her eyes met his, they were soft and a bit misty. "It was rumored that Caitlín O'Conor was with child. Rían Kelly's child, of course."

~~~~~

"Are you certain you're alright?" Claire's voice could barely be heard over Ryan's retching.

He was on his knees in front of the toilet, his arms resting across the top of the open bowl, helping to prop up his forehead in between bouts. The bathroom door opened and he waved her away. "Get out, Claire."

"I will not."

He could hear the water running in the sink and a moment later she shoved a cold, wet washcloth under his face. Grudgingly, he took it and wiped his face.

"Or don't you be remembering how it was me there for you, all those times when you experimented at the pub and came home so fluthered that if Mum or Pup had seen you, they'd have tanned your hide?"

He didn't answer and she flushed the toilet. The spray of fresh water covered his face in a fine mist.

"Thank you," he said. "Now get out."

He didn't move from his position but he could tell she was still there. After a moment, he moved his arm and peeked out to find Claire leaning against the vanity buffing her nails.

"You need some toast and ginger ale," she announced.

"I need some privacy."

"Have you eaten yet today?"

"I'm not hungry."

"That's not what I asked you, now is it?"

He started retching again. When he finished, she shoved another washcloth under him and flushed the toilet again.

"Are you taking these pain meds?" she asked.

He wiped his face with the cloth before glimpsing up. "I suppose if the date on the bottle is yesterday's."

She frowned. "It is. It's no wonder you're ill. You're supposed to be taking these with food."

"I suppose you haven't noticed I'm not dry retching here."

She picked up a glass from the lip of the Jacuzzi. "You weren't drinking and taking these pills, too, were you?"

"Please get out."

"It's a wonder you didn't fall into a coma."

He groaned and put his head over the toilet again.

"I knew I should have come over here last night."

"No, you shouldn't."

"Obviously, your lady friend didn't know how to care for you properly."

"Leave her out of this, Claire. I'm warning you."

She fell so silent that he thought she might have left the room but when he glanced up again, she was still there, staring at him and frowning. He opened his mouth to beg her to leave him be when his cell phone rang. Before he could stop her, she'd gone in search of it.

30

Ryan grabbed the remote control from a fellow officer's desk and turned up the volume on one of the flat screen television sets mounted near the ceiling. It was relatively quiet in the office, which was quite rare. But it seemed with the impending hurricane headed for the North Carolina shores, even the perps were busy battening down the hatches.

Now he perched on the edge of his desk as he watched the weatherman pointing at the projected path Hurricane Irene was expected to take.

"Just six days ago," he was saying, "this system was declared a tropical storm. On that day—August 20—it made landfall in St. Croix." He pointed to the area on the map. "The next day, it made landfall again in Puerto Rico. While it was moving across the island, it strengthened into a Category 1 Hurricane." He pointed to an area between Puerto Rico and the Bahamas. "It was only after it skipped across the Bahamas, making four landfalls there, that it strengthened into Category 3 with sustained winds of 120 miles per hour."

Chief Johnston entered the room and stopped to watch the weather report.

"But after curving north of Grand Bahama, it's steadily decreased. Now we're looking at a Category 1. This might sound like it's less dangerous but we want to warn all viewers that a Category 1 can still produce major power outages and winds up to 95 miles per hour. We're advising all viewers who live in mobile homes along this area to move inland to permanent structures. Expect to be without power for several days…"

"Looks like it's going to hit the coast," Ryan said to the chief.

"Yep."

They watched as the weatherman laid out the projected path. It ranged from a direct hit just north of Myrtle Beach, South Carolina to the Outer Banks of North Carolina.

"Let's hope it passes us before it makes landfall," Chief Johnston said. "We still expect widespread outages and some serious flooding."

They watched for a few minutes as weather pundits made personal predictions. Then the chief said, "Landfall—wherever it hits first—will be tomorrow morning. That much we know."

"Aye."

"So when the night shift comes on duty, your task force is dismantled pending further notice."

"I wasn't aware I still had a task force," Ryan said. The chief raised a brow and he added, thumbing toward the conference room, "On account of the FBI getting involved, you know."

"Why are you here, anyway?" Chief Johnston asked. He casually poured himself a cup of coffee.

"I didn't want to shirk my duties."

The chief half-turned to look at him before turning back to add sugar to his cup. "The real reason."

"My sister wouldn't leave."

"We should all have sisters like Claire."

Ryan nodded. "I suppose you're right."

The chief made his way to Ryan's desk. "The agents have gone in a different direction with this investigation."

"Oh?"

"They believe it's someone in the medical profession. They're starting with surgeons and they're looking for those who have links to both Atlanta and this area."

"They think it's someone who lives here?"

"Or who did live here at one time."

"They're wrong."

"Why are you so certain it's a South African national? He has no priors. There's no evidence to suggest that he has any medical training."

"Why would he need medical training?"

"Come on, O'Clery. Can you imagine how difficult it would be to slash a woman's jugular? Not to mention four of them? And not a single one showed signs of a struggle."

"I admit whoever committed the murders is a professional. But not necessarily a doctor. Could he not have worked in autopsies, perhaps, or in a morgue? Either of those might have given him an education in anatomy."

"But why only here and Atlanta?"

"I can't answer that."

Chief Johnston studied him for a moment. "This APB you've got out on Diallo Delport."

"Aye?"

"The FBI wants to rescind it."

"They want to what?"

"They don't think he's involved."

"Why did he run? Not once, but twice, I might add."

The chief shrugged. "He could have picked somebody's pocket. Stolen something from a convenience store. Driven off without paying for gas. There are all sorts of reasons why a suspect runs. But it doesn't necessarily link them to the crime you're trying to solve."

"I have a gut feeling about this man."

"Gut feelings don't stand up in court. We need evidence."

"I can place him at the theatre the night before the first victim was murdered. I can place him at the doctor's office hours before the second victim was murdered."

"So he watches a play and he goes to the doctor. Neither one proves him guilty beyond a reasonable doubt. And believe me a jury would have a reasonable doubt with that so-called evidence. It wouldn't even be enough for the grand jury to move ahead with a trial."

"But—"

"I need evidence, Ryan. I need something to prove that he was at the scene of the crime. Not at the theatre watching a play before the woman was murdered the next day several blocks away. Not seeing a doctor whose staff member was murdered blocks away several hours later. *At the scene of the crime.*"

Ryan muted the television set and walked around his desk before sitting heavily in his chair. "How am I to gather that evidence while I'm sitting at this desk?"

"I'm not putting you back on the street. You look like you've been run over by a train. In fact, I personally think you need to go back home."

"I can't do that, sir. And it isn't that Claire is there," he added hastily. "I know she's long gone. The girls are only in preschool in the mornings. She's got her hands full with them. It's just that, well, if you must know the truth of it, I don't want to sit at home."

Chief Johnston nodded. "I understand." He finished his coffee and crushed the cup before tossing it into a nearby wastebasket. "There might be something I can have you do."

Ryan felt himself sit a little taller. "Aye?"

"I got an email this morning from the Atlanta Chief of Police. They have a lot of information that might help us." He thumbed toward the conference room. "Might help them. But it's not all electronic so they can't email it. I need someone to go to Atlanta and pick it up."

"Couldn't they overnight it?"

"Some of it's evidence and we've got the chain of custody issue."

"Aye, the chain of custody."

"I need an officer of the law to pick it up and sign for it. And with this hurricane approaching, I can't spare anybody."

"But you can spare me."

The chief leveled his eyes at him. "I couldn't spare you yesterday. But after you decided to skewer a police vehicle…"

He motioned toward Ryan's face, which he was sure was black and blue by now. "There's not a lot else I can use you for."

"Atlanta is five hours' drive."

"So, if you want to get started this afternoon, you can make it down there by nightfall. Check into a hotel; get a good night's sleep. Pick up the evidence in the morning and head back. You could be back here by early afternoon tomorrow. Piece of cake."

Ryan nodded and the chief started toward his office. "I'll forward the email to you, O'Clery."

His phone rang and he answered it on the first ring.

"This is Janice," the caller stated.

"Aye?" He frowned as he tried to place the name.

"I'm doing the autopsies on the victims."

"Ah, yes, Janice. What can I do for you?"

"I'm not finished, not by a long shot. But I was told to contact you if I came across anything that might be of interest to you..."

"And you have something of interest, do you?" He leaned forward.

"Possibly. I noticed a mark on the first victim. Made me curious so I searched the others."

"A mark you say?"

"I found the same mark on each victim. And I believe they were all made by the same device. They were all Tasered."

"That is quite interesting," Ryan said as his mind began to race. "Anything else?"

"That's all for now. Just thought you'd want to know."

"Aye. Thank you."

He hung up the phone. It made perfect sense. None of the women could fight their attacker once they'd been Tasered. He remembered well the lessons on a Taser gun, which required each officer to be struck with it during training. It caused neuromuscular incapacitation, or NMI. It meant that while the victim's brain could register what was happening around her, including watching the killer approaching with a weapon, she had absolutely no control over her body muscles, rendering her completely immobilized and helpless.

It was why, he thought, they had such looks of sheer terror on their faces. If the killer could get close enough to Taser them, they would have dropped to the ground right where they were. Perhaps they had involuntary muscle spasms or went into convulsions. But if he acted quickly and he knew what he was using—which he obviously did—he could slice their throats so quickly that by the time their body might have recovered from the Taser, they were already bleeding out. Between the electrical shock and having their jugulars sliced, none of them stood a chance.

He logged onto his email and leaned back in his chair. Various weathermen and hurricane experts were plastered across the television screens. He turned up the volume on one of the stations while he waited for the chief's email to pop into his inbox. They were forecasting that the hurricane would make landfall between 5:00 am and 8:00 am the following morning. That meant he would be in Atlanta when it struck the coast and on his return home, he would most likely encounter heavy winds and rain. Of course, if it was too intense, he could stop and wait it out or even turn back around and head further inland.

The email popped up and he opened it, read the contents and clicked to print it along with an attachment. He heard the whir of the printer and he wandered to the other side of the room to wait for all the pages to print.

Officer Zuker was making his way into the room and he nodded in greeting as he walked to an empty desk.

The conference room was close by and the agents' voices drifted toward the printer as Ryan waited. They had secured a list of every doctor licensed to practice in North Carolina and had compared it to a similar list from Georgia, which narrowed down the suspects to less than a hundred. Now they were painstakingly analyzing each of those doctor's pasts and any complaints against them, any problems with the medical board or any criminal history.

What a bag of wasters, he thought. He had a suspect and nobody was looking for him.

He was pulling the last of the pages out of the printer when Dr. Gravestone stepped outside the conference room. Seeing him standing there, he nodded amicably but Ryan could see a glint in his eye.

"Working the case, 'eh?" Ryan said, trying to keep his voice cordial.

"Yes. And we're about to close in on the suspect."

"Is that so?"

"We're doing it the *intelligent* way." He stressed the word as he locked eyes with him.

Ryan nodded. When he spoke, his voice was thick with an Irish accent he generally reserved for pub crawling. "I can see that you're makin' bags o' the case like a lineup o' bowsie wasters," he said politely.

Dr. Gravestone puffed out his chest. "Thank you."

"No need to thank me, gent," Ryan said as he started back to his desk. "You've certainly earned the distinction."

Zuker slid his chair partway into the aisle. As Ryan approached, he whispered, "What did that mean?"

Ryan glanced behind him. Dr. Gravestone was making his way back into the conference room. "I'm not quite sure how it would be translated in America," he said under his breath. "But in Ireland it means they're royally botching the case."

Zuker started laughing.

"Not too loud now," Ryan chided. "We don't want them to be on to us." He reached his desk and stapled the pages together. Then he sat back in his chair and started to read them. Something began to gnaw at him. Twice, he stopped and cocked his head as if listening but he couldn't quite put his finger on the source of his discomfort.

Then he stared at the television screens and the continued coverage of the hurricane.

Two murders, nearly two hundred years apart. Both arrived in town with a theatre group.

Second in the string were two nurses.

He didn't yet know about the additional homicides Rián Kelly had worked but he had his suspicions.

What he did know is a hurricane was bearing down on the Atlantic seaboard while he was being dispatched to Atlanta, five hours away. That left Cathleen here alone. And he wouldn't return until after the storm had passed and the damage was done.

He logged back into his email and displayed the chief's forwarded message. The original email had the *"From"* and *"To"* lines completed as well as the subject line. He stared at the sender's name; the label read *"Chief Gary Gifford, Atlanta Metro Police Dept."* It certainly looked official. Before the start of the email itself, the police department's logo was prominently displayed.

He scrolled to the bottom and read the signature lines consisting of the chief's name and the physical location of the Atlanta Police Department headquarters.

On a whim, he switched to an Internet browser and looked up the Atlanta PD. The physical address was the same; so was the chief's name. Then why did he have such an uneasy feeling?

He returned to the email and hovered his mouse over the *"From"* line. A tag line popped up with a generic address. He found that interesting. Even in this small town, the chief's name was part of his address. Ryan's name was part of his. And with Ryan's address, like everyone who worked at this police department, the domain listed the city and state. Wouldn't a city as large as Atlanta be the same?

He picked up his phone, switched back to the Atlanta website, located the police department's main phone number and called. The switchboard answered and he asked for the chief's office. A brief moment later, a woman answered the phone with, "Chief Gifford's office."

"Hello. This is Detective Ryan O'Clery with the Lumberton Police Department in North Carolina. I need to send the chief some information and I was wondering if you'd be so kind as to tell me his email address?"

"Certainly," the woman responded immediately. "It's ggifford at Atlanta g-a dot gov."

He repeated it to her and waited for her to verify what he had was correct. "Tell me," he said, "is there any possibility the chief might have sent me an email from a different address?"

"I think it's highly unlikely, if it's official business."

"Are you sure about that?" He read the address in the email. "Does that ring a bell with you?"

"No, it doesn't," she answered. "And if it's official business, we're prohibited from using a third party email provider like that one; it boils down to security and confidential information."

"That would make perfect sense," he said. "Thank you. You've been most helpful. Tell me, is the chief there where I may speak to him?"

"He's in a meeting but I can leave him a message."

"Fine; would you do that for me?" He repeated his name and gave his phone number. After she hung up the phone, he found himself still holding the receiver in his hand, his mind racing.

Then he slowly rose from his chair, hung up the phone and strode to Chief Johnston's office, where he found him sitting at his desk signing papers.

"Sir," he said, stopping just inside the door.

Chief Johnston glanced up. "You still here?"

"I won't be going to Atlanta, sir."

"Excuse me?" When he looked up again, his face was reddening.

"I thought the email looked a bit suspicious so I checked out the sender's address. It didn't come from the Atlanta chief's office."

"Are you sure about that?"

"I just spoke to his secretary. He has a completely different address. This one is generic and with a third party vendor. I left a message for the chief to call me, just to cover all the bases."

"Interesting."

"I thought so, too."

"Call Deanna Wentworth in the IT Department. See if she can find out who that email address is registered to. If they're within our jurisdiction, we'll make an arrest. And if they're not, we'll pass the information to the correct agency so they can."

"Aye, sir."

Ryan turned to go but the chief called to him and he turned back around.

"Why would someone send an email like that?" Chief Johnston asked.

"I've been wondering the same thing. It would have sent me on a wild goose chase. By the time I'd found out the chief didn't send it, I'd be five hours from home and would have lost a day and a half of work."

"Have Deanna check just to make sure it didn't contain a virus."

Ryan nodded as he thought of the attachment he'd opened. He made his way back to his desk, where he called Deanna. A few minutes later, she was sitting in his chair, running a virus scan and preparing to trace the email.

Ryan tidied up his desk while he pondered this new turn of events. Deanna printed out the email, along with the source code. While she made her way to the printer, an email popped up from Forensics. He opened it and then opened the attachments.

The shoe print found along the river near the third victim had been photographed and a cast made from it. He sent the photograph to the printer.

"I'm leaving," he announced to Deanna as she made her way back to his desk. "When you're done here, could you power it down for me?"

"Anything for you," she said, glancing up at him and smiling.

He patted her shoulder as he walked around her. "Thank you." He made his way to the printer, picked up the photograph, and started down the hallway. He should have been on his way to Atlanta right now, he thought. But that little voice inside him was beginning to tell him he had just altered the course of his life.

31

The motel was still as shady looking as it had been the first time he'd seen it. As he pulled into the parking lot and stopped in front of Delport's old room, Arlo pulled in beside him. While the evidence technician removed his case from the car, Ryan pulled the photograph from the passenger seat.

He didn't have to kick down the door this time. The proprietor herself was waiting on the sidewalk before he had even exited his vehicle, ready to unlock the padlock that had been placed on the door after he busted it. She kept her lips pressed together as if she wanted to say something but was trying to hold her tongue. Ryan wondered if Little Johnny had made bail yet from his drug arrest and then realized he was most likely back at home an hour after being booked.

The room was exactly as they'd left it the day before. It was not a surprise, as he figured few people would be interested in renting a room that could only be locked from the outside.

He turned on the lights and led Arlo to the nightstand, where he held the photograph beside the shoeprint. "Look at that," he breathed. It appeared to be an exact match but he knew the evidence techs would have to substantiate that. "I'll need

2

photographs and whatever else you need to do to preserve this print."

"You got it," Arlo said, setting his case on the bed.

"I'll be outside," Ryan said. "There's a breezeway just outside this door and I'm going in search of additional shoeprints. I saw them yesterday and I'll want you to process those as well."

The sky was growing darker as he made his way down the breezeway and he found himself studying the clouds as they rolled over. It was going to be one hell of a storm. He could feel it. He could also feel the effects of the pain killers wearing off and he hoped Arlo wouldn't take long. Between the whiskey, the pain pills, a hot Jacuzzi and a soft woman, he'd been in great shape last night. Right now, not so much.

But when he emerged from the breezeway, he stopped short. The rains had flooded the back of the lot and any prints he had spotted the day before were now submerged. He silently cursed himself and his carelessness. He should have processed this scene the day before.

He walked along the sidewalk, staring at the waters that rose within inches of the establishment. Glancing at the wall on the far side of the sidewalk, he noticed watermarks. That meant by this time tomorrow, the entire motel could be flooded if they got the rains that were expected.

Not my problem, he thought, as he continued to the edge of the building. But now as he thought about things, he began to wonder about Claire and the girls. Fort Bragg would most likely be on high alert and Tommy could be working. That meant his sister and nieces would be left alone a few miles outside of town.

He stopped when he reached the end of the building and hit speed dial for Claire's number.

"Are you feeling better?" she said by way of answering.

"Is Tommy working tonight or tomorrow?"

"It's his Saturday to work. He's to be in at six o'clock."

"Pack your things."

"What? Why?"

"You're spending the night at my house. You and the girls."

"Why?"

"Can't you do anything without a long, drawn-out explanation?"

"No. Actually, I can't."

"Christ."

"Do not use the Lord's name in vain, Re."

He sighed heavily. "There's a hurricane heading for the coast."

"No."

"Come on, Claire."

"I've been telling you about it for a week now," she said.

"I'm worried about you and the girls. I think you could be left stranded in the county. The waters could rise. They're expecting widespread power outages. You could be in a situation where no one could reach you. I'd feel better if you and the girls stayed in town with me. It'll be the first to come back online if the power goes out. And I know I can take care of you here."

"Okay, okay. One tenth of that explanation would've sufficed."

"So you'll come to my house straight-away."

She hesitated. "I'm just taking supper off the stove. Let me feed Tommy and the girls. We'll be over around eight o'clock."

He glanced at his watch. It wasn't quite five o'clock. "It takes you that long to eat?"

"I'm not going to leave the house in a mess with dishes on the table and food on the stove. I'm going to feed my family, clean things up like I usually do. And it will take me some time to pack the girls' things. I have to count on staying with you for several days. And you might not have electricity or water for me to wash their clothes. This takes some preparation, you know."

His eyes wandered as he listened to her. Something told him she already had made her preparations; she was just that way. On this side of the building, the ground was higher and as he stared across the lot, he realized the water drained away from this side. He heard his name and he turned to see Arlo heading toward him.

Ryan waved the technician in his direction. "Fine," he said, realizing Claire had stopped talking. "Just get there before the hurricane hits."

"I'll be there tonight. I'll see you shortly."

He clicked off his phone and knelt as his eyes roamed the grounds. There was no grass; only weeds that appeared to have been unkempt for years. But as he surveyed the ground, he thought he saw what he was hoping for.

"There," he said, pointing as Arlo approached. "Any shoeprints out there that resemble the one in the room, I need processed."

"You know," Arlo said, "I won't be sure until I get back to the office and compare them with my software, but the print in the room back there sure looked a lot like ones I got in the field where the fourth victim was found."

"Oh, that's grand news," Ryan said. It was all beginning to come together. Now all he needed to do was apprehend Diallo Delport before he killed again.

32

As soon as Ryan pulled onto his street, he spotted the cherry red sports car parked in front of his house. He didn't have to wonder who it belonged to; he knew that car well. He'd paid for it.

He pulled past it and into the driveway, hitting the garage door opener and quickly parking. But before he could close it, he noticed in his rearview mirror that a woman was ducking inside. She was nearly as tall as Ryan and shapely. Her blond hair was long and straight; now it was pulled into a flirty ponytail. But it did not evoke feelings within him of freeing her hair from its confines.

He stepped out of his car and closed the door as she approached.

"Nice car," she said. She looked admiringly at his metallic blue Audi TTS coupe. "Must have cost a pretty penny."

"I'm sure it cost the drug dealer some nice change," he said. "I bought it at auction after it had been seized." He felt the color rising in his cheeks. Buying a car at auction was all he could afford after she'd taken him to the cleaners. It was pure luck that this little baby was available on the cheap.

"I wanted to talk with you," she said, looking back at him and smiling.

He didn't return the smile. "How did you know I'd be home?"

She shrugged. "I took a gamble. They showed a video of you on TV this morning; I figured you'd be in no shape to work. I've actually been by the house several times today, looking for you…"

Lucky me. "This isn't a good time, Sophie."

"Please let me come in. It'll only take a minute."

He considered telling her to contact his attorney but thought better of it. It would only cost him more money. He sighed and led the way to the door leading from the garage into the house.

They walked through the laundry room into the kitchen. He hit the remote. Somehow, he felt more comfortable having noise in the background. His stomach was beginning to feel tied in knots.

She glanced around the kitchen and den. It was her first time in his new place and he hoped it would be her last. He saw her eyes settle on the leather couch and then the flat screen TV and he couldn't help but wonder if she was trying to add up their cost.

Finally, she turned back to him.

He needed a whiskey on the rocks but he didn't want to offer her anything to drink so he stood by the counter and waited for her to speak.

"Listen, Re," she began. Her voice was soft and sensuous, just as it always had been. "I know a lot has happened between us."

She stopped and looked at him expectantly as if she was waiting for him to say something. He wondered if she wanted him to agree with her; commiserate over the misery they'd caused each other, perhaps. He remained silent.

"I've had a lot of time to think things over this past year," she continued. "And I'm sorry I hurt you."

Destroyed me is what you did, he thought. Hurt was too mild a word.

"I was wrong. And if I could take it all back, I would."

He shifted his weight and waited for her to continue.

She took a step toward him and he took a step backward, bumping against the counter.

"I hope you don't hate me," she said.

"There was a time when I hated you," he said. The sound of his own voice surprised him; he hadn't intended to say anything at all. "But I don't hate you now. I feel sorry for you. Sorry that you never found what you were looking for."

She hesitated. "I had what I was looking for, right here. With you. And I was too stupid to realize it."

"I forgive you, Sophie, if that's what you're wanting to hear." She took another step toward him and he held up his hand as if to stop her. "But I'm not the answer. I was never the answer."

Her brows knit together. "But—"

"I wasn't your true love. I was just the one you settled for while you were still looking."

"But I realize now that—"

"Don't say it," he urged. "You might mean it now. But you won't mean it tomorrow. You *shouldn't* mean it tomorrow."

"I don't understand." Her bottom lip trembled and she bit into it to keep it still.

"I thought I loved you," he said. His voice was gentle but he knew even as he spoke that his words would hurt her. "But I know now what real love is. And I know that what we had wasn't ever meant to be."

He walked around her toward the front door. He thought for a moment that she wasn't going to follow him and he wasn't quite sure how he would get her to leave. But when he opened the door and turned around, she was standing just a few feet away from him. "I don't hate you, Sophie. And I hope someday you find what you're looking for."

She started to walk through the door but as she brushed past him, she stopped and turned back. She raised her hands as if she might try to touch him and again he instinctively held up one hand in an attempt to block her.

"Don't," he said. "Walk away, Sophie. While you've still got your dignity."

She started to say something and he turned his attention downward, away from her face, away from the big blue eyes that were welling with tears, away from the pouty lips that quivered. After a moment that seemed to go on forever, she walked out the door.

33

When the doorbell rang a few minutes later, he thought she had returned and he almost didn't answer it. But his feet seemed to have a mind of their own and he found himself in the front hallway with his hand on the door knob.

"Ryan," Cathleen said as he opened it.

He reached for her, pulling her inside the house and into his arms. Before she could say anything else, his lips were on hers. No matter how tight he held her, no matter how long the embrace, he knew he could never get enough of her; she could never be too close for him.

She returned his kiss with a passion he had dreamed about; and yet, this was better than any dream. He felt, for the first time in his life, like he was whole.

When at last their lips parted, he realized he had never closed the front door. And as he held her pressed against him, her hair brushing against his cheek and her soft curves blending with his body, he realized he didn't care.

"I came by a couple of times," she whispered. "I thought you'd be here."

He pulled slightly away from her to look into her eyes. Those flecks of gold enticed him, and when she smiled warmly, the skin crinkled around her eyes in a way that beckoned him to run his fingers over her skin. "If I knew you were here," he said, "I wouldn't have been anywhere else."

Her hand went to his cheek; he didn't realize until her fingers stroked him that he had forgotten to shave. As he stared into her eyes, she kept hers on his face, as if she was trying to memorize every nuance. "It occurred to me," she said, her voice a sexy whisper, "that since I arrived in town, I've had every dinner over here. And I was hoping not to break the habit."

He lifted her off her feet as he laughed. "That's music to my ears, darlin'." As he leaned further back, he had a sudden stab of pain in his spine and he reluctantly set her back down.

"Are you okay?" she asked, her brows furrowing.

"Fine. Better than fine, now that you're here." He closed the front door and led her into the den. "But I never picked up those steaks I promised you. Would something else do?"

"I don't care if we have peanut butter sandwiches, as long as I'm with you."

He started toward the cabinets but she stopped him and pulled him back to face her. "There's no need to hurry. We have all the time in the world."

As he stared into her eyes, he wanted to drop to his knee and ask her to marry him. He wanted to tell her that he never wanted to spend another night alone without her; he never wanted to awaken without his arms around her. He didn't want another moment to pass without her in his life, sharing his life and all that was in it.

But as she sank her head against his chest, he knew he couldn't ask her to marry him because she was married to another. The thought caused his chest to constrict and his breathing to grow shallow. They had to talk about it; this man, this marriage, that was wedged between them.

But not now. He couldn't do it now. He couldn't risk spoiling the moment. He couldn't handle it if she told him she wouldn't get a divorce.

"I want you to stay here tonight," he said.

"You're starting to plan now?"

"The hurricane is expected to hit sometime tomorrow morning, early."

"I know. I—"

"Don't run the risk of being stranded alone in your hotel."

She gently pulled far enough away from him to look him in the eye. "You think it's going to hit here?"

"One model has it hitting north of Myrtle Beach and heading inland, directly over us."

"I see."

"Even if it manages to skirt around us, we're expecting widespread power outages."

"I know."

He chuckled. "Of course you know. You're a reporter."

"We have been covering it for a week now," she quietly chided. "In fact, I've been reassigned."

His heart skipped a beat. "What does that mean, reassigned? You're not leaving?"

She placed her head against his chest again. "Tomorrow, I have to start covering the aftereffects of the hurricane."

He pulled away. "They're not aiming to put you in front of a camera with a rain slicker on, are they, while wicked winds buffet you around live on TV?"

She laughed. "No. That's somebody else's job." Then she grew serious. "I'll go in after the hurricane is through and I'll interview people who've lost their homes—"

"Christ. Isn't that a bit like crashing a funeral?"

"Not—"

"I mean, there are some things that should remain between a man and his God, don't you think? I wouldn't want the worst day of my life broadcast all over the world."

"Like it was yesterday?" She was obviously trying to stifle her laughter but catching the serious expression on Ryan's face, she added, "Some of these people could lose everything. And if I can show them on TV, there's a chance someone else will send them money or clothes or food."

"That really happens?"

"More often than you think."

"Well." He raced through the possibilities in his head. "That's more of a reason for you to stay here. We'll put your car in the garage where it'll be safer. And if you need it, mine is all wheel drive; it'll get you anywhere about town. I can pave the way with the police department to get you where you need to be to cover the story."

"My cameraman—"

"He can stay here, too."

"Just how many bedrooms do you have here?"

"Well, you'll be staying in mine, I hope you know."

"My cameraman has family here. He's not staying at the hotel. He'd be about two miles from here."

"Well, there you have it. We'll make sure you get connected in the morning."

"Will you go with me back to my hotel to get my stuff?"

He kissed her on her forehead. "You can check out completely. Stay here with me. Not just tonight."

"Are you sure?"

"I couldn't be surer of anything in my life."

"Let's go now and get it over with."

Ryan reached for his keys. Taking Cathleen's hand, he led her toward the door into the garage. Then he stopped abruptly. "Oh, I forgot to mention."

"Yes?"

"My sister Claire will be staying here, also. And her two girls."

"Are you serious?"

Ryan thought she lost some color in her cheeks but he couldn't be certain. "Is there a problem with that?"

"You tell me."

"I'm not following your meaning."

"That's five people here. If we lose power, that's five people with not much to do. No television, no stove, food spoiling in the refrigerator…"

"We'll make it work."

"I mean," she said, her cheeks turning red, "if it was just the two of us, we could spend the whole time in bed."

"We could anyway."

"With your sister and two little girls here?"

"Well, it's not like you're a screamer."

"I'm serious."

He leaned against the wall. "Are you saying you don't want my sister and my nieces here?"

"I'm not saying that at all."

"That's good that's not what you're saying."

"I just don't know how comfortable they might be with me being here, too."

"I don't think it's their comfort you're concerned about. I think it's your comfort." He felt like he was staring into her eyes, as if he could somehow read her mind if he looked long enough. "You got along well with my nieces. And my sister will be fine, too."

"I don't think Claire likes me."

"Why? Because of the phone conversation last night?" He made a noise as if to dismiss her concern. "She knows I'm happy with you. That's all that will matter to her."

"If you're sure…"

"I'm sure. Now let's go." As he led her into the garage and helped her into the passenger seat, a small voice began to grow inside him. She was a married woman, he thought. And Claire knows she's married to someone else. And being in the house with four females and no electricity was suddenly becoming worrisome.

34

Ryan poured himself another glass of whiskey and made his way into the den. Rían Kelly's journal lay open on the recliner with a bookmark holding the place where he'd stopped reading.

It was approaching midnight and Claire had not yet arrived. Cathleen had fallen asleep in his arms an hour ago and after a few minutes of watching her sleep and memorizing every degree of her facial features, he had gently extricated himself, slipped on a pair of shorts and headed to the den.

He'd spent the last few minutes reading the journal and now he found himself questioning everything he'd ever been taught. It was as if he was stepping into a parallel world where everything was playing out on two continents across two centuries.

Four women were murdered in Rían Kelly's time; four women with their jugulars sliced. Four women who did not know each other and were not connected in any way other than their deaths. And Rían Kelly, like himself, was determined to find the killer.

Ryan settled into the chair and began reading where he'd left off.

*There are reports of a stranger in the village. No
one remembers when he first appeared and no one seems
to know why he is here. I have attempted on numerous
occasions to speak with him. I have visited Mrs.
Doherty's home where he is purportedly renting a room
but each time he has not been about. I have a general
description which has left me rather curious. He appears
to have no color at all in his body. Though not an old
man, they say his hair is white. Even his brows and
his eyelashes are white. His skin is nearly translucent.
And they say under the right light, they can see inside
his eyes, which causes them to appear pink or purple.
But apart from this, he bears a curious scar across his
face. They say it appears as though one eye is crying;
the scar leaves the middle of the eye and forms a
teardrop. And the scar is raised. I would not have
believed the description, were it not given me by credible
people I've known my whole life. And I could not fathom
why Mrs. Doherty, alone and unprotected, would have
allowed such a man to remain in her home. But then,
I have it on good authority that she's suffered many a
financial setback since the passing of her husband some
ten years past and she might have been desperate to
right her finances.*

He heard a car door slam shut and he reluctantly set aside
the journal. If it hadn't been for the very real murders, he would
have been convinced that someone was playing a cruel joke on
him. His mind was having serious issues coming to terms with
the similarities.

He opened the front door to find Tommy and Claire coming
up the sidewalk, each toting a sleepy little girl. Their border collie
bounded past them and into the house.

"Oh," Ryan said, "I'd forgotten about Henry."

"He doesn't pee on the couch anymore, Uncle Re," Emma
said groggily.

"Well," Ryan said as Tommy headed down the hall with her,
"that's a good thing then, isn't it?"

"I've got a carload of stuff to bring in the house," Claire said.

"I wondered what was taking you so long."

"I got to thinking about the possibility of us being here for days without power and I wanted to plan for every contingency."

"And it all fit in one vehicle?"

Claire rolled her eyes and headed down the hall with Erin while Ryan made his way outside. His jaw dropped when he saw their minivan's windows. They were almost completely blocked by all manner of things.

"I've got a dolly," Tommy said, joining him.

"Did she pack your entire household?"

"You know you can't argue with her." He opened the tailgate and pulled out a hand truck.

As they started removing items, Ryan said, "So, you're to be at work in six hours?"

"Yeah. When I leave here, I'm going to Fort Bragg. I'm expecting a long day tomorrow. We've been getting ready for all sorts of possibilities—downed trees, power outages, the works."

"Us, too."

They carried the first load into the house and set it inside the den. Claire was sitting in the recliner with Rían Kelly's journal in her lap.

"You know there's someone sleeping in your bed?" she asked.

"You didn't wake her, did you?"

"I don't think so. That's not your married lady friend, is it?"

"You're seeing a married woman?" Tommy's jaw dropped. "You, of all people—"

"Thank you, Claire." Ryan returned to the car, where he busied himself with preparing another load to bring in. He was thankful Tommy was quiet when he joined him again. He seemed to be in a bit of a hurry now and Ryan couldn't blame him. It was a forty-five minute drive to Fort Bragg and it was already after midnight.

When the last load had been delivered and Tommy was back on the road, Ryan joined Claire in the den.

"So you've been reading more of Rían Kelly's journal, have you?" she asked. She looked tired. Her eyes were puffy and bloodshot and her voice was strained.

"Who has a copy of that journal?" Ryan asked.

Her eyes widened. "I don't believe there is a copy."

"Somebody's got a copy of it."

"How can you be so sure?"

"Rían Kelly details a serial murder case he was working on just before the storm hit. There were a total of four murders just like the ones I've been investigating this week."

"Well, that's got to be coincidence."

"The first was a woman with a traveling theatre group. In Ireland and here. The second was a nurse or physician's assistant. Same in both places. All four were murdered in the same manner, with a slit across the jugular. Same as my cases."

"That can't be."

"But it is. And just now, just before you drove up, I was reading a description of a stranger in the Irish village where Rían Kelly lived; the description was spot-on for my suspect."

She stared at the journal in her lap. "But how can that be possible?"

"Tell me something, Claire. When you were in college, did you study albinism?"

She combed her hair with her fingers for a moment while she thought. "Only in the sense of the psychological aspects. I was training for social work, you remember."

"I'm just curious, is all, if you have an albino—not just someone who is light skinned or light haired, but a true albino—what is the likelihood of producing a child with the same affliction?"

"What does this have to do with Rían Kelly's journal?"

"The stranger in his village fits the same description as my suspect. Both are albino. Both have a very specific scar on their faces as well, and I know that's not hereditary. So the thought occurred to me, suppose Rían Kelly found this stranger. And suppose he was responsible for bringing him to justice. Maybe the man was hanged. Maybe he spent a lifetime in prison. I don't know yet; I've not gotten that far. But just suppose he had a child. And that child grew up hating Rían Kelly for what he perceived was an injustice. And the hatred was passed down from generation to generation, until someone our age is told the tale. And he decides to repeat every murder with me, since Rían Kelly had no direct descendants. Even going so far as to disfigure his own face to match the scar of his ancestor."

"That sounds mighty far-fetched to me, if you want my honest opinion."

"But the alternative is even less believable."

"I'm tired, Re. I've had a long day and the girls wake up early like they've got built-in alarm clocks." She rose and set the journal on the coffee table.

"Are you absolutely certain there are no copies of that journal?" Ryan asked.

"I don't see how there could be. The content of those boxes I delivered to you were found in Auntie's attic. She'd lived in that house for more than forty years. And no one remembered seeing those records before."

"Forty years," Ryan mused. "There were photocopy establishments back then."

"But it's unlikely they would have had photocopies made. I mean, have you seen how many records there are?" She started down the hall. "That would have cost a fortune. Who has that kind of money? Not our family, that's for sure."

She didn't wait for his response. A moment later, the bedroom door opened and closed.

He sat for a few minutes, thinking about his theory in the semi-darkness. Then he gathered the journal and made his way down the hallway. He found the border collie lying in front of the guest room door. He reached down and scratched him behind his ear. "You're a good pup, Henry," he said as he opened the door and let him into the bedroom. Erin and Emma were sound asleep in a twin-sized bed, holding each other like they were afraid of losing one another while they slept. Claire was in the other twin-sized bed.

"Good night, Claire."

"Night, Re. Thanks for taking care of us."

"It's what families do."

"I know."

He closed the door and continued to his bedroom. It was dark and he hesitated while his eyes adjusted. Then he made his way to the bed. Slipping off his shorts, he slid in beside Cathleen. She moaned softly and her arm immediately wrapped around him. He settled into her and she into him like they'd been doing it forever.

And as he lay there, he contemplated that even if his theory was correct and Diallo Delport was copying crimes first committed nearly two centuries ago, it didn't explain how he could be dreaming Rían Kelly's memories.

35

The murders stopped after the Night of the Big Wind. Most people in the village became too absorbed in rebuilding their lives to give the serial killer and his victims much thought. It wasn't that they no longer cared; but rather, that their own survival had been endangered by a freakish storm that had come without warning and had left massive devastation in its wake.

Only Rían Kelly could not shake the memories. Along with those memories of the week before the storm struck came an immense, nearly debilitating guilt that sank his soul to the depths of despair. Had he been able to solve the first four murders and apprehend the mysterious stranger, he knew in his heart and soul that his beloved Cait would still be alive.

An actress. A medical assistant. A legal secretary. And a young mother.

But it had never been about the first four victims. He knew that now. They were just the means by which the stranger had captured his attention. He goaded him and played his game with him, knowing all the while that the real target was Caitlín O'Conor. And the reason she was targeted was simply because Rían Kelly was in love with her and the stranger despised him.

He didn't know why; he knew he'd never met him before. But he would spend the rest of his life trying to piece the puzzle together.

If he had it all to do over again, he knew beyond a shadow of a doubt that he would not have left Cait alone; not for one single minute. He would have sent a dispatch of his own to Dublin to retrieve the evidence they purportedly had there. Or he would have ignored it entirely. But he would not have left the village.

If he had it all to do over again, when he turned his horse back toward the village and saw Cait standing there by the gate, he would have spurred the steed back to her. He would have dismounted that animal the moment it stopped, swept Cait into his arms and never let her go.

For he knew now that the dispatch summoning him to Dublin was a ruse. No one in Dublin had beckoned him there. No one had any evidence.

But the killer knew it would take him hours to reach the city. And by the time he learned of the deception, it would be too late.

Rián interviewed several in the village who remembered well those final horrific hours. The stranger had departed Mrs. Doherty's home before dawn. His room was left exactly as it had been before he'd arrived just one week prior. Some said they spotted him walking along the narrow road from the village proper; he was heading toward the creek that ran between the hills.

There were only a few homes nestled near the creek. The one furthest to the east belonged to the O'Conors. And on that fateful morning, only Cait was at home when the stranger let himself into the gate.

A tenant farmer working on the adjacent hill would tell Rián that he stopped to mop his brow when he spied the stranger lurking near a window of the O'Conor home. Dropping his farming implement to the ground, he immediately began his descent. When he looked again, the stranger was gone but the window was open.

Though it wasn't yet dusk, the sky turned black as though the end of the world had arrived and he could not see even one foot in front of him. He heard Cait's screams and then the winds began to howl like a chorus of banshees. Struck with terror, the man barely made it to shelter with his life still intact.

No one knew why Cait screamed. She might have glanced out the window to see the skies bearing down and the floodwaters barreling toward her, instantly swelling the creek to the proportions of a river.

Or she might have found a stranger with a tear-shaped scar across his face standing in her home with a weapon meant to slice her throat.

Rían never found Cait's body. Each time one was reported, he journeyed to it, whether it took him a few minutes or a few days. And each time he saw that it was the body of a man or a child or a woman too large or with blond or red hair, he wept. He blubbered like a baby and he didn't care who witnessed it.

He wanted to believe she still lived. That the house was swept away and she was spirited downstream and landed in the safety of kind strangers. But as the weeks turned into months and the months into years, he knew he had lost her forever. And in the black pit that enveloped his soul, he knew it was his fault.

~~~~~

Ryan tossed and turned and cried in his sleep, calling out Cait's name over and over again, night after night after night. Reaching for her in the darkness, he begged God to send her back to him; even if she was only in spirit form, even if he had but a moment to tell her he was sorry and he loved her with all his heart and soul, that he would love her through all eternity.

And if he lived an eternity, he would never stop searching for her.

He thrashed his arms about, calling her name but finding only pillows and bedcovers and himself, tortured beyond human endurance.

Then he heard his name through the darkness.

"Re! Re!"

His eyes trembled as they opened, allowing the twinkling of light to reach him. He realized he was entangled in the bedcovers once again.

"Cait!"

"Re! Wake up!"

"Cait!"

"Re! It's me, Claire!"

His eyes opened fully to find Claire hovering over him, shaking him by the shoulders and shouting his name.

"Christ," he said, sitting up and grabbing for the sheet to cover himself.

She took a step back and he ran his hands through hair that felt too damp. He didn't want to look at her and he drew his knees up and rested his head against them, allowing his massive arms to conceal his face. He tried to quiet the frenetic beating of his heart; struggled to calm his shallow, rapid breathing.

Finally, he said, "What are you doing in my bedroom, Claire?"

She didn't answer and he reluctantly raised his head. She was standing beside the bed, her eyes wide. He could tell by the tremble in her lip and the way in which she stared at him that she was thinking and the longer she stood there, the more uncomfortable he became.

"Well?" he said at last.

"You were crying out in your sleep, Re," she said quietly. Her voice sounded strange to him; hushed.

"Just a bad dream." He said it dismissively. He wanted her to go away, to stop staring at him the way she was.

"I'd forgotten…" she started.

He chewed his bottom lip.

"I'd forgotten how intense those dreams are," she said. "It's been so long since our bedrooms were side by side. I used to listen to you during the night, wishing you would fall asleep, wondering what it was when you closed your eyes, what demons tormented you…"

"What time is it?" His voice was abrupt and thick with sleep.

"Close to 8:30."

Like a wave crashing over him, he realized why Claire was in his house on a Saturday morning. His eyes widened and he looked around the room. The electric clock on his sound system read 8:28. The ceiling fixture in the hallway shone its light inside. They had electricity. He looked upward at the skylight; it was gray outside and the rain was pouring down.

"The hurricane—?"

"It passed us by, Re."

"It's out to sea?"

"No. It made landfall about an hour ago."

"Where?"

"The Outer Banks."

He jerked toward the other side of the bed. "Where's Cait?" She took a step back.

He jumped out of bed, dragging the sheet with him to provide some sort of cover. "Where is Cait?" he asked again.

"She's gone, Re."

He reached for his shorts. He caught his sister's reflection in the mirror as she turned her back to him.

"She left a note."

"How long has she been gone?"

"An hour. Maybe a little longer. I was in the bathroom—"

He was already halfway down the hall. "Where's the note?"

Claire hurried to catch up with him. "On the counter there," she pointed toward the island separating the den from the kitchen. Erin was sitting on a barstool finishing her breakfast and Emma was standing on a stool at the kitchen sink, rinsing off her plate.

Ryan grabbed the note. The words seemed to swim in front of him.

> *Ryan,*
>
> *They're sending me to the coast to cover the storm damage. You were sleeping so soundly, I didn't want to awaken you. And I don't think I would have had the courage to say good-bye.*
>
> *With any luck, I will be back with you by nightfall.*
>
> *I love you,*
>
> *Cait*

"To the coast—what the hell does that mean?" Ryan whipped around to stare at Claire. "There's hundreds of miles of coastline!"

"How do I know?" Claire answered. "I heard her in here talking to the girls. I slipped into the bathroom to make myself presentable and when I came out, she was gone and the note was there."

"She made us blueberry pancakes, Uncle Re," Erin said. "They were frozen and she used the toaster."

"She's a keeper, Uncle Re," Emma added.

Ryan felt sick to his stomach. He moved away from the counter and toward the window, where he watched the rain descending in sideways sheets. The ground was already saturated and the water was pooling toward the back of the lot.

As Claire joined him, Ryan rubbed his forehead. "I've got to go after her."

"Are you daft?" Claire's voice was hushed. "You see the rain, Re. The streets are flooding. It's not safe out there."

He didn't turn toward her but continued staring outside. "I got an email, Claire, summoning me to Atlanta. I was supposed to leave last night."

She stepped toward him and stared at his profile without responding.

"Only it was a fake. The police in Atlanta never sent the email." He turned toward her. "The killer sent it."

"The killer?"

"I don't have proof. Not yet. But I'm convinced he wanted to separate me from Cait. I didn't take the bait. I didn't go. And I thought I would wake up this morning with Cait in my arms and we'd be together." He felt his knees go weak but he forced himself to remain in control. "I could protect her if she was here. But because I didn't leave, he summoned her."

"I don't understand."

"He's after me, Claire. It was never about the other women. It was always about Cait. It was always about destroying me."

"Listen to yourself, Re. You sound like you've—you've lost your grip on reality."

"He's copying the crimes of his ancestor," Ryan said. "The final murder was Caitlín O'Conor. And if I don't get to her before he does, I'll spend the rest of my life living a nightmare."

"Wait until the storm subsides. At least do that."

"Don't you see? I can't. Every minute I'm standing here, the killer could be one step closer to her." He crossed to the counter and picked up his cell phone. He dialed her number while Claire and the girls watched. "All circuits are busy," Ryan said, repeating the recording before he switched off the phone. "I'm getting my things and I'm leaving."

"Don't do this, Re. Please don't. It's not safe. The roads are not safe."

"How did she get out? She drove, didn't she?"

"She's not your responsibility, Re. She's not Caitlín O'Conor." She stepped in front of him, blocking his way.

He gritted his teeth as he put both hands on her shoulders and stared into her eyes. "Do not try to stop me," he said through clenched teeth.

"What are you doing to Mummy, Uncle Re?" Emma climbed down from the stool, her tiny hands balled into fists.

"It's alright, girls," Claire said, her eyes fixed on Ryan's. "Why don't you go over there and turn on the telly? Turn it to the weather so we can see what's what."

As Erin and Emma made their way into the den, Claire said in a low voice, "Take your hands off me, Re. We're not resorting to violence here."

"I've never hurt you, Claire," Ryan said, though he removed his hands from her shoulders. "I'd as soon cut my own throat as hurt one hair on your head." He struggled to find the right words. "But don't you see, Claire? Cait—Cathleen—*is* Caitlín O'Conor."

"What insanity is this? Caitlín O'Conor's been dead and gone for nearly two hundred years."

"I've been dreaming about her my whole life. You know that. You just said it, there in my bedroom. She's here, Claire. I would know her anywhere. I know her body and her soul better than I know my own."

"Do you hear what you're saying?"

"The murders I've been working on—they're exactly the same as those Rían Kelly was investigating. He came to the conclusion—and it's all right there, in his journal—that the killer was after Cait. Only he allowed the two of them to become separated. And when they separated, the killer was free to go after her. I'm not trying to save her from the storm, Claire. I'm trying to save her from a killer."

She took a step back from him. Her eyes roamed the floor and the room but Ryan had the distinct impression she wasn't seeing any of it.

"You can't stop me, Claire. Nor should you want to stop me. If anything happens to her, I'd be Rían Kelly all over again, searching for her the rest of my life. The nightmare would never end."

She looked up as if to speak but Emma screamed excitedly, "Cait is on the telly!"

Ryan and Claire bolted around the kitchen counter.

"Turn it up! Turn it up!" Ryan yelled.

Erin turned up the volume.

"Where is she? Where is she?"

"As you can see," Cait was saying, turning to point behind her, "the southeastern part of North Carolina as well as the Myrtle Beach, South Carolina area were spared from a direct hit. Now they are contending with massive amounts of rainfall as the storm system swirls in a circular motion over an area several hundred miles in diameter. We're expecting flash flooding and we're urging everyone to *stay home*."

Claire turned to stare at Ryan.

"Thank you," the host of the news report said, turning to face the camera. "That was Cathleen Reilly reporting. We'll hear from her throughout this newscast as she makes her way to the Outer Banks in North Carolina."

"The Outer Banks!" Ryan breathed. "What's in the Outer Banks?"

"The hurricane, Re," Claire said quietly. "That's where it came ashore."

He stared at the tube dumbfounded.

"I thought you were dating a married woman," she said.

"Don't start with me, Claire."

"Is this the woman you've been telling me about? Cait is Cathleen Reilly?"

"Aye. That's the woman," he said impatiently.

She stepped in front of him, forcing him to look at her. "Cathleen Reilly is not a married woman."

"What?" His limbs were turning to liquid and he grabbed the back of the couch to steady himself.

"Why did you think she was?"

He felt like he was stammering as he answered, "The chief called her 'Mrs.' And she didn't correct him. I called her 'Mrs.' She didn't correct me, either."

Claire's voice was soft. "Re, she was a reporter in Fayetteville before she went to the national news. A badly wounded soldier was coming back from the war in Iraq—somebody who'd worshipped her from the time they attended school. His dying wish was to marry her. She married him just a couple of hours before he passed. They were married in his hospital room."

"What?"

"It was all over the news, Re. She didn't even remember who he was. But she fulfilled his dying wish. I'm sure he died before the marriage was even consummated. He was injured so badly... She never even changed her name."

He closed his eyes.

"Did you ask her about her marriage?"

"She tried to talk to me," he said, swallowing hard. "And I wouldn't let her."

"It was all over the news," Claire repeated lamely.

He ran his hand through his thick hair. "For more than a year, I've had my head up my own arse. And it's been so dark up there I've not been able to see anything else." He started back toward the kitchen. "Well, I'm seeing clearly now. I'm going after her."

He marched through the kitchen, grabbed his keys off the counter and shoved his wallet into his shorts pocket.

"Re," Claire said, rushing after him, "look at yourself. You're not half dressed."

"Go after her, Uncle Re!" Emma yelled, jumping up and running for the hallway. "I'll get your shoes!"

"I'll get your shirt!" Erin called.

"Don't forget your cell phone," Claire said as tears began to stream down her cheeks. "Go. Start your car."

As he rushed through the door leading into the garage, he caught a glimpse of Claire running to the refrigerator. He didn't hesitate but was in his car and had it started before the garage door was halfway up.

The twins barreled out of the house. Emma was carrying his shoes in the air and nearly threw them in the car with him. Erin was right on her heels, handing him a shirt. Claire rushed them out of the way as she tossed a grocery bag full of bottled water onto his lap.

He'd barely put the bag in the passenger seat before turning back to Claire. "Thank you."

"Take care of yourself, Re. You're all the family I've got left. Now go," she said. As he started to pull away, she yelled after him, "But phone me and let me know where you're at!"

He backed out of the garage at a fast clip. As he continued down the driveway into the street, he paused to put the car in gear. He glanced into the rearview mirror as he drove away. His last glimpse was of Claire standing in the middle of the garage, wiping tears from her eyes, as the two girls jumped up and down screaming, "Go, Uncle Re! Go after her!"

36

The windshield wipers were turned to the fastest setting but they did little to stop the flow of water from pouring across the glass, making visibility nearly impossible. He'd never been to the Outer Banks before and when he used the car's voice control to set the navigation system, he felt his heart skip a beat when he realized how far he would have to travel. His only hope was to catch up with her before she got too far ahead of him so he pressed on, his foot dangerously heavy on the gas pedal.

He tried repeatedly to telephone her, hitting redial every two or three minutes until he'd just about driven himself crazy. A recording announced each time that all circuits were busy. He tried contacting the police department but he realized it was pointless trying to phone anyone at all; it seemed as if everyone was on their phones, most likely checking on loved ones in the path of the storm.

He turned on XM radio and managed to find her television station; as fate would have it, the hurricane's path and devastation was the top news. About thirty minutes into the newscast, the host said, "And now we're cutting to Cathleen Reilly, who is standing by in Dunn, North Carolina."

When he heard her voice, the sense of relief he felt was almost overwhelming. As long as he could hear her, he knew she was okay; neither the killer nor the storm had overpowered her. As she spoke, he tried to find her position on his navigation system. Dunn was straight up the interstate; she was about an hour ahead of him.

He didn't have the advantage of seeing her onscreen so he listened intently, trying to pinpoint her exact location. All he could determine was she had stopped at a truck stop or service station. They were experiencing high winds and downed trees but the eye of the storm was to the northeast—the direction in which they both were heading.

The winds swept his car into the adjoining lane and he silently thanked God that the traffic was so light. Those insane enough to get on the road were either pulling off or stopping under overpasses or they were barely moving at thirty miles an hour. His vehicle was all-wheel drive and though the logical part of himself cautioned against hydroplaning, he kept his foot down hard as he tried to close the gap between them.

She was only on the air for a brief two or three minutes. He tried calling again but received the same recording.

He tried vainly to remain calm, reminding himself of the major differences between Hurricane Irene and The Night of the Big Wind. The first storm had come without warning, sweeping across Ireland as unsuspecting people went about their usual business. They'd had days of warnings about this hurricane even if he himself had ignored them as he tried to capture the killer.

But as the minutes turned into an hour and then two, he began to wrestle with the feeling that his efforts were futile.

He stopped near Wilson, pulling into a service station and gassing up. While the gas pumped, he slipped on his shoes and shirt. Though he longed to get right back on the road, he forced himself to go inside and get a tall cup of coffee and a sweet roll, though he knew when he bought it that he'd be unable to eat. His stomach was too busy roiling. At least the caffeine would keep him awake and hopefully alert.

His hands trembled slightly as he counted out the change. Pointing at the television screen, he said, "Have you heard the latest on the storm?"

"It's bad to the east of us," the woman said. "Hope you're not going in that direction."

"I am," he said. "I'm headed to the Outer Banks."

"Not in this, you're not."

"Afraid so."

She reached for a map and slid it over the counter toward him. "Once you get past here," she said, pointing to an area between Interstate 95 and the ocean, "power is out. You know what that means? Our service stations are closed. They can't pump gas."

"Oh, no," he breathed.

"Your best bet is to fill up before you reach this point— whether you need it or not. Once you run out of gas, it could be days before the service stations are back on the grid."

"Thanks for the warning," he said.

"You're not from around here, are you?"

"Lumberton," he said. "Originally from Ireland," he hastily added when he saw the perplexed look in her eye.

"Don't fool around with these storms," she admonished. "The flooding will be worse than the high winds with this one. I don't know if you have hurricanes in Ireland but around here…"

He nodded, grabbed his coffee and the sweet roll, which he definitely decided would go uneaten, and hurried back to his car. A couple of minutes later, he was back on the Interstate and feeling like he was attempting to drive under a massive waterfall.

His knuckles were white from his tense grip on the wheel. He found the minutes going by and his coffee growing cold as he gripped the wheel even tighter with both hands to keep from lurching around the road as the wind whipped him. A car about a half mile ahead of him careened sideways; he let up on the gasoline and moved to the right, pulling onto the shoulder as he drove past it. In his rearview mirror, he saw it continue to move northward while still remaining sideways.

A tree fell beside the highway, startling him. Then another toppled, the branches seeming to sprout wings as they sailed across the highway in front of him. Despite his urgency to reach Cait, he found himself releasing his firm footing on the gas pedal as trees and debris began to take on lives of their own. They whipped around him and in front of him, causing him to grasp the wheel even tighter as he dodged fragments as small as his hand and as large as his torso.

The road was slicker than slick; even with all-wheel drive, he felt nearly as helpless as if he'd been trying to drive on the surface of a lake. He passed one automobile accident; the cars straddled across the left shoulder and left lane, the inhabitants looking through their windshields with eyes that appeared bulging and shocked. He tried to call the police department or even 9-1-1 to report the accident, but could not get through. A sense of guilt washed over him; he was an officer, he thought; he should have stopped to lend assistance. But he knew if he had, he might be there on the shoulder with them for hours.

And as he passed another accident and then another, he knew everyone was stretched thin—state troopers, rescue, ambulances and wreckers. And as he continued to listen to the news reports, they confirmed his fears: many first responders were forced to wait out the storm before they could get on the road themselves and lend assistance.

Through the rapid swipe of the windshield wipers, he saw the signs for U.S. Highway 64 as his navigation system instructed him to turn right one mile ahead. He could no longer see the shoulder of the road; the water was rising so rapidly that the ditches alongside the shoulders had filled up and the water was sweeping across the highway. He looked to his right as a car came into view, floating as the carload of people opened their mouths in unison as if they were screaming.

He knew he couldn't continue past them, leaving them to drown, and he slowed his car until he thought he'd pulled onto the shoulder. He turned on his flashers and then turned around, expecting to see the car still floating or perhaps the nose pointed downward as the ditch sucked it in. But miraculously, they had reached the interstate once more and were pulling back onto the roadway.

He put his car back in gear and put his foot on the gas, only to find that he was moving sideways, the water now sweeping his car off the road. He fought a growing sense of panic as he battled the steering wheel, trying to will his tires to remain on the ground and continue northward, praying that he would not be stranded here, where he could not rescue Cait. But as the winds and the rain sucked him further off the road, he unbuckled his seatbelt and prepared to swim to safety.

37

Claire had barely risen from the couch all day. With every minute that passed, she thanked the powers that be for keeping the electricity on and the news in front of her. It was a dire situation and she knew she wouldn't breathe easier—couldn't breathe easier—until Ryan phoned to tell her he was safe.

She didn't understand this woman's hold on him; she'd never seen him react so strongly. He'd been enamored of Sophie but that had taken time and even the decision to ask for her hand in marriage had been angst-ridden; she well remembered the phone calls and talks well into the night as he debated whether he wanted to commit to her for the rest of his life.

She'd encouraged him to marry Sophie. She thought the woman might finally move him beyond his dreams, his nightmares of another woman whose name he called night after night, a woman he had never known. She had wondered in those first few weeks and months of marriage if his dreams had continued but neither Ryan nor Sophie had ever mentioned them. She'd thought them gone until this week.

It seemed they had started in earnest after Cathleen Reilly had appeared in his back yard. In between watching the almost constant hurricane updates, she found Rían Kelly's journal in Ryan's room and began reading the entries. With each account she read in his neat, precise handwriting, she felt a chill she couldn't shake and she knew why her brother was compelled to find this woman who looked so much like the one in his dreams. She didn't know what the relationship was between Rían Kelly's nightmarish existence and Ryan's dreams; or what it was about Cathleen Reilly that convinced him she was Caitlín O'Conor. But it no longer mattered.

All that mattered was her only sibling was heading directly into the eye of a hurricane in search of a woman he loved. And she didn't know when this day was done if either of them would still be alive.

When Cait came on the screen, even the twins stopped their constant chatter and watched her. It was obvious the weather was worsening. The further Cait traveled northward and eastward, the more violent the winds became and the fiercer the rains. Twice, Cait mentioned the possibility of stopping somewhere until the storm had abated somewhat but only a few minutes later she was back onscreen and further up the road.

Claire tried calling Ryan repeatedly but couldn't get through. She didn't know if he'd been listening to Cait on the radio or if he was clueless as to her whereabouts. And if she stopped along the way, Ryan could end up driving right past her. While she remained dry and safe in an interstate hotel, he could be catapulting ever deeper into the storm, still in search of her.

"May we have a picnic in front of the telly?" Emma asked.

Claire glanced at her watch. She couldn't believe it was already mid-afternoon. In fair weather, the Outer Banks should have been no more than a few hours' drive, at that. But she had no way of knowing how close or how far away Ryan was to his destination—or if he would find Cait once he got there. It wasn't as if the Outer Banks was a theatre or shopping mall, where one could make an announcement over the intercom. It was nearly two hundred miles long. Finding Cait would be like finding a needle in a haystack—and in a hurricane, to boot.

"Aye," she said. "Get what you want and make a picnic for yourselves."

"Aren't you hungry, Mummy?" Erin said.

"No, darlin'. I'm a bit preoccupied."

She half-listened as the twins planned what they'd have for their picnic. They might have been four years old, she thought, but they spoke as if they were thirty. And thank God, because she was beginning to feel completely paralyzed.

It vaguely registered that Emma had gone into the kitchen and was preparing a snack tray; of what, she couldn't imagine. She turned back to Rián's journal and her frantic, silent prayers.

"Now you see," Erin exclaimed suddenly. "I told you he was in every report!"

Claire's head jerked up. "Who? Uncle Re?"

Emma hurried into the den with a tray of crackers and cookies. "I think he's her boss," she said as she set the tray on the floor.

Claire settled back into the couch and wiped her brow. She was a nervous wreck. And that was so unlike her.

"I would not want a boss who looked like that," Erin said.

"I think he's very old."

"Do you have to be old to have white hair, Mummy?"

"What?" She looked up again.

Erin walked to the television set and pointed while Henry ate her cookies. "That man right there. His skin is the same color as his hair."

"It's not polite to talk about the way people look," Claire admonished.

"But is he old?"

"What does it matter if he is?" Claire asked.

"He's spooky," Emma said. "I would not want him to be my boss. Can I choose my own boss when I start to work, Mummy?"

"If you're a television reporter," Erin said, "then he's going to be your boss."

Claire leaned forward and stared at the television screen. Cathleen Reilly was giving another update on the storm; the banner across the bottom read, *Dare County, North Carolina*. The cameraman was panning behind her as she spoke. Sitting behind the steering wheel of a car not far behind her was a man with white hair and skin so pale he almost did not appear human.

"Girls," she interrupted.

"Yes, Mummy?"

"Are you saying that man has been in every shot?"

"Almost from the very first time," Emma said. "Do you think her boss would drive her around?"

"I think he would make her drive," Erin said.

Claire looked at the journal in her lap and then back at the screen. She blinked and then rose, coming close enough to the television to squat down in front of it and look closely at the car parked behind Cathleen Reilly. The rain was heavy and the winds fierce. When the report ended, she grabbed the remote and rewound the report, freezing it at several points so she could study the man in closer detail.

Then she rose unsteadily and reached for her cell phone. She tried to telephone Ryan but received a message that all circuits were busy. Then she tried the police department, only to receive the same message. It had been that way all day. She was going to insist that Ryan get a landline, she thought. At least it could up the chances of getting through.

As she watched the girls eating crackers and cookies alongside their dog, she calculated the distance between Ryan's house and the police department. She walked to the front of the house, where she peered out at a street that was flooding rapidly. There was scant chance it would reach the house, but it looked too dangerous to risk driving.

She could hear the twins both talking non-stop. She couldn't leave them home alone; that was out of the question. Could she risk putting them in the car and driving across town to the police station? She could be putting all their lives in danger. She couldn't endanger her children. She couldn't. She would never forgive herself if anything happened to them.

Like Ryan couldn't forgive himself if anything happened to Cait.

Her brother or her children. The refrain seemed to mock her. The waters were high and swift and she was not familiar enough with the town if she'd need to take a detour en route to the police station. She tried calling again but still could not get through.

Then she remembered that Tommy had driven them to Ryan's house the night before. Tommy had taken the vehicle to Fort Bragg. She hadn't thought anything of it at the time; she knew Ryan's car was in the garage. But now Ryan's car was gone and she couldn't reach anyone, even Tommy. They were stranded.

But she knew she could no longer sit there and do nothing. She had to act.

38

The tree stopped the car with a jolt, sending it careening back toward the interstate. Ryan hit the button to roll down the passenger side window. The rains drenched the passenger seat within seconds but if the car was sucked into the water, he knew he could be stuck inside, unable to open a door or even roll down a window. At least he had an exit now.

But as the car hit another tree, it pushed it even closer to the interstate and when a third one bumped him, he began to feel like the trees had come alive and were shoving him back to the relative safety of the road. He could barely believe it when he felt the firm asphalt under him.

Before the car spun back to the shoulder in the increasing winds, he applied pressure to the gas pedal, eventually righted the car and continued northward. He was rolling up the window when his navigation system reminded him to bear right and he left Interstate 95 and headed directly east into the storm.

"We have another report from our traveling correspondent, Cathleen Reilly," the host said.

Ryan turned up the radio and leaned forward as if he could hear her voice with more clarity if he was closer.

"The last time we spoke to her, she was in Dare County, not far from the Outer Banks of North Carolina, where the eye of the hurricane came ashore early this morning," the host continued. "And now she—oh." She hesitated. Ryan felt himself holding his breath, waiting for her to continue. After a few seconds, she said, "We've lost contact with Cathleen Reilly. We'll be bringing you that report in a few minutes. This is to be expected, since the storm—"

Ryan didn't hear the rest. He felt as though his insides were dropping into the pit of his stomach like a lead ball. His breath grew shallower until the road in front of him started to blur and he forced himself to maintain a hold on his emotions.

What did that mean, they'd lost contact?

He didn't know much about television reporting and didn't know what it took to connect from a satellite location to a station, especially when the station was hundreds of miles away. He'd seen correspondents report from war zones, astronauts from outer space, even weathermen reporting through worse hurricanes than this.

The cameraman was with her, he reminded himself. She was not completely alone. He didn't know if they'd gone in her compact car or if they had a larger SUV or van, hopefully something with better traction and drive— He tried to stave off a mounting panic that Delport had reached her, that somehow he'd managed to harm Cait. Or as the memory of his own close call surfaced, that they'd run off the road and were perhaps even now fighting for their lives.

He was right behind them, he reminded himself. He began looking more closely at the sides of the road, at the areas just off the highway that were flooding, at the trees leaning precariously as the ground beneath them became soaked and waterlogged, and at the trees that had already fallen like dominoes as the winds gained strength. But even as he looked for signs of a car in the water, he knew that wasn't his primary concern. No; what made his insides feel like they were turning inside out was the gut feeling that Diallo Delport knew where she was, and he was somewhere between Cait and Ryan.

Darkness in August didn't settle in until eight o'clock or later but now it appeared as though it was dusk, the only lights those from his car's headlights. The lights along the highway were darkened, as were all the houses and businesses he could see from the road. And as he drew ever closer to the eastern shore, he knew the water would get deeper, the rains harder and the winds stronger.

The next news report indicated the center of the storm was over the coast of Virginia now, pummeling Virginia Beach and Newport News. But as he stared into the storm, he felt as if he was driving right into the eye of the hurricane.

39

Claire adjusted the raincoat on Emma and stood up. "Now remember what I told you, girls."

"I don't understand why we have to wear our rain slickers if we're to stay in the garage," Erin said. Her eyes had always been large and now they appeared voluminous.

"Unless the rain is going to come into the garage," Emma added, her little brows wrinkled with worry.

"It won't come in. It's just a precaution. Now, don't leave the garage," Claire said, trying to make her voice firm. "Keep Henry here with you. And I'll be right back."

As she turned around and opened her umbrella, her hands were shaking. It was so unlike Ryan to leave her alone like this to fend for herself and the girls. He had always been the strong one, even though he often said the same thing about her. He was her rock and now that she was unable to reach him, she felt like she was sliding down a slippery slope.

The storm hit her umbrella with a vengeance. She hadn't left Ryan's yard before the winds whipped it inside out and she was forced to run through puddles that reached above her ankles as the rains lashed against her, drenching her within seconds.

Please Mother Mary, she prayed as she ran, *please take care of my children.*

She looked back twice. The garage door was open and the twins stood resolutely in the middle of the empty space with Henry seated beside them. Sitting on his haunches, the dog was as tall as they were. She knew their yellow rain coats were hot and if all went as planned, they wouldn't need them. But she found herself in the desperate situation of needing to do something and not wanting to endanger her children in the process.

Her feet sank deeper as she tried to cross a trench between Ryan's yard and the neighbors, sucking one shoe into the soft dirt. She stopped for a moment and grappled through the water to find the shoe. Once she'd retrieved it, she realized it had filled with mud and she removed her other shoe before continuing.

Lord, please protect my children, she mouthed.

She reached the neighbor's front door and looked back again. The girls hadn't moved and for once, she didn't think they were talking. Henry also looked as still as a statue. She waved as if everything was fine but they didn't wave back.

She rang the doorbell and waited. After a couple of minutes, she knocked on the door. Then she pounded.

It hadn't occurred to her that the neighbors might not be home. And now she found herself looking back at the twins and then at the water in the street. This was the only house she could have ventured to where she could still see the girls standing in the garage. To cross the street or continue to another house would mean she'd lose sight of them.

She started to cry, her tears mixing with the rain as it continued to pommel her. She turned her back to the girls so they wouldn't see her desperation and angst. *Mother Mary, please. Please help me.*

She pounded on the door once more and then sobbed openly. Just as she was turning around, the door opened.

"What on earth?" the woman said as she stared at Claire. She appeared to be in her 80's; she was diminutive with perfectly styled bluish-white hair and was dressed in a peach colored leisure suit.

"I'm Ryan O'Clery's sister, Claire," she said, pointing next door.

The woman peeked toward Ryan's house as if she would see him there.

"I need help," Claire continued, her voice shaking. "Do you happen to have a phone I could use?"

The woman continued staring toward the garage before turning back to her. Claire was embarrassed that she'd kept her children standing in the garage in the midst of a storm and hoped the lady didn't think her a neglectful mother.

"Our phone is out of order," the woman said, wringing her hands. "I don't know if anyone in the neighborhood has phone service. The storm, you know." She looked at Claire with genuine concern. "You said someone needs help?"

Claire wiped the tears from her cheeks but they were replaced immediately by more tears that she couldn't seem to control now. She nodded. "I need to call the police. My brother, he works there and—" She looked back at the garage. Seeing the girls still standing there, dutifully watching their mother, she said, "I've got to get back home to my children."

As she turned to go, the woman stepped forward. "You said you need the police?"

Claire glanced back at her and nodded. "Yes, m'm."

"Well, my husband—"

Claire hesitated, caught between keeping an eye on her girls and listening for any lifeline the woman might throw out to her.

"My husband's been listening to the police all morning," the woman said. "He's got a police scanner."

40

Ryan could see the flashing lights at least three miles away. It had been as dark as dusk all afternoon and the closer he'd gotten to the eastern shore, the fewer cars he saw on the road. He found himself straddling the line between two lanes to avoid the deep water that was washing over the road now, ready to suck him into the fields that ran alongside; fields that now appeared like vast lakes.

Though the news reports kept coming and he knew the eye of the storm had already moved north, they still had not heard from Cait. Earlier in the day, they had aired segments from her on a regular basis. But after they lost contact, they mentioned her a few times and then not at all. He wondered if anyone at the station was trying to reach her but in his heart, he knew they would fare no better than he. He'd been trying for hours to get through.

He had tried not to think of Rián Kelly and his desperate attempt to reach Caitlín O'Conor after the Night of the Big Wind, but the image kept popping up until he finally succumbed. Now he could think of nothing else.

It was as if history was destined to repeat itself. Like some twisted joke, he was preordained to live one life after another, finding the woman of his dreams only to lose her again and again to a madman. He second guessed himself over and over; what could he have done differently? How could he have kept Cait at home, kept her off the roads, convinced her that the last place she needed to be was heading into a hurricane?

But how could he have known he would wake up to find her gone?

He did what he thought he had to do. He'd convinced her to stay with him last night. He'd helped her move out of the hotel. He'd thwarted Delport's attempt to draw him away from North Carolina, away from Cait. He thought he was changing the outcome but now Fate seemed to be stepping in and laughing in his face.

He thought he would catch up with her long before now. After all, she'd been stopping on a regular basis. The cameraman would have to set up, certainly, and she would have to wait until they worked her into the broadcast. That surely would take time. He should have caught up with her somewhere along the way.

He replayed the earlier segments again and again in his mind, memorizing where she had been at any given time, checking the navigation system to make certain he was still behind her, that she hadn't gone another route.

Yet here he was, slowing to a stop at a roadblock up ahead. And she was still nowhere in sight.

He dimmed his lights as he approached the yellow sawhorses and the police cruisers, rolling down his window as an officer approached in a raincoat and hat.

"The road's closed up ahead," the officer said, having to shout to be heard through the rain.

"I'm a police detective," Ryan said, showing him his identification. "What's happened?"

"The road's flooded out. No one can get through. And we've closed the bridge."

"When did that occur?"

"Several hours ago."

"Are you saying that nobody has been able to cross to the Outer Banks for several hours?"

"That's right."

Ryan stared out the windshield but it was so dark that he couldn't see much beyond the barricades, even with his headlights on. He glanced to the right, catching another officer walking from a nearby building. Beyond the building were several men working near a Coast Guard boat.

He turned back to the officer. "I'm tailing a suspect wanted for several murders. I have reason to believe he's headed to the Outer Banks."

"Nobody has come through here; I can tell you that."

"Not at all? You've not turned anyone around?"

"Not in several hours. How long ago would he have come through?"

"I didn't believe I was more than an hour behind him, if that."

He shook his head.

"Have you had any media come through? Cathleen Reilly and her cameraman. I've reason to believe the suspect is stalking her."

"Not here, but I understand some media took a boat over to the island just a bit ago. Against our better judgment but what are you gonna do? They're the media… They'd complain on-air that we obstructed free speech."

The second officer reached the vehicle and leaned in to hear the discussion.

"Can you let me through?" Ryan asked.

"Afraid not. It isn't that you can get through if you're careful. The road is washed out. Nobody can get through, including police."

"How will you get to the island, then?"

The second officer spoke. "We're waiting out the storm. We've been telling people for days if they stayed on the barrier islands, they were on their own. Once this storm passes completely, we'll use those Coast Guard boats to get over there. We're expecting the worst."

Ryan glanced again at the boats. The men who had been working near them were walking back toward the building. "Can you get someone to give me a ride across?"

"Too dangerous." Someone started speaking over the radio and he paused to listen. "We'd help you if we could. But our hands are tied. Now, if you'll excuse me…" He stepped away as he turned his attention to his police radio.

He turned to the other officer. "Would you mind if I pulled in over there? I've been driving since this morning and I don't mind telling you, I'm completely exhausted."

"Go right ahead." The officer waved toward the building. "Go on inside, if you want. There's coffee inside and the television is on and you'll even get some food."

"You have electricity, then?"

The officer chuckled. "No. A generator. We have to keep emergency services online, even if we can't respond until the storm is over."

Ryan nodded and started to roll up his window. "Park over there?" he asked, pointing to the parking lot beside the boats.

The officer nodded but before he could speak, the second officer called to him.

Ryan didn't wait but pulled slowly away, veering into the parking lot. Visibility was poor at best and it made perfect sense for him to cautiously locate a parking space that would be out of the way. He peered toward the building; the men he'd seen earlier were not in sight. He assumed they had returned inside to wait out the storm.

He parked the car and turned off the headlights. He could see the two officers who had spoken to him; they were a short distance away but the only reason they were still visible was they were caught in the flashing lights.

One officer pointed in his direction. They were discussing him, he thought. One could be telling the other that he was an officer on the trail of a killer. The other could be debating whether to allow him to pass.

He looked at the Coast Guard boats. But if it was determined to be too dangerous for anyone to venture to the barrier islands, even on a boat, what were the chances of them allowing him through the barricades? Slim to none, he thought. And the officer had said the road was washed out. It was impassable.

The only way across was by boat.

He reached to the roofline and flipped the switch so the interior would not light up when he opened his car door. He slipped his cell phone and his wallet in his pockets.

The officers began walking in his direction. Now they were moving into the shadows, out of range of the flashing lights.

He took a deep breath, opened his door and ran.

He didn't take the time to close his car door. In seconds, he was boarding the boat and pulling the ropes off the cleat. He worked quickly, hoping he was still cloaked in the shadows created by the driving storm.

But as he looked in the direction of the two officers, he knew they'd spotted him. Their mouths were open as if they were shouting, although their voices were being carried off by the wind. Now they were running toward the boat and he knew within a few seconds, they would be upon him.

Without the ropes holding the vessel in place, the winds rocked and buffeted it, pushing it away from the shore and then back again. He raced to the wheel, hoping the key had been left in the ignition.

The officers reached the dock as he found the switch. A gust of wind pushed him just beyond their reach and he turned the key.

The boat sprang to life. He grabbed a pole to help push him further away from shore but it wasn't needed. The wind was driving him further east toward the barrier islands.

Quickly, he grabbed the wheel and opened the throttle. The waves were rushing in on him, crashing over the sides of the boat, as he set his direction due east. He struggled to maintain control but found he was at the mercy of the winds and the storm.

Behind him, he knew the officers were notifying the Coast Guard and soon everyone in that building and accessible through emergency lines would know he had stolen the boat. But as the waves buffeted him, he began to realize that getting caught was the least of his worries. Surviving long enough to reach the barrier islands would be a far greater challenge.

And he had to hope once he'd landed that he could find Cait before it was too late.

41

Claire opened the door from the laundry room to the garage as the police cruiser pulled inside. She'd been standing at the front door, anxiously waiting, shifting her weight from one foot to the other as the minutes crept past. When she saw the cruiser heading down the street straddling the middle of the road as the waters churned at the edges, she felt as though she'd stopped breathing. It seemed like a monumental request to ask another human being to get out in this storm, perhaps risking his own life to get to her, and she hoped he wouldn't think her a hysterical woman.

The officer was on his radio and didn't immediately exit the car. Behind her, Claire heard the girls talking in the den, their voices too low to make out their words. Their raincoats were hung in the laundry room, dripping into the laundry tub.

Finally, he opened his door and climbed out. "Mrs. Erickson?"

"Claire. I'm Ryan's sister."

"Officer Zuker," he said.

She led him into the den, where Emma and Erin jumped to their feet upon seeing him.

"Our Uncle Re is a policeman," Emma said boldly. "Do you know him?"

"Yes, I do," Officer Zuker said politely. "He's a good man, your Uncle—Re?"

"A nickname we have for Ryan," Claire explained. "Anyway, as I was telling the lady I spoke to at the police department; Ryan has been working a series of murder cases."

"Yes. I'm aware of them."

"I suppose the whole town is." She smoothed back her hair. She'd managed to comb it to make herself more presentable but it was still wet from her excursion next door. "He had a suspect, a man with white hair, white skin—an albino."

"Diallo Delport."

"Aye, well, I didn't know the name. He thought—well, he thought that this suspect was going after Cathleen Reilly, the reporter."

Officer Zuker's expression seemed to change somewhat and he looked at Claire more intently. "Cathleen Reilly?"

"Cathleen Reilly, the reporter."

"I know who she is. Go on."

"He took off after her this morning. She was heading to the Outer Banks and he was convinced this man was going to follow her."

"Did he say why he thought that?"

She shook her head. "He doesn't tell me details about his investigations."

Zuker looked disappointed.

"But," Claire added hastily, "we've been sitting here all day, watching the reports of the hurricane. And my girls here, they noticed a man who appears to be an albino in just about every news report that Cait—Cathleen—has appeared in."

"Really?" Zuker looked at the television and then at the girls.

"Aye. Emma, can you show him?"

Emma picked up the remote and punched a series of buttons. "I bookmarked the news reports," she said as one popped up on the screen.

Zuker and Claire exchanged glances. "I don't know what it means, either," Claire said.

"It means," Erin said, "that we can mark a scene in a show and then go straight to it. And see," she pointed, "there's the man in the car behind Cait."

The officer moved closer to the screen and leaned in. It was raining heavily in the piece, which was helping to obscure the man sitting in the car. He might have been across a narrow street or parking lot from the location where Cathleen was reporting from.

"Here's another shot," Emma said, punching another button. The screen changed instantly. Cathleen was still talking about the storm but it was apparent that she had changed locations. The same car was in the background and they could see the man's profile more clearly.

"There are several more," Emma continued as if she was conducting a presentation in a board room. She switched from one to the other, proving their point that the man with the white hair was clearly following the same path to the eastern shore as Cathleen Reilly.

"That's the suspect, alright," Zuker said finally. "Can I get the tape?"

"What tape?" Claire asked.

"You're videotaping all of this?"

"It's on the hard disk," Erin said, "inside the cable box."

"The news station would have it," Claire offered.

"It's also on YouTube, Mummy," Emma said.

"We checked it," Erin added.

"Officer Zuker," she added, trying to keep her voice from trembling, "my brother went after Cathleen. I've not been able to reach him by phone, I suppose due to the storm. I've been terribly worried all day."

"And you say he's gone to the Outer Banks?"

"Aye. I suppose Cathleen had an hour's start on him. He'd hoped to catch up with her. But seeing this man in each report, I—I don't believe he has. Otherwise, he would have made his arrest. Or so one would think."

"Do you think something's happened to Ryan?"

Claire motioned for him to follow her. "Thank you, girls," she said over her shoulder. "That was very helpful." When they reached the kitchen, she turned toward him. "I'm frantic with worry. Is there anything you can do?"

He looked at her for a moment and then looked at the girls. "Are you okay staying here?" he asked finally. "I mean, if you've got food, water, electricity… Or would you like to come with me back to the station?"

42

When the boat slammed into the shore, Ryan didn't even know he had reached land. His muscles ached from wrestling with the wheel; even with putting his whole body behind his efforts, he'd been no match for the driving winds and relentless rain. He'd long ago lost track of his location, if he ever knew it at all; and now he hoped he hadn't just landed back where he'd started from.

As he peered over the side of the boat, he realized he'd crashed into debris from what appeared to be a destroyed home. There were pieces of decking floating away from shore only to be pushed back onto land as the wind whipped around, as if it couldn't quite make up its mind. A sofa was floating a short distance away as well as scores of clothing, shutters and siding, floor lamps, appliances, pots and pans… It looked as though a bomb had exploded.

When a doll floated past him, he thought of Emma and Erin and swallowed hard. He had no idea how many might have remained on the barrier islands to wait out the storm and how many might, at that very moment, be fighting for their lives.

The vessel jostled back and forth like a flimsy toy boat in a bathtub. Each time he thought he could jump ashore and try to secure it, he was pushed somewhere else. No amount of steering or maneuvering could outwrestle the storm.

Finally, he cut off the engine and jumped into the water. He immediately regretted his action as a two by four slammed into his head. He went under and found himself struggling to reach the surface as debris closed in around him. The waves were wicked; tall and wide and violent. And even when he managed to break the surface and gasp for air, it was short-lived as he fought through housefuls of wreckage.

He half-swam and half-walked the few yards to the shore. He had no idea how long it had taken him; it seemed as though he would take one good step forward only to be rocked backward by the next roiling wave.

When at last he felt sand beneath his feet and the water behind him, he moved inland as far as possible before stopping beside a house and holding onto the fragments of a deck while he caught his breath. His lungs felt filled with water and he coughed and sputtered, the act burning his lungs and his nasal passages.

Then he tried to get his bearings.

He didn't know what he'd expected to find. It seemed ludicrous now, to have thought he would arrive in the Outer Banks to see Cait providing her news report and all he'd have to do is whisk her back home. As he stared first in one direction and then in another, he felt as alone and isolated as if he'd landed on a deserted island—one over a hundred miles long.

From the debris littering the shoreline and the waters, he came to the conclusion that he must be several blocks inland— or what had been several blocks inland the day before. Now it was oceanfront property. He tried to adjust his sight to the murky darkness. It couldn't be nightfall yet it was nearly pitch black. There were no lights anywhere, in any direction. The sounds were deafening, though; the vicious winds, the ruthless rains, the assortment of noises as rubble crashed into each other before being swept into the waters, only to be pummeled back onto the shores a few moments later.

He walked past a few houses, his body bent nearly double as he struggled against the wind; walking in the opposite direction was no better. It was swirling all around him. He was soaked through. In a moment of clarity, he reached for his cell phone and wallet. Miraculously, they were both in his pocket but he was certain the cell phone was ruined. He pushed the button on the front and was surprised to see the face light up, though the screen was wet.

He knew she was unlikely to answer but he dialed Cait's number anyway. Receiving the same message as before, he checked the battery level and then returned the phone to his pocket.

Ryan looked at each house as he passed; some were in worse shape than others. Some were buckling, the second floor already touching the ground at one corner while still suspended at the others. Others looked ready to collapse completely at any moment.

When he found one that appeared to be in better shape, he climbed the stairs until he could go no further and then peered in every direction, hoping the height would offer him the advantage of seeing further. But with the gloom of the storm, it was futile.

He climbed back down and continued moving, calling out periodically for Cait. He knew his voice was lost on the winds as soon as it escaped his lips but he had to try.

He climbed up two more decks and entered a house for a short period of time; the storm had blown out the windows but it was a roof over him, no matter how rickety. After a few minutes, though, he determined he was safer outside than within four walls that kept groaning as if they might fold inward on him.

Listening intently for sounds of voices, he heard none even as he walked block after block. He had no idea how far he'd traveled; when he turned around, he didn't recognize the houses and debris he had just passed by. The Coast Guard ship had long ago disappeared and he suspected it had never completely come ashore.

He was thirsty, which came as a surprise; with all the rain and the ocean water surrounding him, he thought the water might have soaked right through to his insides. But he found himself tilting his head upward to allow some of the rainfall to moisten his lips and roll down his throat as he thought of the bag full of water bottles left in his car.

Periodically, he pulled out his cell phone and continued trying to reach his office or Cait or Claire, to no avail. The storm had somehow managed to sabotage even that.

He'd begun to realize he was totally alone and the futility of trying to find Cait now seemed overwhelming. He felt ludicrous. His thoughts alternated between hoping she was safe; perhaps holed up in a hotel on the mainland, to trying to find her before it was too late.

He stumbled over something in the roadway and he tried to catch himself before he fell. He'd become accustomed to the garbage that appeared to be everywhere. The road itself looked like it was made of sand; it was covered so thickly it was nearly impossible to see the asphalt. He'd dodged chairs and bicycles and all manner of household items. But this object had seemed to come out of nowhere and he cursed as he instinctively reached to the offended foot. He hoped he hadn't broken a toe.

He turned back to the big black object protruding from the sand, wondering how he could have missed seeing it as he approached. He started to turn back around and continue moving—in what direction, he had no idea—but something pulled at him deep inside.

Returning to the object, he knelt in front of it and began to push the sand away from it.

As he brushed away the grit and the muck, a long black lens emerged. His heart began to beat faster as he worked more feverishly to free the item. Soon, an entire lens and part of the housing came into view.

He knew before he saw the call letters emblazoned on the side that it belonged to a news station. It was too large and too bulky to be a personal video recorder. But when he stared at the letters, his heart felt as though it might explode from his chest.

Cait had been here.

43

Both girls settled into Ryan's desk chair, their eyes riveted on the television screens in the police station. Though there was barely an empty chair in the room, it was almost eerily silent. Then the rains began to dissipate and officers began springing into action, loaded down with calls that had arrived during the height of the storm but which they couldn't respond to until the danger to themselves had passed.

Claire placed their raincoats over Ryan's trash can but they still left puddles beside his desk. She smoothed her hair and listened while Officer Zuker spoke to Chief Johnston.

"He did what?" the chief said.

Zuker murmured his reply; though Claire leaned in to listen, she couldn't make out his words.

Then the chief strode to his office, Zuker on his heels.

A moment later, she heard the chief's voice again. "He did *what?*" This time, it seemed that everyone in the room turned to look in the direction of the chief's office. Several nervously looked at Claire and the girls, and she busied herself with getting juice out of the cooler she had hastily thrown together just a few minutes earlier.

It might have been only five minutes that she waited but it felt like an eternity before Chief Johnston returned to the room. He walked purposefully toward her. She fought the impulse to wring her hands as he approached the desk and motioned for her to step to the side, a short distance from the twins.

"Good news and bad news," he said, taking a deep breath.

"Lord," she said, grabbing the closest desk to steady herself.

"The good news is," Chief Johnston said, "Ryan made it to the bridge that connects the Outer Banks to the mainland."

"He made it," she repeated as her knees wobbled under her.

"The bad news," he continued as others in the room stopped talking to listen, "is he stole a boat belonging to the Coast Guard."

"Why?" Claire breathed. "Why would he do that?"

"The road was washed out before he could get onto the bridge. And the bridge has been closed in both directions. He must have been pretty determined to reach the Outer Banks…"

His voice faded and Claire tried to grasp his meaning. Finally, she said, "He stole a boat so he could reach the islands? Did he make it?"

The chief stared at her for a long moment before answering. "We don't know."

"Lord have mercy," she breathed, her knees giving way beneath her.

Officer Zuker rushed to her side, wrapping his arm around her to catch her. "We have to believe the best," he said.

"I've spoken to the State Police," Chief Johnston said after a moment. "Rescue workers probably will not make it to the island until tomorrow morning."

"Tomorrow morning!"

Zuker pulled a chair behind her and gently helped her into it.

"Anything could happen before tomorrow morning," she said. She tried to keep from crying but her lip continued to tremble. "Please," she begged, isn't there anything you can do?"

"Mummy!" Emma called out. "Cait is on the telly again!"

Claire jumped up from the chair, rushing to the television screens as the others joined her. Cait was speaking and the caption across the bottom of the screen read, *"Dare County, North Carolina."*

"There," she said, pointing to a car behind her, "that's him. That's the man Re described to me."

The chief leaned in, peering at the man in the vehicle. "That's our suspect," he said. "That's Diallo Delport."

"That was the last time we heard from Cathleen Reilly," the host said. "That segment was originally aired a few hours ago as Cathleen neared the bridge connecting the mainland to the Outer Banks."

"That wasn't a live report," Claire breathed.

"We're asking anyone who has seen Cathleen Reilly since this afternoon to call our news station. We've lost contact with her and…"

Claire turned back to the girls. Ryan was missing. Cait was missing. And the killer was there, perhaps with them both. Her legs felt as though they were on autopilot as she made her way back to Ryan's desk and laid her hands on the back of the chair.

Chief Johnston and Officer Zuker spoke quietly for a few moments. Somewhere in the recesses of her mind, she registered the words "every segment" and "that's our man" but all she could think about was the nightmarish words in Rían Kelly's journal. She silently prayed that Ryan was physically alright but as soon as the prayer was said, she found herself praying as much for his emotional state as his physical state.

He had to find Cait. And she had to be alive.

She barely registered a man moving behind her until he stopped in front of Chief Johnston. He waved several pieces of paper in front of him, excitedly reporting, "Detective O'Clery was right."

"What have you got, Arlo?" the chief asked, reaching for the papers.

"At two scenes, we got clear footprints. The soles are an exact match for prints found in the motel room where Delport was staying. See this?" he pointed to an area on one photograph. "It's worn down in that one spot. The guy stands on that edge, walks on that edge. It's impossible for two different people or even two pair of shoes—to contain that exact amount of wear in that precise location."

"Detective Haliman," Chief Johnston said, motioning for a detective to join them.

"There's more," Arlo went on, "we picked up a few items at the first and second scenes, hoping they would have some evidence… There is a partial print on one item that matches Delport's thumbprint exactly."

"What's the item?"

"Gum wrapper. It was found not far from the first body."

The chief nodded. "Detective Haliman, notify the FBI task force of this evidence. Get word to the media that we're looking for this suspect. Call the news station in Atlanta and ask for copies of each of Cathleen Reilly's reports. We need the exact date and time stamps on them and the precise locations. Also find out when they last spoke to her and where she was. Also where she was headed. She had to have had a more precise location other than the Outer Banks—that's about two hundred miles long."

He hesitated as he rubbed his chin in thought. "Contact the State Police as well as the FBI. Make sure they know O'Clery is somewhere around the Outer Banks and he's going to need reinforcements. Get Cathleen Reilly's picture to them, also, with instructions to let us know when either of them has been located. And get as much as you can on Delport."

He turned back to Claire, who had been listening intently. "We may not know anything until morning," he said in a softer voice. "The storm is moving past us here but it's still strong in the Outer Banks. Rescue workers and law enforcement won't go in until the storm's danger has passed. You're welcome to stay here. Or if you and your girls think you'd be more comfortable somewhere else, let Officer Zuker know and he'll take you wherever you want."

"I'd like to stay here for a time, if you don't mind," Claire said. "I have the strongest feeling that Re is in danger. He needs help." She began to cry but she didn't try to regain control. "If you must wait until morning, I'm afraid you'll be too late."

"Is there anything you're not telling us?" Chief Johnston asked.

She shook her head. "No. It's just that Re and I have always had this close connection. I've always known when he needed me. And I'm feeling it more strongly than ever before. He's in danger," she repeated. "And I'm afraid for what might happen to him."

44

He found the body in the middle of the road.

He couldn't have missed it if he'd tried. He stood over it, trying to hold his emotions at bay and examine the scene from the detachment of a professional cop. The winds had subsided and the rain was steady but no longer pouring down in sheets. Pieces of wood had been dragged into the center of the roadway; it had obviously occurred within the past hour or perhaps two, as the swath of sand was still visible where the heavy decking had been dragged. If it had been the storm that had pushed it inland, he surmised, there would have been no clear line in the sand and other debris would be in the road as well.

But it was only three pieces of wood, constructed like a rough teepee with the body of the cameraman propped up in front of them.

He was meant to be found. That much was evident.

He knelt in front of him. His eyes were wide and open; the expression held within them proof that his final moments had been spent in terror. His throat had been sliced over the jugular, the same as the others. And now Ryan knew he'd most likely been Tasered, rendering him helpless as he watched Diallo Delport approach with the knife that would take his life.

The cameraman would know, more than most, what was to come. He'd covered the murders in Atlanta and at least two in North Carolina. He knew he would bleed out while still paralyzed from the Taser. And here, on this island that appeared deserted, there would be no one to help him, no one to come to his aid.

He looked past the man's shoulder to the road that lay ahead of him. He had to assume that Cait had been with him; it wouldn't have made any sense that they would have separated. Had the cameraman intentionally come between Cait and Diallo, allowing her to get away? But where would she have run afterward? Where could she have hidden?

He studied the ground just beyond him. It was too murky to see whether there were footprints in the sand. If Cait had left any, they would have led Diallo straight to any hiding place. If there were none there, what would that mean for Cait's fate?

He pulled out his cell phone, pushing the button to access the built-in flashlight app. He pointed it toward the area behind the cameraman, searching for footprints, but the light seemed woefully inept. He stood up and clicked the button to turn it off. The screen was blank, the phone off, and he started to return it to his pocket when he caught a reflection in the screen. He leaned in and moved the phone until the reflection grew larger. As it drew closer, pale skin and white hair came into focus.

He whipped around as Diallo Delport's arm flew toward him, the blue light of the Taser lighting up the area between them. He threw up his forearm, catching Diallo's at the elbow. The Taser sailed out of his hand, landing on the ground a few feet away.

Diallo made a move toward it but Ryan landed a solid punch to the man's jaw as he turned, catching him unawares. Diallo staggered backward and then came at Ryan with a guttural roar.

He was taller than Ryan by a couple of inches and heavier by a good forty pounds. He struck Ryan first on his cheekbone, sending him reeling backward. As he fought to regain his footing, he struck him again in the face. Diallo held both hands in front of him like a boxer in the ring; a smile on his face showed that he relished the opportunity to fight.

As his arm flew forward again, Ryan ducked, landing an uppercut that wiped the smile from Diallo's face. But Diallo responded with a violent punch to Ryan's abdomen. As he doubled over and tried to catch his breath, he could see the larger man rushing for the Taser. He stumbled after him, managing to catch one leg with his foot, sending the man sprawling into the sand.

The rain was pelting them as they continued to fight. Diallo kicked him twice, each time sending him stumbling backward. While he managed to stay on his feet, he couldn't get between the killer and the Taser and each time Diallo rolled and tumbled closer to it.

Ryan stayed close behind. He grabbed Diallo's leg and tried to drag him further from the Taser, but the man was heavy. And as he pulled him toward the center of the road, Diallo grabbed a piece of decking and swung it at Ryan, catching him on the shoulder. A cracking sound reverberated through the air and Ryan dropped Diallo's limb as he stumbled backward. Diallo kicked him in the abdomen, and Ryan fell to his knees.

He could see Diallo rolling and crawling toward the Taser. He knew he had to stop him. He tried to come to his feet but the pain in his abdomen caused him to gasp and he realized he was having trouble breathing. He fought to regain control as he managed to rise unsteadily to his feet. The man seemed to swim in front of him and he lunged for him as Diallo grabbed the Taser.

Ryan grabbed Diallo's forearm with both his hands. Ryan was a large man; tall, broad shouldered and muscular. He'd been in many scraps, most of them while making arrests of uncooperative criminals, and he had yet to lose a fight. But Diallo was different. He seemed oblivious to the pain and no matter how hard Ryan pushed against him, trying to dislodge the weapon, he only smiled more broadly.

They were nose to nose now as they lurched and tottered back and forth across the road. All Diallo needed was a split second to touch Ryan with the Taser and it would all be over. He forced all thoughts of Cait out of his mind as he fought for his own life.

He managed to slip his leg between Diallo's and with one swift kick he knocked the larger man off his feet. As he fell, the Taser flew out of his hand, landing a few feet away. Now they both raced for the device.

Ryan's foot reached it just as Diallo's hand was closing over it. He managed to kick it out of his hand and they repeated the scene a second time and then a third.

Ryan grabbed a metal pole in the debris and swung at Diallo, catching him on the side of his head. A smaller man or weaker man might have been knocked out but to Ryan's amazement, it didn't seem to faze him.

He struck him again and again, pounding him with the metal until the pole, bloody now and bent, could no longer reach him. As Diallo staggered to his feet, Ryan grabbed the Taser.

Now they circled one another, their eyes locked. Ryan pressed the button twice, sending blue shocks through the air. He jabbed at him but each time, Diallo jumped back, dodging the weapon.

As they zigzagged from one side of the road to the other, turning in circles that grew closer and then farther apart, Diallo abruptly turned and ran.

Ryan raced after him, each breath he took causing sharp pains in his chest and abdomen. He was hurt; that much was clear. But he couldn't stop. He had to see this thing through— which meant killing Diallo Delport before he managed to kill him.

His foot hit something hard and he glanced below him to see his cell phone, the screen cracked. Swiftly, he reached down and grabbed it, shoving it into his pocket. In the fight that had ensued, he'd never even realized he'd dropped it. And now it seemed ludicrous that he was expending the time to retrieve it.

The larger man reached a beach house that had been battered by the storm. It was elevated, the ground level originally intended to park vehicles under the house. But the pilings were collapsed, causing the entire house to list dangerously as the waters swept in.

Ryan could barely see in the gloom. He caught a glimpse of Diallo's pants as the man ran up steps that didn't seem as if they could support him. As Ryan closed the gap and followed him upward, the steps pulled away from the house and they both were forced to hang on while they swung wildly around.

Then Diallo jumped into the house through an opening that appeared to be caused by sliding glass doors that had imploded in the storm. As the steps swung back around, crashing into the side of the house, Ryan made a leap for the same opening.

Diallo met him at the edge with a kick that sent Ryan reeling backward. The Taser flew from his hand into the depths below as the water rushed in. He couldn't remain on the steps; that much was clear. He could hear the wood cracking and splintering beneath him and in another moment, he knew he was likely to crash into the raging water.

He made a desperate leap for a window that gaped open, the curtains fluttering into the wind and the rain. The glass punctured his palm as he grappled for the ledge. He roared in pain, his voice carried with the wind, as he tried frantically to find a foothold. He couldn't let go of the ledge or he would fall into the water and debris below but to keep hanging on meant his hand was becoming impaled in the glass.

Finally, his other hand found the splintered ledge and his foot anchored him against the wall long enough for him to pull himself up and into the house.

Every manner of household items was piled around him. Urgently, he ripped the largest glass fragment out of his hand as blood spurted. A yell that sounded like an injured animal escaped his lips as he grabbed his shirt at the shoulder seam and ripped it. Feverishly, he rolled the material around his palm, trying to stem the crimson tide.

He wiped rain and perspiration from his brow as he fought to get his bearings. The sound of the storm surge lapping against the house was deafening and as he tried to move through the room, the floor listed dangerously.

As he made his way into the hallway, he heard a thunderous crack behind him. Looking behind him in horror, he watched as the room he'd just stood in crumpled into the water.

He raced toward the other side of the house, intent on jumping out any opening he could find to get back on solid ground. As he turned the corner in the hallway, he saw Diallo's arm a split second before it flew out; catching him with such violence that he stumbled backward against the far wall.

Diallo was upon him, beating him relentlessly. For the briefest of moments, Ryan saw his sister's face, the twins, and his beloved Cait. He would die here, in this house, on this beach, in this storm.

The thought had no sooner entered his mind than he was pushing back, matching Diallo blow by blow. The men staggered backward and forward with each punch and counterpunch as the drywall cracked around them.

Somewhere it registered in Ryan's mind that he could see the sky; that it was raining down on them there inside the house; that furniture was beginning to pick up from the ground and float until it banged against the walls.

The sounds were ear-splitting; the noise made by the storm and the waves intermingling with the collapse of the house around them and their own primal roars as they tried to kill one another.

His arms felt as if they weighed a ton apiece. Each time he lifted his fist, it grew heavier. Blood spurted from his face and his fists. Diallo's clothes were covered in muck and rainwater and blood and he knew he looked no better. They staggered into one another as they fought like boxers holding in a ring.

He didn't know how much longer he could stand his ground but he knew if it came to it, he would have to die fighting.

A deafening crack caused both their eyes to widen as the house split in two. Ryan stumbled backward as the floor beneath his feet fell away. But as Diallo was whisked downward, he thrust his hands out and grasped Ryan's arm.

As Ryan went down his leg lodged between the wall and debris, preventing the larger man from pulling him into the swirling waters below. He felt like his arm was being wrenched out of the socket as his body lay prone on the floor. He stared into Diallo's face beneath him as he dangled out of the side of the building.

"Where's Cait?" Ryan yelled. His voice was dry and hoarse and he repeated it again to make certain Diallo heard him.

Despite his dire situation, Diallo smiled. "She's gone, Ryan O'Clery," he shouted. "She was always going to die."

Diallo inched his hands up Ryan's arm to climb back into the house. He could feel the debris around him shifting and knew in a few more seconds, he would be swept out with him. He frantically grappled with his feet, trying to get a foothold on which to hang on.

When he looked back, a massive wave was rolling toward them. It was taller than the house and appeared as though it was blocking out the sky as the frothy waters rushed in.

"Why?" Ryan shouted.

Diallo's voice crackled as if in laughter. "Just one more payment in the debt you owe my family!" he shouted as the wave crashed into the side of the house.

The impact knocked Diallo's body against the house and then Ryan stared in horror as the man was swept out to sea, his hands still outstretched as if to grab onto him once more. Ryan lodged one arm against a wall and the other behind debris in a desperate attempt to hold on as the water rushed in. Within seconds, he was completely underwater.

He seemed to float and for the briefest of moments, he thought he could end it all right there. He could simply let go and let the waters take him where they will. Underwater, his muscles became weightless and the sounds of the storm were drowned out. He sank ever deeper as the house collapsed around him, sucking him into the murky depths.

45

Claire kissed Emma on her forehead and leaned over to kiss Erin.

"When will Uncle Re come home?" Emma asked tiredly.

"Maybe tomorrow," Claire said, fighting back tears.

"Will we go home then?" Erin asked.

"Yes. We'll go home tomorrow. Now go to sleep." She watched as Tommy kissed the girls. Though Ryan's spare bedroom contained two twin beds, both girls had insisted on sleeping together in one. Now they appeared ready to succumb to sleep in each other's arms.

Tommy moved into the hallway and waited for Claire. When Henry was settled at the foot of the girls' bed, she joined him, closing the door behind her. Once she was out of sight of the twins, she placed her head on Tommy's shoulder and burst into tears.

"Everything is going to be okay," Tommy said, rubbing her back.

"How can you say that?"

He didn't answer but his eyes reflected her pain.

"We've not heard a word from Re," she cried. "I know something has happened to him. I can feel it."

He took her hand and led her to Ryan's bedroom, where they sat on the edge of the bed and held each other. "Ryan is a strong man and a smart man," Tommy said gently. "He'll know exactly what to do to stay safe."

"He said to me that the killer was after *him*," she said. "It's too much, this driving into a hurricane and knowing the killer is going there, too."

"But law enforcement knows everything now," he said, combing her hair off her forehead and running his thumb over her tear-stained cheek. "Chief Johnston has notified everybody— FBI, State Police, the local jurisdictions on the Outer Banks. At first light, the helicopters will go in and make an assessment from the air. They may very well spot Ryan then. And even if they don't, rescue workers will be on the island. They'll be going door to door, checking for survivors. They'll find him, Claire. I know they will."

She used the back of her hand to dry her eyes. "I don't know what I'd do if anything happened to Re."

"Nothing will happen to him," Tommy said. "Now, why don't you take a nice, long bubble bath? Then we'll sleep in here. Tomorrow morning, we're sure to hear word."

She nodded tiredly and stood to remove her clothes. She pulled her cell phone out of her pocket and stared at the screen for a moment. "Phone service has been back on for hours."

"Here. But maybe not on the Outer Banks."

"The tech support guy at the police station told me to text him," she said as if she hadn't heard Tommy. "He said even when you can't get through with voice you can often get through with text messages. I've been texting him every few minutes. But there's been no response." She felt completely drained.

"I'll be up for a bit. I'll continue texting him. When his phone goes back online, he'll respond."

Claire looked at Tommy with tired eyes. "I'm so glad you're here. It was tough hanging on for the girls' sake."

"I know. I'm here now. And I'll be with you tomorrow."

"Was there damage at Fort Bragg?" she asked.

"Yes. Trees down. That kind of thing. But you know," he said, his voice brightening, "Fort Bragg is a staging center for FEMA's relief efforts. All day I worked with getting trailers in place filled with water and food and generators, all sorts of supplies, and by first light, they will be headed toward the Outer Banks."

"Oh?"

"I was detailed to it for part of the day. So I know firsthand, Claire, that they're preparing to go in tomorrow. Even Army helicopters are assigned. Once we have daylight, things will happen fast. You'll see."

Tommy stood and wrapped his arms around Claire. It felt good to have his shoulder to lean on, she thought. He was a good man; a good father and a good husband. And he knew how close she was with her brother; if he was concerned for him, he would certainly be making plans to head for the Outer Banks this evening so he could be there at the first light of day. The fact that he was confident Re was alright said volumes. She had to believe it, too.

The alternative was too painful to consider.

46

The first rays of dawn were just a promise along the distant horizon. Ryan sat on a section of steps that had, just the day before, led to the second floor of a beach house. Now it was partially collapsed, the area underneath meant for parking vehicles turned into an accordion of debris. He'd been sitting on the steps for just a few minutes, waiting for the sun to rise and knowing before its rays lit the beaches, he would have to follow through with his plans.

It had been the longest night of his life.

After he'd managed to swim out from under the house as it was swept into the Atlantic he'd searched frantically for Cait. He'd gone house by house calling her name until he reached what he thought was the end of the island. Then he'd turned around and headed back down the same route, checking each house again until he reached the opposite end. Only then did he realize the Outer Banks had been split, the main road and everything on the east and west side of it, washed away.

Sometime around midnight his phone began to beep with missed phone calls and text messages that were arriving several hours after they had been sent. Most were from Claire and the

Police Department, though there were two from the State Police and one from the FBI. Tommy had begun texting as well sometime during the night.

His first priority would ordinarily have been to call Claire and assure her that everything was alright. But it wasn't alright. And it would never be alright again.

So he'd walked and thought the rest of the night, pausing at different times to sit on the beach or on stacks of debris, watching the waves that crashed into the beaches, listening for sounds other than the wind and the rain and the ocean.

Sometime during the night, the rain stopped and for the briefest of time he stared upward at the heavens, looking at the stars and the moon, before realizing their appearance had also lit up the Outer Banks. He'd turned fresh eyes to his surroundings and saw for the first time the devastation the hurricane had wrought.

He could only imagine Rían Kelly's thoughts when he journeyed home from Dublin to find his village wiped out. As he looked around him now, at the rubble of destroyed homes and businesses and remains of lives strewn around him, he felt as if he was there in the Irish village and it was 1839 again.

And he was searching for Cait against all the odds, praying and hoping that she survived and they would be reunited.

Now as he sat on the steps of the decrepit house and stared at the ocean waves and the first promise of light, he tried to piece together what had happened in the last seven days that had so completely altered his life.

Diallo Delport was a descendent of Rían Kelly's killer; of that he was absolutely certain. He didn't know why the killer from Rían's time was intent on murdering Caitlín O'Conor and destroying Rían. And he didn't know if the man had been caught and tried and hanged for murder. But he suspected that he had been. And he suspected the killer had told a different version of events to his family, perhaps embellishing it with a perceived wrong committed by Rían. The story was handed down, generation after generation, until Diallo Delport decided to reenact the crimes.

He suspected all of this but he had no proof. And now, in the big scheme of things, evidence no longer mattered.

What he couldn't quite wrap his mind around was how Delport had found Cait. All his religious training contradicted what he wanted to believe: that Cathleen Reilly was the reincarnation of Caitlín O'Conor. And that he, Ryan O'Clery, was Rían Kelly. And then, he realized, Diallo Delport wasn't just a descendent of the original killer's; he *was* the original killer.

How else could he explain his dreams? These dreams had been with him since his earliest memories. How could he have been all of nine years old and having dreams that alternated between a great love and a tormented soul? How could he explain dreaming of situations that he later read in Rían Kelly's journal? Even the dragonfly birthmark had been in his dreams. Claire had said herself that the journal had been tucked away in their aunt's attic for decades; long before either of them had even been born.

Perhaps we're destined to live one life after another, he thought, repeating the same episodes lifetime after lifetime, into infinity.

Then what grievous sin could he possibly have committed to cause himself so much pain and suffering, lifetime after lifetime?

The dreams had been clues; he was convinced of that. When he first laid eyes on Cathleen Reilly, he'd known her instantly. He'd memorized every inch of her face in his dreams and even the slightest variation he would certainly have noticed. And that first night had been everything he had ever imagined possible.

He'd had plenty of women, especially after coming to America where he found his Irish accent an aphrodisiac to American women. He'd given pleasure and he'd received it, countless times. But he'd never experienced anything like he had with Cait. Their souls were connected. He knew that now.

He'd known it days ago.

He'd trusted his instincts to lead him to the killer and he'd found him because he wanted to be found. Perhaps if he had worked longer hours or harder hours, he might have been able to apprehend him after the first or second murder, sparing the lives of others—and of his beloved Cait. Perhaps if he had taken him into custody the day he met him at the motel, Cait would be alive now. If he'd managed to catch him as he chased him through the county…

He rubbed his forehead with a hand that was coated with grime and grit. His head ached; his whole body ached. The rag he'd tied around his palm was soaked in dried blood and dried saltwater that still stung and he was covered with scratches, cuts and bruises.

He had what-if'd himself all night. And like it or not, what was done was done. There was no going back.

He had tried to alter events. Especially after spoiling Delport's plan to send him to Atlanta on a wild goose chase, he thought he'd gained the upper hand.

How was he to know that Cait had plans to leave before he'd awakened, a decision that would end her life and alter his and those closest to him?

The sun would soon be up and time was growing short. He heard his cell phone beep and knew Claire or the Police Department was sending him yet another text message, a message he would not be answering.

He had decided as he walked countless miles throughout the night that he would not end up as Rían Kelly did. He would not spend the rest of his days searching for a woman he would never find again; he would not become some pathetic figure that generations after him would still be discussing in hushed whispers. He would not spend his nights in feverish dreams that would awaken him to dampened beds, a tear-soaked face, and anguish the likes of which he could never purge. He would not spend his days as if he was sleepwalking through life, a shell of a man who once was but would never be again.

He had decided in those wee hours of the morning as he'd gazed upward at the moon and the stars that he would join her in death.

He'd thought it through. And if he allowed himself to drown in those crashing waves that rollicked toward him like Fate herself, his life insurance policy would be upheld. Claire was his beneficiary and in death he was worth more than in life. The money would go far in getting the twins their college education. It would be the only positive factor in this whole sordid mess.

If he committed suicide, the life insurance would be null and void; but not if he managed to make it look like an accident. And he knew he could. What better time to drown than in a hurricane?

It was why it was so important that he die now before the sun rose. Once the light of day reached the Outer Banks, the beaches would be filled with rescue workers. The chance was too great that someone would witness his death. And he couldn't risk having a witness.

He stood up. He knew exactly where and how he would end it. He'd been watching the waves crash against a pier that had partly collapsed. He would make his way to the end of it, wait for the next big wave, dive in and allow it to sweep him into the ocean.

Perhaps he should have died when the house crumbled in on him, he thought. But he had still held out hope then that he would find Cait alive. And now he knew it was futile. She was gone. And in a short time, perhaps if there was a merciful God, he would be reunited with her on the other side.

His cell phone beeped again and he instinctively reached for it. He knew he wouldn't answer it; it would be far better for Claire to think he died in those early hours than suffering through the night. It was time to leave the phone on the beach so she would know he'd been here; they would find the phone even if they never found his body.

But when he looked at the phone, it didn't show a missed call or text message. And when he scrolled through those he'd received during the night, there hadn't been one within the past hour.

The beep sounded again and he realized with a start that it was not his cell phone he'd heard but someone else's.

He looked toward the horizon; the sun was coming up. Within a few short minutes, it would be daylight. He looked in the direction of the pier and at the waves crashing against it. And then he looked toward the road where the cameraman's body still sat exposed, propped against the wood.

At the sound of the next beep, he was walking around the house, trying to peer through the wreckage to the area below the first floor of living space. He used the flashlight app on his cell phone to shine some light, albeit weak, into the section where the sound was originating. He managed to make out a boat that had been parked below the beach house.

He moved some of the debris out of the way, the effort causing his strained muscles to throb. He was still a few feet from the boat as a voice inside him was growing frantic that the sunrise was swift and he was wasting time. He shone the light toward the wreckage once more as the metal on the boat reflected it back.

He heard the sound of a helicopter in the distance and turned to determine its location. The rescue workers were arriving, even if he couldn't see them. It was time to go.

He glanced once more under the house and was turning to leave when something caught his eye. He flashed the light in that direction and tried to make out what he'd seen. He gasped instinctively when he saw it; it was a lady's foot dangling over the edge of the boat, wedged in between the vessel and the beams that had collapsed over it.

As he stared, the beep sounded again and he knew beyond a doubt that it was coming from inside the boat. He bent down and crept toward it, looking for some sign of movement.

"Hello!" he called.

No one answered.

But as he drew closer, he realized the ankle was tattooed with a dragonfly.

"Cait!" he bellowed. "Cait!"

He ducked back out as the sounds of the helicopter drew closer, waving his arms in the air to get their attention. But he couldn't wait. He had to reach her and he had to do it now.

The beams were heavy; it was all that continued to hold up the rest of the house. And as he began frantically clearing the wreckage, the house began to shift and groan. "Cait!" he screamed. "Cait!"

Jesus. If only she would answer him; if only she moaned or groaned or did *something* to let him know she was alive.

He ducked out again, his eyes searching the skies for the helicopter. It was light now, the rays heralding what would surely be the start of a hot, humid day. He turned in the direction of the cameraman and then in the opposite direction. A group of rescue workers were securing a boat along the newly formed shore. He shouted until he was hoarse but no one appeared to have heard him.

He turned back to the house. He had to reach her. It was all up to him.

Again, he ducked under the house and half-crawled toward her. He had no idea how long it was taking him. It felt like the longest moment of his life. When he looked over his shoulder at the debris he had relocated, it amazed him that he'd been able to move any of it. But as the house grumbled and shifted, he knew he wasn't working fast enough.

Frantically, he pulled on supports until his palms were raw; he pushed and shoved them with every ounce of strength he had left in him. He wasn't even aware that he was crying until the tears spilled onto his shirt and mingled with the sweat.

He called her name until his voice was barely over a hoarse whisper.

When he reached the side of the boat, he was afraid to look inside. She was dead, he told himself. She couldn't have survived. If she'd been alive, she would have answered him. But she hadn't even moved her foot as he'd struggled to reach her.

And if she was dead, he would lie down beside her and somehow die right along with her.

He leaned into the boat, pulling debris away from her, calling her name.

A beam had fallen diagonally across the boat and now as he struggled to move it, he saw the blood. He noticed it first on the wood and then as he managed to shove it a few inches from her, he saw the wound on her forehead.

"Cait!" he yelled. He was inches from her face and yet she didn't move.

He didn't know how he got into the boat. He was half-crouched beside it one moment and the next he was inside and kneeling beside her. He brushed her hair away from her neck, desperately searching for her jugular. It had not been cut. He found her wrist and tried to find her pulse but couldn't. Then he placed his head on her chest.

The slightest movement pushed his head upward a fraction of an inch. At first he thought it was his imagination but his head came back down and then moved upward. It was slow and barely perceptible but it was there. He moved his ear along her breasts and there, near the hollow, was the tiniest of heartbeats.

"Cait!" he yelled. "Cait! Hang on, Cait! Hang on!"

He climbed out of the boat and reached back in to pull her out. "Don't give up, Cait," he begged. "Don't give up. Stay with me, Cait. Stay with me."

Somehow he managed to crawl through the wreckage with Cait in his arms. She was covered in dirt and muck but the wound on her head hadn't split her skull. He hung onto that knowledge as he emerged from under the house to see the rescue workers moving toward him.

"Help!" he yelled. "Help!" But even as he shouted, he knew his voice was drowned out by the sound of the helicopter, crisscrossing the island.

As he carried Cait farther from the house and into the open, one of the rescue workers looked in Ryan's direction as he studied the helicopter's path. Ryan raised an arm in the air, waving it and yelling, his voice scarcely more than a hoarse, dry croak.

His legs suddenly felt weak and unstable and he dropped to his knees with Cait still in his arms. As he cradled Cait's head, begging her to stay with him, pleading with her to hang on, his tears streaming over her face as he knelt over her, he was barely aware of the helicopter circling him overhead and the rescue workers rushing to their aid.

47

One year later

The office was buzzing with ringing phones and an array of voices that ranged from whispers to shouts. A steady stream of witnesses and suspects were led past Ryan's desk, some en route to the interrogation rooms and others to chairs beside officers' desks where they would give their statements and file their complaints.

Ryan glanced up from his paperwork periodically to catch the latest news report on the television screens or make a quick assessment of the activity occurring around him before returning to his work.

"Have to admit," Officer Zuker said from the desk nearest his, "I miss not seeing Cathleen Reilly on the news reports."

Ryan looked at Zuker briefly before glancing at the television sets. He turned back to his work without answering.

"Oops," Zuker added, "Cathleen O'Clery."

"Don't you have work to be doing?" Ryan asked without looking up.

"Nope. I'm just biding my time until tomorrow comes."

"And I suppose when you make Detective, you'll try giving me a run for the money, 'eh?"

Zuker laughed. "Not for a while. First, you'll have to teach me everything you know. *Then* I'll give you a run for your money."

"Well, here's your start," Wanda said as she approached Ryan's desk and slipped him a piece of paper.

"What's this?" Ryan asked, looking at the address.

"Homicide."

"Oh?" Ryan stared at the paper. "Why is this address familiar to me?"

"Remember the guy who kept beating his wife? Cut her up once with a broken beer bottle. She refused to press charges. Then he locked her in an old refrigerator and she almost suffocated. Still wouldn't press charges. Broke her nose—"

"Oh, of course I remember her." Ryan rose from his chair, shaking his head. "He finally did her in, did he?"

"Nope." Wanda waited until he looked her in the eye. "She finally had enough. Shot him while he slept."

"And he's dead?"

She nodded. "She unloaded a full clip. Guess she wasn't taking any chances. She's already confessed and they've got her in a squad car. But I knew you'd want to handle the scene."

Ryan glanced at Zuker, who was already on his feet. "Let's go."

They strolled through the police department and emerged in the parking lot under a hot sun. They had almost reached Ryan's car when they heard a police siren approaching fast. It was unusual to hear a siren this close to the station; usually when police cars approached the station, they already had their suspect in custody.

A minivan careened around the corner and headed straight for the parking lot. Two little girls were hanging out the windows, one in the front passenger seat and the other in the back seat right behind her. Both were shouting but Ryan couldn't make out what they were saying.

A police cruiser was right on their heels, the lights flashing and siren blaring.

"What the bloody hell?" Ryan said as the minivan lurched to a stop in front of him.

"Get your seatbelts on, ladies!" he bellowed at the twins. He turned a ruddy face to Emma. "And what are you doing in the front seat? Why aren't you in the back where you belong?"

The police officer jumped out of the cruiser at the same time as Claire bolted from the driver's seat.

"Have you gone completely daft?" Ryan yelled.

"I can't make it to the hospital!" she shouted over the hood. "Hurry, Re!"

He stared at her, his mouth open. Then a movement caught his eye in the back seat. As Erin retreated from the window, Cait's head popped up.

"Get in here and deliver these babies!" she shouted at the top of her lungs.

Ryan sprang into action. "Christ!" he yelled as he raced around the car. "They're not due for another month!"

"Tell that to the babies," Claire screamed. "The O'Clery girls are coming now!"

"Christ!" he said again. He threw open the back door to find Cait lying in a puddle on the back seat. "Jesus!" He pointed at the police officer. "You! Give us a police escort to the hospital. Zuker," he yelled as Officer Zuker rushed around the car. "You're driving this thing. Claire, get in the front with Emma."

He had no sooner moved into the back seat than Zuker closed the door behind him, jumped behind the wheel and took off behind the cruiser.

"How far apart are the contractions?" Ryan asked.

"Less than a minute," Cait puffed. "You'll be delivering the first one any time now," she added through clenched teeth.

Claire turned to peer over the back of the seat. Catching Ryan's eye, she smiled. "Looks like the O'Clery twins are about to arrive."

A NOTE FROM THE AUTHOR

The Night of the Big Wind is considered Ireland's greatest natural disaster. It occurred on January 6, 1839 as a cold front slammed into warm air that was following on the heels of a snowfall. The rapid changes in weather from cold to warm to cold again resulted in gale force winds that some say swept the Atlantic Ocean from the western shores of Ireland all the way to the Irish Sea.

The hurricane force winds and relentless rains resulted in several hundred deaths, thousands left homeless and thousands of livelihoods ruined. In north Dublin, one of the last places to be hit before the storm reached the Irish Sea, between 20% and 25% of the homes were destroyed or damaged. But the real devastation occurred with the storm surge; as the ocean washed over Ireland from west to east, creeks and streams that were far inland were instantly turned into raging rivers that swept away the poorly built homes of the least fortunate and even damaged castles that had stood for centuries.

Irish folklore had long predicted that the Feast of the Epiphany (January 6) would mark the end of the world and when they heard the roar of the winds, saw the floods, felt the storm and witnessed its devastation, many thought that Judgment Day had arrived.

At least 42 ships were lost at sea. Nearly every county in Ireland witnessed the devastation. The dead in cemeteries in Carrickfergus were forced to the surface. Gort and Loughrea suffered total devastation. In Kilkenny, many homes were lost to fires as a result of lightning. In Longford, barely a house was left standing. The list goes on and on and as a result, The Night of the Big Wind has entered mythical status in Ireland.

Hurricane Irene was the first major storm of the 2011 hurricane season, reaching a peak of 120 mph winds and Hurricane 3 status. It was downgraded to Hurricane 1 status before it slammed into the Outer Banks of North Carolina on August 27, 2011. It then reemerged in the Atlantic and struck again in southeastern Virginia. Becoming a tropical storm, it wreaked havoc all the way up the eastern seaboard, eventually causing widespread flooding and devastation in Vermont and New Hampshire and turning into an extratropical cyclone before moving into Canada and eventually out to sea.

Hurricane Irene caused at least 56 deaths. Damage that occurred in the Caribbean, the United States and Canada exceeded $19 billion dollars, making it one of the costliest hurricanes in history.

Cape Hatteras, Ocracoke, Rodanthe and Duck in the Outer Banks were completely cut off from the mainland and the Outer Banks suffered five complete breaches of Highway 12, the major artery from north to south. In one stretch of Highway 12, a 900-foot section of the road was destroyed. Debris was washed 150 yards inland and some buildings showed water marks as high as four feet. The winds and surge were so violent that it sandblasted the paint off the top of the Currituck Beach Lighthouse in Corolla.

Other Books by p.m.terrell

Black Swamp Mysteries:

Exit 22 (2008)

Vicki's Key (2012)

Secrets of a Dangerous Woman (2012)

Dylan's Song (2013)

The Pendulum Files (2014)

Other Books:

Kickback (2002)

The China Conspiracy (2003)

Ricochet (2006)

Take the Mystery out of Promoting Your Book (2006)

Songbirds are Free (2007)

River Passage (2009)

The Banker's Greed (2011)

About the Author

p.m.terrell is the pen name for Patricia McClelland Terrell, the award-winning, internationally acclaimed author of more than eighteen books in four genres: contemporary suspense, historical suspense, computer how-to and non-fiction.

Prior to writing full-time, she founded two computer companies in the Washington, DC Metropolitan Area: McClelland Enterprises, Inc. and Continental Software Development Corporation. Among her clients were the Central Intelligence Agency, United States Secret Service, U.S. Information Agency, and Department of Defense. Her specialties were in white collar computer crimes and computer intelligence.

A full-time author since 2002, *Black Swamp Mysteries* is her first series, inspired by the success of *Exit 22*, released in 2008. *Vicki's Key* was a top five finalist in the 2012 International Book Awards and 2012 USA Book Awards nominee. The series has several main characters whose lives are forever intertwined through events or family ties: Dylan Maguire, Vicki Boyd, Brenda Carnegie, Christopher Sandige, Alec Brodie and Sandy Stuart.

Her historical suspense, *River Passage*, was a 2010 Best Fiction and Drama Winner. It was determined to be so historically accurate that a copy of the book resides at the Nashville Government Metropolitan Archives in Nashville, Tennessee.

She is also the co-founder of The Book 'Em Foundation, an organization committed to raising public awareness of the correlation between high crime rates and high illiteracy rates. She is the organizer of Book 'Em North Carolina, an annual event held in the real town of Lumberton, North Carolina, to raise funds to increase literacy and reduce crime. For more information on this event and the literacy campaigns funded by it, visit www.bookemnc.org.

She sits on the boards of the Friends of the Robeson County Public Library and the Robeson County Arts Council. She has also served on the boards of Crime Stoppers and Crime Solvers and became the first female president of the Chesterfield County-Colonial Heights Crime Solvers in Virginia.

For more information visit the author's website at www.pmterrell.com, follow her on Twitter at @pmterrell, her blog at www.pmterrell.blogspot.com, and on Facebook under author.p.m.terrell.

20521732R00156

Made in the USA
Middletown, DE
29 May 2015